D0426037

The Wish
~ AND THE ~
PEACOCK

Other Books by Wendy S. Swore
A Monster Like Me

The Wish

~AND THE~

PEACOCK

WENDY S. SWORE

SHADOW
MOUNTAIN

© 2020 Wendy Swore

All rights reserved. No part of this book may be reproduced in any form or by any means without permission in writing from the publisher, Shadow Mountain®, at permissions@shadowmountain.com. The views expressed herein are the responsibility of the author and do not necessarily represent the position of Shadow Mountain.

Visit us at shadowmountain.com

This is a work of fiction. Characters and events in this book are products of the author's imagination or are represented fictitiously.

Library of Congress Cataloging-in-Publication Data
CIP data on file
ISBN 978-1-62972-608-3

Printed in the United States of America
Lake Book Manufacturing, Inc., Melrose Park, IL

10 9 8 7 6 5 4 3 2 1

To brave kids everywhere—
Don't be afraid of change. You can do hard things.
Find what you love and work hard to reach your dreams.
I believe in you.
And don't forget to make a wish.

CHAPTER ONE

Hide-and-Seek

Finding lost things on the farm is the world's hardest game of hide-and-seek. I've been searching for Dad's favorite shovel for weeks, but it's not in the pump house, by the corrals, or in the toolshed. The chicken barn, the horse stalls, and the canals were all duds too—I already checked.

Lots of times, grown-ups blame kids when stuff goes missing, but Dad never did. He might ask for help finding it, but he never blamed us—probably 'cause he knew *he* was the one who lost it most of the time.

Best I can figure, he must'a been working with his shovel somewhere, got called away on another job, and left it right where he was. And since Dad's worked every inch of our eighty-acre farm, I've got a whole lot of footsteps to follow.

Some days it seems all I do is look for lost things.

I ought to run over and pour feed for the pigs, but the sun's just barely leaning toward the horizon and Mom's still busy with somethin' in the house, so I've got gobs of time to check the potato cellar—just in case Dad left his shovel there. Besides, the calendar says it's time to air out the cellar this week. Might as well get that done while I'm at it.

The heels of my boots sink into the ground—still soft from the spring thaw—and my dog, T-Rex, pads along behind me. When I was little, he'd be on ahead with Dad, scampering after every little bug, wagging his whole body instead of just his tail, but now I slow my steps to match his meandering stroll and glance down into his deep brown eyes. "You think he left it in the cellar? We haven't looked there yet, have we?"

T-Rex wags his dusty red tail and bumps his head against my thigh so I can scratch his floppy ears. Usually he follows my little brother, but Scotty must'a run off too fast this afternoon, so T-Rex shadows me instead. Dad called him a houndy-boxery-something-or-other because breed never matters as much as heart—and of that, T-Rex has plenty.

As long as a football field, the cellar's spine looms high overhead like an A-frame cabin blanketed with a thick layer of soil.

T-Rex and I round the dirt bank and drop into the shadow of the solid end-wall, where clumps of wild daffodils greet us like baby chicks nestled in tufts of grass beside gigantic, truck-sized double doors.

We ignore the big doors—they're bolted shut from the inside anyway—and I unlatch the person-sized door in the corner. T-Rex follows me inside.

I blink against the gloom.

The belly of the spud cellar is a whole different world, right down to the air we breathe. It's rich and earthy, as if digging down between dirt walls uncovered new pockets of clean air that no one ever breathed before. Like force fields against snow or blazing heat, the earth walls keep it nice and cool inside, no matter the season.

Dad, Scotty, and me spent loads of snow days inside here, playing ball with potato sacks for bases—anything to get the wiggles out.

A plywood mat-board Dad made for my robotics team leans against the left wall, half-hidden by shadows and covered in so much dust I can almost pretend the practice course is part of the soil.

Almost.

It used to be my favorite thing: building mini-robots for competitions. I'd imagine how someday I'd build somethin' to make our farm run better and easier, somethin' that would help us get jobs done quick, so we could play together more.

But that was before. When I had time to pretend.

I flip on the light switch, and hanging lamps flicker to life in a long line down the ceiling. Dozens of huge metal tubes big enough to crawl through lean against one wall, but no one ever climbs inside—way too many spiders. Outside pipes are for water, but these pipes move air under and through the spuds when the whole place is filled with mountains of potatoes.

The shadows between the pipes hide a pitchfork propped against the dirt, but no shovel.

Maybe it's leaning against something else?

My tiny puddle of hope shrivels up as I try to imagine where else the shovel might be. There's not much inside the cellar right now other than the pipes, a few cabbage heads left-over from last year, and a couple machines.

I walk around the potato piler, with its long-arm conveyor belt rising up almost to the rafters, and circle around the scooper hog, its conveyor belt pressed to the ground ready to lift new spuds right off the floor. It might seem like a waste to keep such big machines around, gathering webs and dust when we only use them one month a year, but when the spud trucks come rollin' in, we need every bit of help we can get.

Deep in the cellar, T-Rex sniffs here and there, poking his nose into every little mousehole he finds. Silly old dog is always on the hunt for mice. He sees me looking and wags his tail.

I'd wave back, but my disappointment weighs on me dang near as much as the dirt overhead. I take a deep breath and let it out real slow.

Without mountains of spuds, the cellar seems enormous, and me no bigger than an ant bonking around inside a rabbit hole. The space feels lonely, waiting empty all year—this year most of all—but Dad always said the emptiness was a promise of things to come as long as we're willing to do the work.

Speaking of work, I've got a job to do.

I eye the crossbeam resting on thick iron brackets bolted to the back of the double doors. Dad could've lifted the crossbeam right off, but my twelve-year-old arms can't quite heft the whole bar at once, so this might take a bit of doing. If I can't lift it, I can always ask Grandpa—except I hate asking for help.

I've got more responsibilities this year, but I don't mind. I said I would look after things, and I will. It's my job. So it doesn't matter if I'm tired, or too short, or not strong enough. I'm doing it, and that's all there is to it.

Bracing myself against the dirt floor, I wedge my shoulder under the rough board and lift one end of the crossbeam up with my whole body. It's almost too tall for me, and I have to tippy-toe to push the thick board over that last metal lip so it slides clear of the bracket. I set down the one end, and the other end pivots up like a teeter-totter. A few minutes of tugging, shoving, and grunting later, and the beam falls to the ground in a poof of dust.

When I rest my fingers against the great wooden doors, I can almost hear Dad's voice in my ear saying, "Give 'er a nudge, Paige, and let the light in."

The greased hinges give way at my touch, and afternoon sun slices through the darkness.

At least I can mark one job off the calendar.

"T-Rex! Let's go. C'mon, boy!" My voice peals with metallic echoes through the pipes, the sound bouncing off the far wall and rushing back changed, as if my invisible twin stands at the other end and hollers back at me.

C'mon!

C'mon!

Boy!

Boy!

A rustling starts in the rafters among the giant beams way down the roofline, and T-Rex whines, watching the ceiling.

Did raccoons get in here?

I hurry to check, but thirty feet in, something white, wide, and fast flies through the trusses right above me. Light catches on feathers, and I crouch, watching the barn owl bank against the rafters and wheel back the way he came. Wind whispers across his wings, each beat making only a breath of sound.

Hoping to see the owl's mate, I watch the spot over T-Rex's head, but either his mate isn't in here or she's hiding real good, because nothing else moves.

At the far end of the cellar, the lone owl drops beneath the wide joist beams—each one as strong as a telephone pole—and glides straight for me. A ghost in the dark.

Graceful, powerful wings whoosh over my head, close enough to feel the breeze from his flight as the raptor bursts from shadow into daylight and soars. Had I lifted my hand, I could have touched him, felt the soft down of his underbelly, or maybe the sharp sting of his claws.

I watch him spiral up and up, circling the farm with its island of trees, until his pale feathers blend with the sky and disappear.

How he managed to get in, I have no idea. Maybe a hole through the straw that lines the ceiling boards, or a crack in the far wall? Either way, no one but me has been here all spring. Owl pellets litter the ground where T-Rex ambles back to me, and I wonder how long our owl's been alone.

Part of me wants to spread my arms and fly after him—to

leave the work and worry of the farm behind. With a strong enough wind, maybe I could follow him all the way up to heaven.

If only it was that easy.

T-Rex nudges my leg, pulling my head from the clouds, and my feet settle deep in the dust. I scratch his ears before heading for afternoon chores.

I wish that owl all the luck in the world, but I know where I belong, and it's right here on my farm.

I was born here, like my dad, and his dad before him. My great-grandfather built our white farmhouse and wraparound porch from old railroad cars and army barracks that he took apart board by board, bending nails back into shape and saving every scrap of wood. It might not have cost much in money, but it was paid for with sweat.

As I near the railroad-tie fence that marks the pig pasture, the pigs squeal and come running, their pink-and-brown ears flapping and their noses wriggling as they lift their bristly chins. Seems they're always chewing on somethin', but it looks more like smiling to me.

I dump mash into their trough and spread it out along the line. "Dinner! Here, pig, pig."

They dig in with happy snorts and grunts while I drag another sack from the shed. Another few years and I'll be able to shoulder the bag like Dad, but for now, a bag-shaped furrow erases my footprints as I haul it right up next to the trough, grab my pocketknife, and slice open the corner.

But before I can pour more mash into the trough, a car

turns off the road onto our gravel drive and rolls toward the house.

I squint at the car. It's some low-riding fancy thing that would high center on a molehill. In late summer and autumn, folks come 'round for corn and such, but it's too early for vegetables—they've only just been planted.

Nothin' to do but go find out.

After scooping a few handfuls of mash into the trough, I haul the whole bag up and dump it in, then snap my fingers at T-Rex, who snores softly on his pillow of dandelions. "Someone's here."

His droopy eyes blink up at me, and his tail thumps a couple times, probably hoping I didn't mean it.

But that long, black car is already pulling up to the house, so I let T-Rex nap and jog toward home.

While I'm still threading between outbuildings, Mom steps out onto the porch and waves at the visitor—she's like that, always trying to make people feel welcome. Then I catch sight of a lady dressed in suit nicer than any Dad ever had.

Tall and slender, the lady glides up the steps on high heels the likes of which our farm has never seen. A silk scarf smothered in paisley drapes over one shoulder and trails down her back, and pearls peek from around her throat. With black hair cut short as a boy's on one side, the rest spikes up near the top, then falls in a sleek, hard angle down her other cheek. With suit lines sharper than porcupine quills, she steps onto the porch as if she owns it.

Holding the door for the stranger, Mom fades into the

background with her soft, plaid shirt worn loose over frayed jeans. "Come in. We appreciate you taking the time to meet with us."

I puzzle over that as I walk past the cars to the front gate. Why would Mom call a fancy lady like that over for anything?

My eye catches on the words scrawled across the side of the lady's car in elegant gold writing.

Miss Dolly Mazer
Real Estate Agent
Trust me . . .
And your home is as good as SOLD!

I look from the words to where Mom welcomes the lady into our home—a dove welcoming a viper into the nest. I'm not sure what's going on yet, but everything in me says this Miss Dolly means bad news.

The two disappear inside, and the screen door snaps shut like the jaws of a gopher trap.

CHAPTER TWO

Stained-Glass Windows

It's been two weeks since Mom opened the door and let Miss Dolly into our lives.

Two weeks of me watching that Cadillac come down the drive and park in a spot we keep open for friends—except she's no friend. She shows up with her hair all done up, shiny high heels, and outfits so nice dust wouldn't dare touch them.

Every time that shiny black Cadillac slithers down our lane, it seems a little slicker, a little more poisonous, like the oil in the paint might ooze right off the car and snap at our boots.

I almost feel bad that our little van has to park so close to it.

Mom named our van Patches on account of how it has a different-colored door and rear hatch than the rest of the car—like a patchwork quilt. Mismatched colors or no, it runs just fine, so when a new spiderweb of cracks appeared in the rear window last year, we named them Spidey and didn't worry about it. We thought we had all the time in the world to fix the window.

But we didn't.

I suppose it fits us even better now. One more bit of broken to add to the pile.

Every time Dolly comes, Mom and Grandpa send me and Scotty out to do chores. And every time I come back, she's got them listening to her twisty words all full of "Trust me. Believe me. I'm here to help" nonsense.

At first Mom and Grandpa told me to never mind when I asked why Miss Dolly was here. Then they mumbled some dumb story about "getting information."

That makes no sense, 'cause I got Dad's calendar. If there's anything they want to know, I can look it up, and I told them so. It says when to plant, trim the trees, and lay out pipe. Everything we need to run the farm is on the calendar, all ready to go. But more and more Mom and Grandpa only have ears for Miss Dolly.

I talked myself blue, but it was like I never made a sound.

When she steps out of that sleek black car, I half expect to see a bloodred hourglass stamped on the back of her fancy dress seeing as how she's weaving her sticky-sweet words around my family's brains. And once their heads get all muddied and confused, she sinks her fangs in and gets them to do exactly what they want.

Mom always says you know a person by what they do— and after a few long talks, Dolly pretty much got Grandpa and Mom to flush our whole lives right down the toilet.

They agreed to sell our farm.

I'm sure they don't really want to, 'cause Dolly's visits suck the joy right out of their souls. Yet they still open the front door and let her in instead of giving her the boot like they should.

I don't understand it.

I flick my red braid over my shoulder and peek through the window at my mother packing boxes in the horse barn.

The horses nicker, puffing soft breaths with their velvet noses, and wait for her to stop and scratch their forelocks like always, but she doesn't. She's not even singing. Not a hum. Not one note.

It's unnatural.

She stretches her back and turns her head, and I duck.

Grasses brush my sides as I crouch beneath the windowsill, my shoulder braced against the rough wood. A ladybug crawls up my jeans to the hole in my knee, the tiny feet tickling my skin. My little brother, Scotty, could tell me what its scientific name is and its genus and a million other facts he's stuffed in his nine-year-old brain, but for me, it's just a nice little ladybug.

It spreads its spotted shell wide, little wings whirring faster than I can see, before it lifts off to the sky.

I grasp the windowsill, the weathered red paint flaking off under my fingers, and peek at Mom again as she stands beside the stalls with her hand on a harness. The horses bend their necks, straining to touch her, but she ignores them and lets the harness fall against the wall.

Our buckskin mare, Queenie, whinnies in frustration and watches Mom with trusting eyes that shine almost as dark as her mane. With a white snip on her nose and tan cheeks, she nickers and talks, expecting Mom to talk right back, let her out, and saddle her up to go somewhere other than the pasture—but Mom doesn't.

Queenie's lips flap and wriggle, reaching for Mom's shirttail to yank her near enough to scratch forelock and ears and make things right again. But Queenie can't reach, so she tosses her head and snorts.

She doesn't understand it either.

Brainwashed. That's the only explanation that makes any sense at all.

Without Mom's chatter or singing, my ears fill with the quiet rustling of leaves from cottonwoods high overhead, gentle trees towering skyward in our own oasis in the high desert. A breeze rolls off the eastern hills, smelling of juniper and sage, and I breathe it all in. Years past, we'd ride those hills 'most every day, a grand view of the Tyhee Flats stretching out below us to the west all the way to the American Falls reservoir. With Pocatello to the south and Fort Hall to the north, we can see it all since our farm perches on the side of these hills halfway between.

Sometimes kids at school roll their eyes when I say something's to the north or south 'cause they don't think that way, but with all the sunrises we see, I don't remember ever *not* knowing which way was east. Out here, my skyline is made up of mountains and horizons, not skyscrapers and rooftops.

T-Rex pads up beside me, and I sneak away from the window before he can whine and give me away. He leans against my leg as we walk and lifts his chin so I can scratch him better, which I do without hardly looking. But I have to check again, because something long and blue sticks out the side of his mouth.

"Whatcha got, Rex?" I snatch the slobbered end away from him and hold up the prettiest feather I've ever seen. It's longer than the chickens' feathers, for sure, and filled with far more colors than a goose could ever hope to have. Just to be sure I'm not dreaming, I touch the gold-and-black eye mark surrounded by electric blue-and-green wisps.

"Paige?" Scotty whispers from the doorway of the chicken barn, his hand beckoning in quick curls. "C'mere!"

I cradle the feather in my hand, careful not to crush it, and slip across the yard with T-Rex on my heels.

Scotty is three years younger than me, but if he has something to show, it's usually worth a look. After a few blinks in the gloomy dimness of the barn, my eyes start to adjust. Feed sacks line the wall by the coop door, where rustling feathers and soft clucks coo from inside—which is wrong, since the hens should have been let out to pasture by now, but that's Scotty's job. A few more steps in, I peer into shadows and search out the corners of the room, but Scotty is nowhere. Not on the equipment, not by the carts, and not by the tool rack.

"Mew." Our orange cat, Scuzbag, peeks out from his perch atop the wall of straw bales stacked along one side of the barn as far back as the coop—except he's not alone. A second set of yellow eyes glares from the shadows, the body so black I can barely tell where its fur ends and the shadows begin. Its eyes close, and it disappears, like magic.

T-Rex huffs and sits on his haunches, gazing up at Scuzbag, or maybe looking for the other feline that vanished from one blink to the next. I know all the cats on the farm by name, and that's not one of ours.

My steps falter and shivers race across my shoulders. "Scotty? Are you in here?"

"Up here!" His blond head pokes over the side of the straw stack by the door, and he's grinning as wide as a horse. "Wait till you see what I found!"

"Did you find Dad's shovel?" Never in a million years would I have thought to look on *top* of the straw stack. Around it, sure, but on top? I try to think of some reason he'd need it up there, but can't.

Scotty laughs. "No. This is better. Way better."

"Says you." I set my feather on the ground and clamber up the side of the barn using the sideways slats as ladder footholds until I flop over onto the prickly mass of straw, bits of it already slipping inside my torn jeans and jabbing my socks.

"So what's the big deal—" I suck in a breath at the blue lump lying in front of Scotty's knees.

The lush blue-and-green tail feathers shimmer in the pale light filtering through the barn wall, and I gasp when a tiny, feather-topped head swivels on its slender neck to stare right back at me.

I always thought owls were the prettiest birds out here, but a peacock? It's like digging for spuds and finding gold.

"Can we keep it?" Scotty gently strokes the wing.

The bird struggles to rise, but falls still again.

"It's hurt. The leg, I think. Or maybe a wing. I can't tell yet. It's male though, definitely."

"It's beautiful," I murmur. Ducks are like that too, with the boys all gussied up and the girls plain brown and boring. "Where'd it come from?"

"It was here. Right here." He pats the straw. "He came to us for help."

"It might be lost." Could it have flown all this way from the Pocatello zoo? No, I don't think so. That's miles away. Clear south of town.

It ruffles its tail and catches a sunbeam, the feathers shining brighter than stained-glass windows.

I almost forget to breathe. Dad always said nature was chuck-full of miracles, and now we've got a straight-up miracle sitting right in front of us.

"Mom will know what to do. I'll go get—"

"Wait." Scotty grabs my sleeve and holds fast. "I heard them talking today. They're going to sell the animals. *All* of them."

"All the pigs and cows?" That happens every year when we take livestock to the sale.

He shakes his head, his gray eyes serious behind the smattering of freckles across his nose. "Them too, but they meant the chickens and geese. Even the horses."

"Queenie?" My stomach sinks like it's being dragged under by the plow. "They wouldn't. Mom would never—" But I know he's telling the truth because I know they're selling the farm, and where would we put the animals even if we did keep them? In one of those tiny postage-stamp-sized yards in town? Maybe on the back porch of some microscopic apartment somewhere? Dad used to say people in towns lived like ants, packed in tight with a million places to go but nowhere to stop and breathe.

My throat chokes right off at the thought of him. If Dad were here, he'd never let this happen. Miss Dolly could say her magic words all day long and he'd just laugh at her. *Sell the farm? Not on your life. Don't let the door hit you on your way out.* But he's not here.

And he won't be ever again.

Mom and Grandpa aren't thinking straight, and they haven't been ever since Dolly came. My lips pinch as I try to think what they might do to our peacock. Sell it? Take it to the zoo? Would Dolly demand roast peafowl for dinner? A fancy meal to go with her fancy outfit. Just thinking it makes me shudder. I shake my head, blink hard, and look Scotty straight in the eye.

"You hold the peacock down, and I'll check for breaks. We're gonna do this on our own."

CHAPTER THREE

Chickens Are Terrible at Sharing

Gentle as can be, I slide my fingers over the bones in his legs, wings, and ribs. His feathers are soft and silky, like new wheat that's only ankle-high. They cover my hands as I work. At last I sit back. "No breaks that I can find. That means a tiny fracture, or maybe a sprain, but nothing we can splint. Our best bet is to keep him quiet and fed."

Scotty and I set about making a cage from the panels of our old rabbit hutch. The cage is partly to keep the peacock quiet and partly to keep him safe in case a raccoon or skunk comes by and decides he wants a tasty treat.

While I tie off the last corner, Scotty brings water and food pans filled with chicken scratch and a little cat food, for good measure. Geese and turkeys need the extra protein, so a real wild bird like this has got to need more than grain for dinner. The peacock doesn't seem to mind the fuss too much—either because he's weak and tired, or maybe because he knows we're trying to help.

The graceful neck extends as the peacock pecks at the feed, his tiny black crown of feathers bobbing. I could watch him all day, but the chickens cluck louder and a couple of the hens squawk like all this waiting is the rudest thing ever. All their fuss breaks the spell, and miracle or no, chores are waiting.

"C'mon, let's let the chickens out. We can come right back when we're done."

Scotty lingers by the cage. "Remember when we nursed the goose back to health with Mom?" He tugs on his collar like he does when he's nervous.

"I remember." Outside of horses, the birds have always been Mom's favorites.

"That took weeks. Maybe a month before it could walk again."

"Yeah, but he got better, didn't he?"

"What if we don't have enough time to make him better?" he asks.

"I don't know. Maybe we can stall—or change their minds." But I don't believe it, 'cause I already tried, and it was as much use as standing in a creek, telling the water to go back up the hill.

"Have you seen Momma? Is she making lunch at the house?" Scotty's eyes drift past mine.

"Maybe. She was at the horse barn before. Let's get the chores done quick and see. The best thing for a stressed animal is to let it be. We don't know what he's been through, but it's gotta be somethin' big for him to end up here. We'll check back later."

We scuttle back from the peacock and climb down to let the hens out of the coop. I don't have to look to know the whole flock stands by the door, their pea-sized brains almost overloaded with excitement for the pasture waiting on the other side.

When I pull the sliding door up, an explosion of feathers erupts from inside, and I can't help but smile at the way the girls come charging out into the sunshine, their wings beating like crazy. None of them really fly, but they hop and run around flapping their wings, pretending as hard as they can. It's all happy coos and clucks until a Rhode Island Red scratches up a worm—then they're after her faster than hawks on a hare.

She dashes to the far side of the pasture, worm flapping like a tiny pink flag out the side of her beak. But White Leghorns are faster, and one snatches half the worm right out of the red's mouth. The rest of the girls switch from chasing the red to the white, and off they go until another one finds a bug and it starts all over again.

Mom calls them characters, but I think they're more like drama queens. Always preening, squawking, and strutting around. I admit, chickens may be cute, but they're terrible at sharing.

When we get our chores done, we hunt around for Mom.

T-Rex helps too, sort of. He follows and finds good piles of straw and grass to lie on, watching us with droopy eyes while we look. He's supposed to guard the whole farm, but I think he decided pups like us need more looking after than most. Difference is, now we watch out for him too.

We find Mom standing between stacks of empty pots with her back against the horse barn wall, eyes closed. Under her freckles, she's as pale as Grandma's porcelain dolls—this year more than normal. Her ponytail is loose, having given up for the day trying to hold her strawberry blonde hair up off her shoulders. She's real pretty, even times like now when she doesn't care how she looks.

Mom and me have got two skin tones: white with freckles, or burned with more freckles. That's why we wear long sleeves and the widest cowboy hats we can find all summer. We've even got matching sombreros if the wind would ever quit.

Scotty's the lucky one. He can tan some if he wants—not as much as Dad, but still. Even a little tan is better than none. All Dad ever had to do was *think* about sunshine and he'd wake up three shades darker.

I open my mouth, but close it again, 'cause I don't know how to say the things I need to say:

Are you really gonna let Dolly sell the horses? Do you know the thought of losing Queenie—or anyone else—feels like jamming a crowbar in my chest and prying up my heart?

Even if I did figure out how to say everything all knotted up inside me, I'm not sure she'd hear me. Not really.

Her eyes flutter open, and she smiles at us like she's waking from a dream. "Hey, darlin'. What's going on?" She pulls us into a hug, each of us tucked under a wing.

I point at the upturned pots. "Calendar says we're supposed to transplant tomatoes this week. Can we get some starts from McKee's?"

Scotty nods. "They have baby goats in the petting zoo there. We should go."

"We're not getting goats." Mom kisses the top of his head, then leans in to kiss mine, but I pull back.

"But we can get tomatoes, right? We need seeds and stuff, too. Radishes need to go in, and beets, carrots, peas. . . . It's time to plant."

The longer she waits before answering, the harder it is to breathe, like my lungs can't work without the right answer.

"I don't know, honey. Maybe we don't need a garden this year."

I wave my hand like it's no big deal. Except it *is* a big deal. "Don't worry. Me and Scotty can plant it ourselves. Maybe Dad left some seeds from last year. We can check. You don't have to help if you don't want to. I know what to do."

Gardens are a promise. With planting comes harvest—but you gotta be around to do the work. The calendar says radishes take twenty-two days to grow. Less than a month. What does it mean if Mom doesn't even want to plant those?

"How about we go for a walk instead?" Mom says. "The three of us. We haven't been up to the hills yet this spring."

That's not the answer I wanted, but at least she wants to do something other than study for her nursing school or hide in her room. Heck, I'm excited she wants to do anything at all.

"Can we take the horses?" Scotty asks. "You could ride Queenie."

She shakes her head before he finishes speaking. "I can't. Not today."

But she could, if she wanted to. "You wouldn't have to ride," I say. "We could walk them with their lead ropes. They haven't been anywhere but pasture and barn since—"

Mom pushes away from the wall. "I need to work on something in the house. You both see if your grandpa needs help. Okay?"

She doesn't wave, or look back, or say goodbye. Standing together, we watch Mom disappear into the house.

"Paige, why does Mom hate the horses now? Did Queenie do something bad?"

"No, Queenie didn't do anything."

His fingers twist, and he drops his gaze to the ground. "Did we?"

"What?"

"Did we . . . do something? Is that why?"

"No. It's not your fault. C'mon. Let's go check our peacock."

His question rings in my head as we walk to the barn, even though I try to ignore it. I already know the real answer.

If it's anyone's fault, it's mine.

23

An hour later, a car engine purrs up the lane, and T-Rex growls.

The Cadillac is back, and I glare at it. No one will talk to me about what's going on, and I can't fix it until I know what's broke. I'm done with being in the dark. I tug Scotty's sleeve. "Let's go."

Dolly's up the stairs and inside before we can get to the house, so I pull Scotty down beside me to huddle against the wall under the open dining room window. The grown-ups have already started talking, Grandpa with his garbled voice, like he's holding a mouthful of chick feed in his cheeks and has to talk through the crumbs. Then my mom's sweet voice—too quiet and hollow without the music that should be there.

Drowning them both out is Dolly with her list of must-do's, and you'll-see-I'm-right's, and trust-me-I-know-what-I'm-talking-about's. I swear it's like the snake on that jungle movie saying "Trust in me" all the time with its eyeballs full of swirls and colors. Maybe that's how hypnotizing works—just say "trust me" a hundred thousand times till people's brains turn to mush and they give in.

Miss Dolly says she moved here because her husband is a professor at ISU. I'm not sure exactly what a psychology professor teaches, but it sounds awful sneaky, and I bet he taught her everything he knows.

"How soon can you empty out the barns?" Dolly asks, and something clinks—maybe Mom's china tea set. The thought of Dolly's poisoned lips touching those special cups makes me sick. We'll have to wash them with turpentine to get all the lipstick off.

"You want the equipment out?" asks Mom.

"Of course. And everything else as well. They must be vacant to show properly, trust me. The animals have got to go. The smell alone would turn prospective buyers away."

"But it's a farm." Grandpa clears his throat. "Wouldn't they expect it to smell like one?"

Dolly laughs. "No. Buyers want the ambiance of the country but none of the distasteful reality. You'll need to remove the manure and replace it with fresh straw, of course. We want those barns smelling sweet! By the time I'm done, this'll be the prettiest farm in Idaho. Of course, if we get lucky and have a developer take interest, all that wouldn't matter, and the payoff would be far larger."

Payoff?

I grit my teeth at the way she talks to him. Grandpa knows more than she'll ever hope to learn, and she talks to him like he's a child.

"I'm glad to see the packing is underway," Dolly says. "The more you can pack up or throw away, the better. Now that the papers are in order, I'll post a sign. We'll be more aggressive after you've done what I've told you. Don't forget. I'll be back."

The screen door bangs open, and she glides down the steps to her fancy Cadillac. Just before she gets in the car, her phone rings, and she whips it out.

"Hello?"

Scotty and I peer through the bushes beside the house while she waits, her long, electric-green nails thrumming against the hood of her car. If I'd seen her in town, I'd have thought her pretty, with her black hair all fancy like a runway model, penciled eyebrows, and shadowed eyes same as you'd see in the movies. But when she talks, a giant mole, or maybe a wart, bobs at the corner of her mouth like a bug trying to decide if it's gonna jump in or not. I wish it would. I bet a beetle down her throat would make her quiet down and leave my family alone.

"I'm just leaving. I'll be back to the Pocatello office in twenty minutes. No, they didn't back out. Like I told you, with all the development for the new Siphon I-15 exchange, and the Northgate Project, this is prime real estate. This is exactly the sort of place you're looking for." She laughs again—more of a soft cackle really—then slips inside her car and revs the engine before heading out to the road.

What kind of a person laughs about ruining someone else's life? We're just another juicy fly she's caught in her web. She might look like a movie star, but all that face paint and those fancy clothes can't make up for an evil heart.

Scotty and I watch as she stops at the end of the lane and hauls a big white board out of the trunk and over to the poles her goons installed the day before. I cringe at the whir of her electric drill that whines like a demonic mosquito drilling holes in the heart of our farm.

"That must be the 'For Sale' sign," Scotty whispers. "I hate that thing. They'll never let us keep the peacock now."

He's right. If Dolly wants everything cleared out, it's just a matter of time before Mom and Grandpa discover our blue-feathered secret.

"What will we do?" Scotty says. "How do we farm without the farm?"

Dolly drives off, her sign bright and cheery at the end of the driveway, and the whole thing swirls in my head until one thought is louder than all the rest. *We need a plan.* If we make the barns smelly enough, maybe no one will want our farm, ever. I bet a couple gophers stuffed in Dolly's car would make her think twice about coming back—or maybe slugs in her tea?

Dad said it was my job to watch over the farm while he's gone, and he'd never want this. Never in a million years. He's not here to protect our family from being caught in Dolly's web of lies, but I am.

A war plan starts to take shape in my head, and then I'm running to the toolshed, my braid bouncing against my back as I weave around the tractors and over tufts of grass.

"What?" Scotty races beside me. "What are you gonna do?"

I spy what I need and wrench the wood saw off a peg. "I'm gonna cut that sign right down to the ground."

We skirt the house and slip down the lane.

Righteous fury swells inside like an irrigation pump shooting hot water straight through my chest. How dare she laugh about taking our farm away? How dare she break my family all to bits? She may fight dirty with fancy cars, fancy words, and

27

fancy clothes, but there isn't a farm kid ever born alive that doesn't know how to fight dirty right back. She thinks she's got us whipped, but this farm girl's got a thing or two up her sleeve, and I've not lost the fight yet.

I leap over a side ditch and lift my saw overhead like a sword. "C'mon! We're going to war."

CHAPTER FOUR

Facts Are Facts

Miss Dolly's enormous face takes up most of the sign, and she's grinning with perfect white teeth like she's *so* proud of herself. Well, when Scuzbag drops a half-eaten mouse on the porch, he's mighty proud of himself too, but that doesn't mean I have to like what's left behind.

The rest of the sign says *BARGAIN SALE! Eighty Acres of Prime Commercial Land with House and Outbuildings.*

Bargain sale.

Reading it makes my stomach twist like I drank a whole glass of curdled milk.

I might not be allowed to drag Miss Dolly out by the ankles in real life, but I can topple her graven image in nothin' flat.

I crouch to set the blade against the base of the sign, but Scotty grabs my arm. "Don't move."

"Aw, man. Not now, Scotty. This is important!"

29

"It'll only take a minute." Scotty holds on tight, but leans over me real slow, then pounces with both hands cupped down on the ground. "Got him!"

"What do you need another grasshopper for? We've got work to do." I get to sawing back and forth, a thin furrow growing beneath my blade. "Watch the road."

"It's not a grasshopper. It's a katydid." He peers between his fingers at his new prize. "Hello, little Microcentrum rhombifolium. Don't be scared. You'll be with your family."

"Looks like a grasshopper to me." Wood flakes salt the grass by my knees as I draw the saw faster across the sign post, the metal rasping against the wood. A couple minutes later, I break through the first post and set the teeth against the second.

Scotty taps my shoulder. "Someone's coming."

I hide the saw deep between two clumps of weeds before scrambling to my feet. "Who is it?"

"Dunno." Scotty steps back to give me a clear view of a shiny red Dodge Ram as it comes up the road.

I don't recognize the driver, but he's got sunglasses and a tiny, fancy hat like he's some kinda FBI secret agent. Scotty waves, being neighborly, but the man doesn't wave back—which proves he's a stranger. Everybody waves here. The stranger looks this way and that, like he's got no idea where he's going at all. When he gets right up beside us, he slows down to give Dolly's stupid sign a long once-over before rolling on by.

"Shoot." I was hoping no one would notice the sign before we cut it down, but that chance is gone. I dive for the saw. "Let's get this done."

For someone with such a fancy car, Miss Dolly sure does use wimpy posts for her signs. I don't even break a sweat sawing through. If Dad had posted a sign, he woulda used pressure-treated wood or a railroad tie—something that would last past the first hard gust of wind.

When my saw bites through the last bit of wood and the whole thing topples over, Scotty giggles. "Timber!"

For good measure, we kick gravel and weeds over what's left of the poles till it looks like any other patch of weeds along the side of the road.

It took barely ten minutes to take the sign down, but hiding the thing is a whole lot trickier. I send Scotty on ahead to watch for Grandpa and Mom while I carry the board on my back like a flat turtle to the canal and drop it in.

Good thing we did, 'cause Scotty hisses a warning. "Another car. I think it's Mrs. Pruitt."

"Gosh dang." Of all the luck. I drop the saw and double-check that we've covered our tracks the best we can. I'm mostly sure a car can't see inside the canal from the road, but it still sets my teeth on edge when Mrs. Pruitt's rusty station wagon rumbles over the last rise and slows down. Like always, she almost breaks her neck from gawking so hard.

We plaster neighborly smiles on our faces.

"Think she'll stop?" Scotty talks through his smile, and I do the same.

"I hope not." I wave, cheerful-like, and breathe a sigh of relief when she rolls on by. "Ugh. Why'd it have to be her?"

That lady couldn't keep a lid on a jar if it was bolted down.

Hopefully she didn't notice anything, 'cause if she did, it'll be all over the county before supper.

Dust envelops us as she rounds the corner, and I grab the saw. After that, it's easy to walk along the canal as the board floats hidden beside us.

Near the house, Grandpa waves from the south field, where he's been fighting with the tractor. With the saw tucked tight against my back, I wave. Nothin' to see here. Just minding our own business. We walk on.

At the culvert where the canal tunnels underground, we grab the corner of the sign and drag it out, dripping wet.

"Should we carry it the rest of the way?" Scotty asks.

"Nah, this is fine." I drop it facedown and drag it so Miss Dolly's polished smile can kiss every rock, weed, and twig on the way to the burn pile. I smirk, imagining all that dirt getting stuck between her teeth.

The screen door bangs open, and we drop the sign in the high grass as Mom steps onto the porch and spots us. "Paige? Scotty?"

We keep walking all natural but veer toward the house. "Yes, Momma?" I say.

"Have you done the chickens and pigs yet today?" Her wandering gaze slides away from us and over the field, like she's looking for something but can't remember what it is.

"Yes, ma'am," Scotty reports. "Did them first thing, and I checked the cows."

"Oh, cows. Right. Good job, hon." She half turns away, picks up one of my old robots from the windowsill on the porch, and starts fiddling with the arm piece without lookin' at what she's doing. "I keep thinking I'm forgetting something."

She sure is forgetting something, like how delicate my robots are. Course, I shouldn'ta left it out like that, but there was only so much I could carry that day. I keep thinking I'll bring it in and finish it when I have time, but time's like a lit fuse, and no matter what I do, it keeps getting shorter.

"Is it your homework? Maybe you got a test tomorrow for nursing?" Scotty asks.

"Oh, I'm studying, but I could swear there was something I should—" Her head snaps up, and she stares long and hard across the fields before turning back to the house and disappearing inside with my bot.

The screen door slams after her.

"Did she remember what she forgot?" Scotty shades his eyes. "Is it a test?"

"It was just her heart pulling toward the field again. It's normal time for Dad to come in."

I think losing someone you love is like having a puzzle all put together nice—maybe your most *favorite* puzzle in the whole world—and then someone goes and takes out half the pieces. You might could tell what the picture was, but it won't ever be the same again.

I sigh and try to ignore the gnawing hole inside me, but I'm missing a fair number of pieces myself.

I lift up the corner of the sign again. "C'mon. We're almost there."

Each year, we gather all the leaves, twigs, and Christmas

trees, and pile them higher and higher until New Year's Eve. Then, at the stroke of midnight, Dad would tuck a firework he'd saved from the Fourth of July down inside, make a wish for all of us, and light the wishfire. Like a giant birthday candle to welcome in the New Year.

We make our own wishes, too.

Mom, Scotty, and me make our wishes by blowing on s'mores cooked over the wishfire then eating the warm, gooey, delicious mess. Grandpa likes to gaze up to heaven through the fiery pinpricks of ashes riding the winter breeze and send his wish on to Grandma. Dad always pulls a stone out of his pocket, whispers his wish to it, then tosses it deep into the heart of the fire. He picks a new stone every year when he plants the first crop, and then carries it with him in his pocket like a lucky penny.

Last year, we almost didn't light the wishfire, but Grandpa said there was no use in letting a perfectly good burn permit go to waste. But as it burned, all I could think of wishin' for was a time machine. I filled a bucket of water and set it in the snow, in case we needed it. At least Scotty was happy—especially when I said he could have my s'more.

Seeing as it's only April now, the pile is only a little taller than me.

After pulling a few branches off the pile, Scotty and I shove the sign as far as we can underneath the brush. The edges of the board scratch deep ruts into last year's ashes, pushing charred pieces of wire, hinges, and rocks aside.

A double bump on the edge of one of the blackened

stones catches my eye, and I pluck it out of the ashes. Flat and smooth, it rests in the palm of my hand, a scorched heart-shaped stone.

Scotty peers over my shoulder. "Is that Dad's lucky rock?"

"I think so. From two winters ago."

I should put it back—keep it safe in the ashes like a penny in a wishing well, but my fingers close around it, and I can't quite make myself let go. I slip it into my pocket. "Come on. Let's hide the sign."

We sprinkle grass, twigs, and leaves all over and chuck big branches over the mess so it's impossible to see where the old pile stops and our new camouflage begins.

"Should we light it?" Scotty nudges a lump of dead grass with the toe of his boot.

Light the wishfire early? That's crazy. "Nah, we'll light it on New Year's like always."

"Unless we aren't here." His voice is so soft, I don't think he means for me to hear, but I do, and neither of us talk for a while after that.

༄ ༄

Later, we scramble up the side wall to check on our peacock again.

A thin line of white outlines his bright black eye, which watches us carefully.

If he could talk, what would he wish for? Maybe he wishes he landed somewhere else, somewhere with his family.

I tilt my head, and he does too.

Probably he'd wish he never got hurt at all. He'll probably heal in a few weeks. That's way better than the hurts on the inside that seem to go on and on. Well, being alive means hurting sometimes, so we make do with what we've got.

Scotty flops down beside me, and after a while, his brain starts leaking facts again. "Did you know peacocks live in India? That's on the other side of the world."

"Nope. I've only ever seen them at zoos."

"Did you know girl peacocks are called peahens?"

"I know about normal hens and geese and ducks. Doesn't seem that much different. Just prettier feathers. I can guess the rest."

He pokes a blade of grass through the peacock's wire cage and lets it go when the bird snatches it and gobbles it whole. "They're a whole different species. Guessing isn't good enough. What if we're wrong? We gotta *know*. I bet there's books on peacocks. We could share."

"Books are your thing, not mine." That's way too much sitting still. I get antsy if I don't have something to work on, like my bots, or an engine, or even caring for one of my animals. I mean, who doesn't like a good long scratch while they're munching on hay? My cows love it, and it's just as much fun for me to watch them flutter their eyelids as I dig my fingers in and find that perfect spot. "Did you check Milkshake when you checked the cows today?"

Scotty purses his lips. "I saw her, but she was kinda back from the trough, so I didn't get a good look."

Shoot. I was so distracted with the peacock I clean forgot

about Milkshake. I roll up and scoot to the side of the stack. "I better go check. It was my job anyway, not yours. It's okay. You don't have to come."

"Wait!"

But I don't wait. I run across the farmyard feeling like a fool. I don't have time for mistakes like this. No matter what else is goin' on, I gotta get everything done. I can't let myself be tired or distracted. Farm work can't wait. Reaching for the top rail, I jump up to lean over the corral overlooking the herd. "Milkshake!"

Scotty's small hands grab the rail beside mine, but I pretend not to notice and keep scanning for my favorite cow.

"You read books to study about robots for Lego League. What if the peacock needs something special? We don't even know how much we don't know."

I groan. Once he starts looking stuff up, there's no stopping him. "I'm not in the league anymore. Remember? I can't do it anymore."

"But you love it. What about your robots?"

"It doesn't matter what I want. That was kid's stuff. I've got real-life things I gotta do now. Besides, we've had loads of birds. It's probably the same as caring for a turkey."

He hangs both elbows over the rail, and I can almost see his analytical brain kick into gear. "You *are* a kid. Twelve is a kid, not a teenager. There's no 'teen' hanging off the end of your age—you know, thirteen, fourteen, like that. And you don't know if peacocks are like turkeys. That's a hypothesis, not a fact. You can't just say things and make them facts because you want them to be. You need evidence to support your conclusion."

"Evidence? Like what?" I tap my finger on the rail, then holler over the herd again, "Milkshake! Come on, girl!"

Milkshake sways into view, her rusty-brown, swollen belly pressing out half-again farther than the rest of her as she ambles up to us. The other cows have dropped their calves already, but Milkshake didn't take as fast as the rest, so she's still carrying.

"Evidence like facts from a zoologist." He leans over and scratches Milkshake's ears while I hop down, pluck some fresh grass, and pass him a few handfuls.

"Here, keep her busy for a minute."

Milkshake's long, sandpapery tongue snakes out and curls around Scotty's bundle of grass, sliming his fingers as she pulls it in. She starts munching while I climb inside the corral to check her.

"Her udder is filling up, but her behind's not swollen yet. Maybe a couple more days before she calves?" Dad would know for sure, but I give it my best guess. I scratch her back and press gently against the bulge in her side. The calf inside bumps back at my soft nudges. "Almost time to meet you," I whisper and run my hands over her thick hide. It smells of dust, cut grass, sweat, and manure.

City folk like Miss Dolly might think that manure smells bad, but to me, it's just part of who Milkshake is. Demanding that a cow not smell is like telling the rain not to make mud. Rain is wet. It just is.

"Books are excellent sources of information," Scotty says. "They're credible and more reliable than the internet. They're . . ." He scrunches up his face. "We *have* to have books."

I sigh. Sometimes, he's more focused than a hen after a worm. "I know. But I have a lot to do. Maybe you can look up all that stuff and tell me if you find anything real important."

Milkshake rubs her big forehead against my jeans as I climb out, asking for one more good scratch before I go. "Don't worry. I'll be back to check on you." I rub her head and smile.

"I could tell you—or I could write you a note!" He lights up like Mom just gave him a whole day free in the library.

"Sure. Write all the notes you want."

Chores done, we head in to wash up. We leave our shoes on the porch beside T-Rex, who snores softly from his nest of old sleeping bags. I used to spend loads of summer hours snuggled with him, my head pillowed on his side, his steady heartbeat and breath soothing against my ear. Scotty still naps with him sometimes, but if the sun is shining, I got work to do.

Scotty shoots a hopeful glance toward the kitchen, but no pans of sizzling bacon, casserole, or biscuits and gravy wait for us on the stove. Between her nursing school and whatever she's doing in her sewing room, Mom's usually gone even when she's here.

He sighs and stares at the closed door of Mom's room, where the hum of a sewing machine whirs inside. "I'm gonna starve to death."

"I'll make dinner."

"Can we have pizza?"

"Only if there's some in the fridge already."

The way he rushes to the kitchen, I almost feel sorry for him when he checks the shelves and bottom drawers but comes up empty. With droopy shoulders, he trudges to the stairs. "There's no pizza."

Potatoes it is. I might not be the best cook in the world, but potatoes are a no-brainer. All I gotta do is wash off the dirt, stab them a few times with a fork, toss them in the oven, and ta-da! Dinner is served.

We've been eating an awful lot of potatoes lately.

Once I get the spuds in the oven, I clear some mail off the table and drop the letters in the basket on top of the piano before setting the table. Scotty's plate and mine go on one long side of the heavy wood table, with Mom's plate across from us, and Grandpa's on the far end. There's room enough for Scotty or me to slide around to the head of the table where Dad used to sit, but neither one of us does. None of us sits there. We never talk about it, but it's *Dad's* seat. That's all there is to it.

When Grandpa comes in from the field, his face and hands smudged black with oil and grease, I call Scotty down to eat and knock on Mom's door.

Inside the room, the whirring stops. "Yes?"

I lean my forehead against the door. "Dinner's ready."

"I'll be right out."

She makes it to the table about the same time that Grandpa shakes the last drops of soapy water off his hands and eases into his chair. I load my spud with butter and bacon bits, because: bacon. Does there really need to be another reason?

"Did Miss Dolly get that sign up on the road?" Mom sprinkles salt over the potato on her plate.

"I thought she stopped at the end of the lane on the way out." Grandpa points his fork at Scotty. "Did you see a sign?"

Scotty opens his mouth, but I kick his foot and head him off. "There's no sign there now," I say.

"Maybe she forgot," Mom says.

I shrug as Scotty stares at his plate. Technically I told the truth. There is absolutely no sign at the end of the driveway right now. All we gotta do is keep quiet, but I know the truth is teetering on the edge of Scotty's tongue like a bucket of water about to spill over. The way he's squirming, he's probably half chewing his tongue off to keep it all inside.

"Well, I suppose another day or two won't make much difference." Mom sighs. "Miss Dolly left a message that she'd be by in a couple days to survey the property. Changes are coming soon enough."

Everyone tucks into their food, and I stab my potato with my fork. Changes might be coming, but if I have anything to do with it, it'll be Miss Dolly who has a change of plans and not us.

CHAPTER FIVE

Royal Turkey

With Mom either studying or sewing in her room, and Grandpa picking up tractor parts in Blackfoot this morning, it's up to me and Scotty to get the animals fed before school, but we only need a couple bales today—just enough for Milkshake, since I pulled her away from the main herd and put her into the barn to keep an eye on her.

Good hay is still green inside the bales, but dry all the way through without any mold. Sometimes wet bales are heavy so we can tell, but other times we cut the string and have to jump back as white mold spores explode up from the blackened insides. It works the same for people. You never know what's going on inside just by looking. Sometimes you got to wait for them to open their mouths before you know what's happening in their hearts. I bet Miss Dolly's insides are blacker than black, no matter how gussied up the outside is.

Scotty and I lift a bale between us, push it onto the tailgate of the truck, and shove it as far as we can, which isn't very far, 'cause even good bales are pretty heavy.

"Climb up and roll that one farther in." I pull a few bits of hay from my shirt and drag another bale closer to the truck. That's the worst part about loading hay. Just when I think I've got it all out, *bam*, another piece of hay pokes through my socks or down my shirt. How it always ends up in my underwear, I have no idea. The good news is that our neighbors live too far away to notice me twisting all over with an arm halfway down my pants, trying to pull out the sneaky bits of hay.

Once we get the bales loaded, I open the door and jump in the truck. Dad started me driving garden tractors when I was five—course he could walk faster than it could go. He figured if I was big enough to help fix machines, I was big enough to drive them, so I've been driving the farm truck since I was tall enough to see over the dashboard and still reach the pedals at the same time—just not very far or fast.

I start the truck and ease it over to the barn in first gear. There, we half-drag, half-roll the bale to Milkshake's stall, where her blue ribbon from the Eastern Idaho State Fair hangs nailed to the post.

"I got your breakfast!" Scotty cuts the twine with his pocketknife and grabs a slice of hay.

Dried leaves and stems crackle under my fingers as I toss the alfalfa flakes into the manger, where they break apart into soft piles.

A dirt bike grumbles up to the barn entrance as our nearest neighbor boy, Mateo, rides in and toes the kickstand down, his overstuffed messenger bag of newspapers swaying as he dismounts.

His dark hair is blacker than a brand-new tire and he can slick up into a sweet fauxhawk when he wants to, but after riding his paper route, it's more like a crazy-haired guinea pig stuck on his head than anything. Still, it's just long enough to touch his lashes—not that I'd look at his eyelashes, because gross. I mean, he's definitely not ugly, but we ran around in diapers together, so who cares if he has dimples or muscles or whatever. He's just Mateo. And we're friends. That's all.

"*Hola*, Mateo!" Scotty waves before tossing a scoop of grain onto the hay.

"*¿Qué onda*, Scotty?"

"*Nada*." Scotty grins. He doesn't know a whole lot of Spanish yet, not even as much as me, but once he's decided to learn something, it's a done deal. Besides, Mateo likes to let him practice.

"Is she calving?" Mateo grabs the top rail and runs a hand over Milkshake's side.

"Not yet, but soon." I scratch her forehead as she roots around in the hay. Like a kid eating dessert before supper, she goes for the grain first. Only thing she likes better than grain is potatoes, which she pops like candy. *Crunch!*

"Oh, almost forgot. I saw this on the side of the road." Mateo pulls a white stone out of his pocket and passes it to me like it's no big deal.

Tiny sparkles glint from the translucent surface as I turn

it over and hold it up to the light. "Wow, that's a nice one. Quartz, maybe?"

"I think so. Thought you might like it for your collection."

I tuck the stone into my pocket, but I keep my fingers wrapped around it a little longer. Mateo doesn't bring rocks, shells, arrowheads, or crystals every day—not even every month—but it's nice when it happens. I think he saw my dad pocketing a rock one time and that got him started.

He scans the barn, his dark eyes lingering on half-filled boxes along the wall. "So, when are you moving?"

I stiffen. "Who says we are?"

"It's in the paper." He slides a paper out of his bag and opens it to an ad with a picture of our farm and information about an open house and tour of the property next week.

"Give me that." I almost rip the thing out of his hand. How dare Miss Dolly put a picture of our home in the paper! Old Mrs. Pruitt's probably dancing a jig and drooling over the juicy news already. I check the dates listed in the ad. "A week? This is happening in a week?"

"That's what it says. If you'd ever read my texts, you'd know that already."

Since the accident, texts always feel dangerous, as if by sending them, I'll hurt the person on the other end. "I left the phone at the house."

"Dead?"

"Probably." I shrug.

He fake-whispers to Scotty, "Why does she even have a phone?"

Scotty shakes his head. "If *I* had one, I'd text you back."

They stare at me, and I scowl at Scotty. The traitor. "I don't text."

"I know," Mateo says, "but I thought . . . Never mind. Where are you moving to?" He holds a hand out for the paper.

"Nowhere." I toss it back to him. "It's not gonna happen."

He keeps his gaze on Milkshake. "It's in the paper. I think it's probably gonna happen."

"Just because it's in the paper doesn't make it so. It's that Miss Dolly. She's talked Mom and Grandpa into selling, and it's nuts. They've all lost their minds."

Mateo rolls the paper and tucks it carefully into his bag. "My dad told me this might happen."

"It won't." I smooth a flyaway hair off my cheek and let the rest of my braid slide, bump by bump, through my fingers. "We're gonna stop it."

"We're going to war." Scotty hops off the stall and gathers up cut twine.

"War, eh?"

I pretend not to hear the disbelief in Mateo's voice. "Yeah. You know that sign you *didn't* see at the end of the road? That was the first shot."

"We cut it down," Scotty whispers.

"Shh!" I snap.

Mateo smirks. "You think cutting down a sign will make it go away? You can't stop it."

My shoulders bristle like a rooster puffing its feathers. "Can too."

He leans against the stall, arms folded. "Oh yeah? How?"

"We got a plan." Scotty grins. "I've been catching grasshoppers for days."

"Your mom isn't stupid. She'll catch you, and then what? You gonna lie to your mom?"

"Course not." I wouldn't have to lie if I could just show Mom that I can do this.

"Won't your mom ask for help with the open house? You really gonna tell her no? *Vivas in las nubes.*"

Scotty pauses in his cleanup. "Paige lives in the clouds?"

"More like—she's dreaming if she thinks she can change something like this."

"Watch me." I sidestep him and stalk to the truck. "We *are* fighting this. Come on, Scotty. We've got stuff to do." That's no lie. Another hour and we'll be late for school.

"Aw, don't be like that." His arm drops to his side.

"Mateo, this farm is my whole life. I'm fighting for my family. You can help, or you can go away."

I feel him standing there, watching me open the truck door and jump in, but I don't say anything. What else is there to say? It *is* a war, just as real as the ones Grandpa talks about— except the war zone is right here at home. We have to win. And Mateo's supposed to be on *my* side.

He walks real slow to his bike, but neither of us start the engines. Finally, he sighs, steps over, and leans against my door. "Maybe I can help."

"You mean it?"

He puts his hand over his heart. "No lie."

His words are better than ice on a hot day. With his hand on his heart, his promise is as good as gold.

"Okay," I say, "that sign has got to stay down. Miss Dolly wants the farm bad. There's no way she's gonna let it go easy."

"Sign down. Got it." He nods. "What else?"

"When people come over, we need to make them think things are awful here. That no one in their right mind would ever want to live on this farm."

His lips curl into a sly smile, and I poke his arm. "No one *other* than us. Shut up."

"I didn't say anything." He raises his hands. "I was going to ask, though—can I bring a hanging basket over here for my mom? My dad bought a big one for Mamá, but we need to hide it until her birthday. You think you could take care of it for a week or two?"

"Yeah. Put it in the greenhouse."

"Sweet. Anything else you want me to do?" Mateo adjusts his messenger bag full of papers.

"You can help catch grasshoppers," Scotty pipes up.

"I'll keep an eye out for them. I bet Kimana would help, too. You should ask her at school." He straddles the bike. "Oh! I almost forgot. I saw a fox down at the grove by the irrigation pump. It ran across the road and ducked right under the mainline. I thought you should know."

"I hope there's not another den. I'll keep an eye out. Thanks."

He waves. "See you at school."

We start our engines, and I watch in the rearview mirror

as Mateo disappears behind the garage, a dust trail rolling up behind him.

On the seat beside me, Scotty repeats Mateo's words, memorizing them. *"Vivas in las nubes."*

I park the truck behind the house and grab cat food from the back porch. Scotty scampers ahead to the chicken barn, and by the time I get there, he's already lying on top of the straw stack, his hand outstretched.

"Pass me the food."

I hand it up to him, then climb the side wall. Our peacock watches me until Scotty slips the food inside its cage, latches the door, and backs off so the bird can eat.

"Did you know peacocks can live for forty years?"

"Nope."

"And a family of peacocks is called a pride—or a muster, or an ostentation—depending on the source." Scotty lies back onto the straw, his head pillowed on his arm. "Oh, and they kill snakes."

"What? Like little ones?"

"Yup, big ones, too. Peacocks defend their territory and kill intruders—even poisonous snakes."

"What about black widows?"

He tilts his head. "They eat other spiders, so maybe? Probably? I'll look it up."

I watch the peacock's slender neck dart down as he eats, every move graceful. How would he protect his family? Shake his pretty tail at the intruder? I try to imagine the shimmering

49

feathers moving to fight a snake, and I can't do it. "He seems too fancy for fighting."

"Did you know peacocks symbolize rebirth?"

That one seems odd. "Why would a peacock ever want to be reborn? They're perfect as is. Look at that tail. How could he ever hope to have something better than that?"

"It's symbolism. I didn't say it makes sense. In Spanish, he's a *pavo real*—a royal turkey—and they *do* fight intruders." He rolls the *r* and draws the word out so it sounds like *pavo rrrey-al*.

"I told you it was like a turkey," I tease.

"It's not a turkey. It's nothing like a turkey. You really should get a book about him."

"Ugh, Scotty. Not again." I pick a piece of straw out of the end of my braid. Usually, I don't mind the red color, though Mom says it's probably gonna darken to auburn when I grow up, but teachers *always* notice me because of it. There could be a whole room full of kids perfectly willing to volunteer, and who gets called on? Me. The one person trying to blend in with the desk and catch up on a little sleep.

Scotty sticks his fingers through the cage and pets one of the peacock's tail feathers. "No, really. You can't know things unless you read them."

"I'm sure you'll tell me whatever there is to know soon enough."

"But—"

"Stop! Okay? Just stop." I see his fingers flutter, so I soften my tone on purpose. "I told you to write notes if you want me to know something."

"You could pretend it's a manual," Scotty says. "Except for a peacock instead of a tractor."

The peacock eyes me and bobs his head as if to agree. *Sassy little thing.*

I flop beside Scotty on the straw. "If we're keeping him, we should name him."

"How about Pavo Cristatus? That's his scientific name. *Cristatus* means he's got feathers that stick up on his head."

The peacock ruffles his feathers and makes a funny *click, click* noise.

"I don't think he likes that. You want to name him 'Turkey with Feathers on His Head'? You're grounded from naming things." I pick at the straw and toss a handful over the edge. "I like the first name you told me—*pavo real.* Let's call him Royal."

"Royal?" Scotty tests the word, and the peacock pauses its eating and stares back at us.

Good enough for me. "Royal it is."

"Paige? Scotty?" Mom's voice floats through the cracks in the barn wall, and we slide down off the stack.

"Coming!" I holler. We head for the house, but halfway there, I notice T-Rex staring across the field toward the road, where a red truck idles, stopped on the road. I bump Scotty. "Hey, is that the same truck that passed by the other day?"

He climbs a rail fence and peers over the top. "I think so. What's it doing?"

I squint but can't quite make out the driver. Is he staring right back at us? Are those sunglasses—or binoculars?

Slowly, the truck eases forward and picks up speed before disappearing over the rise.

"Do you think he's lost?"

"No." I glare at the dust trail he's left behind. "Ten bucks says he's Miss Dolly's spy. Come on, we better hurry."

When we reach the house, Mom holds the back door open and steps aside to let Scotty rush in under her arm. "You've only got a few minutes before we need to go. Are you ready? Backpack? Breakfast? Jacket?"

I slip past her. "I'll be ready in a sec."

Three minutes later, we're settled into the van, with me riding shotgun and Scotty in the back. Country songs play over the radio, guitar riffs and tunes sweet as spun sugar. Mom taps the wheel with the beat a few times—a habit from before—but like always, the music leaks right out, and her fingers fall still.

We used to always take the bus, but that was when Dad finished up morning chores. Now there's not enough morning daylight to do both, so Mom drives us.

Mom's phone chimes from where it's tucked into her purse. I glance at her hands; she keeps them on the wheel.

Good.

Mom turns onto the highway and heads toward town. "I'll need you both to come right home and help clean up."

"Clean what?" Scotty looks up from his textbook.

"A little of everything, I guess. Miss Dolly called. She's bringing someone by to see the farm this afternoon."

"Someone like who?" I pull the tie off my braid, pluck some straw out of the weave, then smooth and rebraid it before wrapping the band again.

"She didn't say. Probably an inspector or something. Whoever real estate agents need to get approval from."

"Great." It's probably the same person she called on the phone that first day when she talked about her big payoff. Whoever it is, if he's a friend of hers, he's no friend of mine.

"Honey, even though things are hard, we need to make the best of it. We'll have a lot of people coming to the farm over the next couple weeks. I need to know I can count on you to welcome them."

I glance back at Scotty, who mimics opening a jar and shaking it out, then clasps his hands against his face like he's screaming before giving me a thumbs-up.

Covering my laugh with a cough, I smile back at him. "You bet, Mom. We'll welcome the heck out of everyone."

CHAPTER SIX

Beads and Books

Scotty's already got his backpack on when Mom pulls into the drop-off loop in front of Tyhee Elementary, but instead of hopping out, he sits sideways with a knee on the seat and peers out the rear window, his fingers tapping the door handle as he watches kids spill out of the cars behind us. "That's Austin's car."

"Well, run out and meet him." Mom glances in the rear-view mirror at the line of cars behind us.

"If I get out, I have to walk around to the back of the school." He glances at the teacher on morning duty. "It's the rules. We can't wait in front."

"Honey, we need to go. People are waiting, and we can't make Paige late."

"Wait one second." He taps a little faster and squints at the car. "One second."

I watch in the passenger side mirror as a kindergartener with a huge backpack jumps out of her van. She teeters when she hits the ground but doesn't fall. Good thing too, 'cause with a backpack that big, she'd be stuck worse than a beetle on its back.

"Scotty . . ." Mom warns.

A husky boy with an Avengers T-shirt and three long black braids hops out of a car and slams the door before looking around.

"Bye, Momma!" Scotty jumps out, darts through the crowd, and runs right up to his friend. They bump knuckles and start to walk around the side of the school toward the playground.

I notice that Scotty's shirt has a tear in it, and both knees in his jeans are ripped open. He always looks like a farm kid, but today he's rocking the ragamuffin look. If Mom was paying attention, she'd probably take him home to change, but she's already watching the cars in front.

"Paige!" Scotty turns and waves.

I roll down the window as Mom starts to pull out. "What?"

"Check your library. For books . . . that *I* want to read!" He stares at me, hard, so I can't mistake what he means.

I can't imagine why there'd be books about peacocks at my school, but I wave out the window anyway. "I will!"

As we wait our turn to pull away from the red-brick building, Mom shakes her head. "The way he talks, you'd think we starve him for reading material, but he brings home a new armful from school every week."

I shrug. If Scotty had to choose between books and breathing, he'd probably go for the books. When teachers turn him loose in the library, he prowls the aisles like a fox raiding a henhouse full of fat, lazy chickens. He eyes the books hungrily, caressing the spines, and snatching one, then another, till he's plucked so many off the shelves, his arms can barely hold them all. His fingers twitch quicker than a rabbit's nose as he cracks them open one by one, a feeding frenzy of words. He savors them too. Sometimes I catch him repeating the words just to taste them rolling off his tongue—the longer, the better.

Hippopotomonstrosesquipedaliophobia?

Dee-licious!

Reading's never been that way for me. Sometimes the words squiggle around like tadpoles in my head, 'cause I keep thinking of chores, or robots, or calves, and before I know it, I've read the same line three times without understanding a word.

Mom used to always push me to read more—which mostly made me read less—until Dad had the transmission all tore apart on the Deere 4850 and asked me to read him the manual so we could figure out how to put it all back together. It was slow going, 'cause I was little and the words were big, but I did it. And I've read every manual since.

I guess for me, reading's a tool I can use if I need to, but most of the time I get around it. Why use a drill if all you really need is a screwdriver? Same thing.

The closer we get to town, the closer the houses sit next to each other. They're nice houses, but when *land* is what's needed to grow food and keep everyone fed, it's a whole different feel.

Neighborhoods gobble up field after field, farm after farm, ruthless and relentless in their need for more open spaces.

A yawn catches me off guard, and I cover my mouth. Mornings are always hard for me, because from the minute I leave the farm, there's seven hours of school ahead. Seven hours wasted where I could be getting things done. I smooth my pants and stop when my hands run into a bump in my pocket.

Dad's wishstone!

I curl my fingers around the stone, rub the smooth surface, and watch them come away sooty. Suddenly the day doesn't seem as long as it did before.

By the time Mom drops me off at Hawthorne Middle School, there's only fifteen minutes before the bell rings, so I make a beeline for the library in the basement and slip inside.

With the phone to her ear, the librarian smiles and waves at me, the overhead lights sparkling on her silver bracelets and rings. Mom still wears a wedding ring, but Dad never did, 'cause he didn't want to lose a finger in an engine. He only ever wore his once—on their wedding day. It's been sitting safe in a black velvet case in his dresser drawer ever since.

I wave at the librarian as I walk past the long wooden counter and head straight to the computers against the back wall. I type in "peacock," then blink at the list of books that comes up. With the cursor highlighting one book after another, I narrow it down to *Sojourn, An Exploration of India* by Annie Alaina Evers, and *Wild Nature Child* by Ellie May Shelby.

After I've found the books I'm looking for, I spy Kimana tucked in a corner table of the library, her long, straight, black

hair spilling over her shoulders to her waist as her clever fingers
work on her latest project. She used to work on her beading
projects only at home, but her beadwork started selling real
good, and she's trying to save up money for a special jingle
dress, so she uses whatever bits of time she can find to make
more.

"Hey, Kimana." I plop down in the chair across from her.

She looks up from her work. "Hey."

"Did you finish those pretty moccasins already?"

"Yeah." She holds up a lined piece of white cloth with rows
of tiny blue beads making a diamond shape. "Sold them yesterday. I'm doing bracelets this week."

"How far do you have to go?" I flip to the back of the *Wild
Nature Child* book, searching for an index.

"I'll finish this by tonight, and I've got another piece of
hide ready to go at home. Hutsi says she'll make another pair
of moccasins for me to bead next week after she takes these
to Fort Hall Trading Post." Kimana threads a string of blue-
and-white beads on her needle and scoots the line down like a
jeweled caterpillar.

"No, I mean, how far till you can buy the jingles and everything for your regalia?" I flip through the last few pages in
the book and grimace. No index. Do they expect me to read
the whole thing?

"Maybe another couple of months? I've been trading for
some of it." She thrusts the needle up through the cloth right
beside the beaded string and sends it back down on the other

side, securing the line of beads in place. "Did you see sign-ups for next year's Lego League are open?"

I turn a page in the book. "I'm trying not to think about it. Did you sign up?"

"Paige, you have to sign up. The other teams murdered us last year after you dropped out. You're the best builder on the team."

"Yeah, but you're the best programmer. You can do it without me. I bet your competition was epic."

"Epically embarrassing, sure. For real, we can't win without you. Last year's robot had three arms, but they put them all on backwards and it couldn't even flip a ball. All I could program it to do was wave at the judges on our way to last place."

"Oh, come on. It's not that bad." I laugh.

"It's worse." She shakes her head. "So much worse."

"Whatever." I watch her lay the beads down row by row, her second needle and thread looping over top to secure the small spheres, each as brilliant blue as Royal's feathers. Her precision is what makes her such a good programmer. She lays down line after line of code and makes something wonderful.

As for me, given the choice between needle and thread or duct tape, I'll take the tape every time. It holds shoes together, doubles as a Band-Aid, catches flies, removes splinters, patches a hose, cures warts, gets cat hair off your clothes, and if a fence nail catches your jeans and rips the holy living daylights out of your pants, duct tape will save the whole world from having to see your underwear.

Pages flip under my hands, but none of it's what I'm looking for. "Do people ever use peacock feathers for regalia?"

"Peacocks? Not that I've seen around here. Their feathers make pretty earrings though. Why?"

I lean close. "We have one."

She stills halfway through a stitch. "What?"

"We found a hurt peacock—well, Scotty did, but we're taking care of it together."

"A real one? Where is it?"

"On top of the straw stack in the chicken barn. Wanna come over? I could show you."

"For sure, but I better check with Hutsi first. You could have dinner with us, and I could come see it when we're done. I could text you—" She grimaces. "I mean, I could call you or your mom after I ask."

Kimana's grandma is the *best* cook, so normally, I'd be there in two flicks of a cow's tail, but . . . "I can't. Remember the real estate lady Mom invited over? She put an ad for our farm in the paper."

Her hands still again. "You're moving?"

"No. Not if I can stop it."

Kimana waits, watching me with deep brown eyes. She's always been a good listener. Other people might needle and pry to find out what they want to know, but Kimana just waits till I spill my guts all on my own. It's like her superpower.

I scan a few more pages of the book for information about peacocks, then flip it shut. "It's a mess. I don't get how Mom and Grandpa can let this happen. Heck, they're *helping* it happen, and nothing I say matters. It's like Miss Dolly's got them both hypnotized or something."

I watch for any sign that Kimana thinks I'm being ridiculous, but she only waits, so I rush on, the words spilling out and piling in a heap between us faster than grain from an auger. "Mom and Grandpa listen to everything she says, no matter how crazy it is. They're selling all the animals—even Queenie—and throwing stuff out. Strangers are coming to the farm next week." My finger taps the table. "Next week! To our farm—to my *dad's* farm. Looking in our barns, poking at our animals, snooping through our stuff, and walkin' right into our house like it's some kind of dollar store."

The librarian clears her throat and raises a bejeweled finger in warning.

I hadn't realized I'd raised my voice, but sitting there, saying it all out loud makes it so real. "I have to stop it, Kimana. I *have* to. It feels . . . it feels . . ."

I lift my face to the ceiling, searching for the right name to give this tangled mess of barbed wire jammed inside my chest. I take a breath and meet her gaze. "It feels like I'm losing him all over again. And I can't. I just can't."

"You don't think he'd want your mom to sell? It's a lot of work."

"No way. The farm was his whole life—*my* whole life."

"It didn't used to be your whole life. You've got robotics trophies to prove it. Same as me." Kimana glances at the clock and strings another line of beads. "Maybe your mom and grandpa have reasons you don't know about."

"I've got Dad's calendar. Everything that matters is already on there. This is something different."

"You said Dolly's making your mom sell the horses? Wasn't she rodeo queen?"

"Yeah, the same year your mom was Shoshone-Bannock Queen at the Festival. Mom *loves* our horses. How can she even think about selling them? Selling *Queenie*?"

"Do they act hypnotized the rest of the time? Like zoning out or acting weird?"

"I dunno. Mom zones out sometimes, for sure. I swear I've tried talking to them, but it's hopeless."

"Maybe they just need more time to snap out of it. Could you get them to stall?" Her fingers swish tiny beads around inside an old mint tin before threading a few more crystal-blue beads on her needle.

"Mom won't stall, but I think I've got a plan to slow things down."

I slide the librarian a glance to be sure she's not listening and whisper while Kimana lays down a couple more rows of beads.

"We're gonna make it so people think the farm is the grossest, most awful place ever. Scotty and me have some ideas."

By the time the bell rings, Kimana's design is looking awesome, and I've got a new ally.

"Besides," I say as I help her put some beads back in the tin, "if you don't help me, I'll never get to come back for Lego League, and you'll be stuck with a three-armed robot forever."

Kimana laughs, then gathers her things and tucks the beadwork into a pouch before stuffing the whole thing into her backpack. "I can't ride home with you because my brothers have practice riding for the Relay race, and Dad's on patrol, so my Hutsi needs me. But maybe I can come over later." Kimana stills. "Wait—I forgot, I can't."

"Why not?" I glance at the clock. The last thing I want is to be late for Mr. Collier's class. He gives detentions, and nobody's got time for that.

"My dirt bike won't start."

"Did your brothers look at it?"

"Not yet. They've been too busy with rodeo stuff. Maybe Sunday."

Sunday is way too long to wait. "Maybe *I* can fix it faster."

"Don't stress if you can't. If my brothers can't do it, my dad will eventually." She waves as she walks out the door. "See you at lunch!"

"Definitely." I set the books on the counter by the librarian. "Do you have any books on taking care of peacocks? These didn't have anything."

She looks up from her work and considers me for a moment before her fingers click on her keyboard faster than the needle on Mom's sewing machine. "Let's see. No peacocks, but we do have several books on pheasants."

Wings, feathers, beaks—it's nowhere near the same, but Scotty can fill in whatever I don't know.

I shrug. "I'll take it."

CHAPTER SEVEN

Fertilized Brains

The chaos of hundreds of feet, excited conversations, and slamming lockers fills the gray-tinted hallways with more ruckus than a whole herd of cattle as I slide through the crowd to my first-hour class on the second floor—social studies with the newest teacher in school, Mr. Collier.

He's a nice enough teacher, except for when I fall asleep in class, which is sort of every day. It's not like I sleep very long. Grandpa would say I'm just resting my eyes. I still listen . . . most of the time.

I keep making lists in my head of all the things I should be doing on the farm—things my calendar says should already be done—and school and the rest sort of blurs together.

My steps slow by the classroom door when I catch sight of Mateo a half dozen yards down the hall. He's leaning against Jessica's locker, her blonde head tilted close to his as she cozies in and shows him something on her phone. Glitter sparkles on her perfectly round nails, which match her fancy shoes.

You can tell a lot about a person by their shoes. You know where they've been, and where they're headed. Expensive or hand-me-downs, shoes take you places, but if they're too pretty to step off the pavement, all they'll ever see is a world bound up by cement. Ten bucks says Jessica never walked a dirt road in her life. If you ask me, all that shine looks way out of place next to Mateo's worn sneakers.

Still, seeing them together makes something inside me deflate like a slow leak in a tire. I duck inside the classroom and squeeze past a knot of girls by the door. Grabbing a Chromebook off the metal cart beside Mr. Collier's desk, I make my way to the back of the class, drop my backpack under my desk, and slump into my chair under a poster of Coretta Scott King, first lady of the civil rights movement. On either side of her, paintings and photos line the wall all the way around the room. Woven rugs, face masks, and iron tools hang below the portraits on pegs and wires. It's sort of a mini-museum, with stuff from all over the world stuck to the walls. Mr. Collier has a picture of himself suited up in a black belt with trophies hanging behind his desk.

If someone said Mr. Collier was some kinda real-life Indiana Jones ninja, I'd believe it.

"Hey, Paige." Mateo slides into the seat in front of me and shrugs off his jacket.

"Hi." I curl my fingers under the edges of the Chromebook to hide my bitten nails. Even if they were long enough to bother with glitter and stuff, the paint wouldn't last past the first day of chores.

The bell rings, and all six foot five inches of Mr. Collier steps through the doorway. He gives a couple quick claps, and his voice, deep as a diesel engine, rolls right over the chatter and shuts it down.

"Welcome, class. Find your seats." He pulls the door shut behind him.

He takes off his sports coat, folds it, and drapes it over the back of his office chair. With a sweeping gaze, he rolls up his sleeves over his dark-brown arms. "Please pass up the review questions for chapter twenty-seven."

Students dig through backpacks, and a flurry of papers flows toward the front of the class.

Right. Homework. I knew I was forgetting something. I open the Chromebook for a mini-barricade between me and the front of the room and keep my head down as Mr. Collier collects the piles of papers from the front of each row, taps the edges of the stack to make them all even, and slides them into his drawer as gentle as a hen tucking eggs in a nest. With that done, he adjusts his gold-rimmed glasses and scans the room.

"All here, I see. Excellent. Get ready to type or write down some notes. Whichever method you prefer."

Most of the class open Chromebooks and power them up. Three-ring binders and spiral notebooks flop onto desks as the rest of us dig for pencils or pens and hold them at the ready. I pull out my notebook, write the date at the top, and set the pencil down. Hanging onto it while he's talking is sort of like holding a hammer over a nail just in case you want to hit it someday. If I hear something I want to write down, I will. But there's no point pretending I'll write loads down. We both know I won't.

He plucks a pen from the side of the interactive whiteboard and taps the screen.

A graph slides into view with numbers and percentages, and Mr. Collier circles a 46%. "This is the average grade from your tests last week."

The class groans, but he raises a hand. "I get it. I do. A new teacher partway through the year is an adjustment, but that doesn't change the fact that your grades matter."

Arms folded across his chest, he paces across the room. "I won't change your test grade, but I *will* give you an opportunity for extra credit."

Mateo flashes a smile at me, and I scrunch my nose back at him. He gets way too excited for grades.

Mr. Collier walks back to the board and pulls up instructions with "May 4th" written at the top. "Each of you will find someone in history whose story speaks to you. Name someone—anyone you remember from history."

Emily, the blonde beside me, raises her hand, and Mr. Collier nods at her.

"Einstein."

"Sure. Anyone else? Throw them out. Let me hear it."

"Lincoln!"

"Alexander Hamilton."

Mr. Collier raises his fist. "'I'm not throwing away my shot!' That's right. Who else?"

"George Washington."

"Elvis."

"Ben Franklin!"

"Lady Gaga!"

He holds up a hand. "All good examples. My daughter would probably add Beyoncé to that list, but those are people we hear about all the time. I'm interested in the stories you *don't* hear—and I want to know how they relate to you."

He points to a painting over his head of two Asian women holding a tiger skin with some kind of writing on it. "These are the Tru'ng sisters of Vietnam. When their people were suffering under China's rule, the sisters killed a man-eating tiger and wrote a declaration against injustice on the hide. They recruited more than thirty-five women as generals for their rebellion and drove China out of Vietnam in AD 40. Ever heard of them?"

We shake our heads.

"I thought not." He taps the pen against his hand and walks to another poster. "Over here, we have Sybil Ludington: a young woman who, in 1777, rode more than twenty-five miles from New York to Connecticut *in the dark* to warn people the British were coming—that's longer than Paul Revere's famous ride. Sixteen years old, folks, and she saved entire towns." Hooking a thumb in the pocket of his pressed, gray slacks, he points to a photo of an African American girl in midair over a high jump. "Alice Coachman. In 1948, she became the first black woman to win an Olympic medal."

Next to me, Jacie bites her lip, her fingers flying on her keyboard like this will be on a test, but Jeff in front of her plays a game on his phone under his desk.

Mr. Collier taps the wall under a black-and-white photo of a girl standing beside an enormous stack of papers almost as tall as she is. "Margaret Hamilton headed a team that wrote the navigation codes that got Apollo 11 to the moon and back."

He stands below a photo of samurai armor and swords. "And then there's my personal favorite, Yasuke. The first non-Japanese man ever to become a samurai . . . was an African slave. As the story goes, he was enslaved as a child and spent his life in chains. So, imagine for a moment what it must've been like for a man who never had choices, power, or freedom to have the chance to wield a katana—and do it with enough skill to be named samurai."

Murmurs roll around the room, and Mr. Collier smiles. "Yes, he was fierce. Now think of how Yasuke's story would resonate with an African American student of martial arts, like me." Mr. Collier steps back into a fighting stance, his fitted dress shirt pulling tight over his arms.

Some kids laugh, others nod as he relaxes and walks to the back of the room, pointing to picture after picture. "Take the time to read all these names. Sojourner Truth, Fredrick Douglass, Booker T. Washington—they all made an impact on history. There are so many to choose from, why stick to the same names you already know? So now, let's try again. Who can think of someone in history that we don't hear about every day?"

Silence fills the room, and students glance at each other for a few heartbeats before Mateo raises his hand. "Chief Pocatello?"

"There you go. How many of you knew our town was named after a Shoshone chief?"

Mr. Collier walks up the aisle beside us and stops beside Jeff's desk, his hand open and waiting. Jeff sighs as he stops his game and sets the phone in Mr. Collier's hand.

"Research," Mr. Collier says, like he's announcing a grand prize at the fair. "Find someone who speaks to your own personal story. You've got three weeks to do this report—and none of that time will be in class—so listen up to the requirements."

For the next ten minutes, Mr. Collier lays out the rules of what he expects and then lets us search on our Chromebooks for who we might use for our reports.

When the bell rings, kids rush to return the Chromebooks and hightail it out the door.

"Paige? A word, please?"

"Yeah?" I veer toward his desk and adjust the strap on my backpack as he steeples his hands and waits for the last of the students to clear the door.

"You didn't turn in your assignment today."

"I forgot." Between Milkshake, chores, and Miss Dolly, it's a miracle I remember school at all.

"That's another zero you can't afford." He turns to his computer, fingers clicking on the keyboard. "And I haven't seen your reading log this month at all. Are you at least reading the assigned chapters?"

My silence is answer enough.

He watches me and shakes his head. "You're a farmer, right? Imagine that your brain is a wide-open field. Your brain is growing new connections, new experiences, and you want this crop to be the very best it can be. Reading books is what makes that ground fertile."

"Books are like fertilizer?" Wait till Scotty hears about this.

"Well, maybe I didn't make the best metaphor, but you know what I mean."

I stare at the pencils on his desk, because I don't know what to say. I'm sick of people telling me what I should and shouldn't do. Mr. Collier doesn't know me any more than Miss Dolly does. I already know what's important, and I'm taking care of it. The farm is running, the animals are fed, and the crops are watered. The rest is just stuff that gets in the way.

"Paige, I'm only saying this because I care. Trust me."

My head jerks up at his words, and I hear Dolly's voice overlapping with his—just another fancy-dressed person trying to boss me around. I lift my chin. "You know what too much fertilizer does? It stinks."

Mom would have my hide for that sass, but I can't take it back. I don't want to, either.

"Enough. Like it or not, your grades matter. If you don't pass this class, you'll have to retake it. Fail enough classes and you'll have to retake the entire grade. If things don't improve real fast, I'll have to call your parents. Would your father approve of these zeros?"

My father? My whole body rocks back as his question cuts deeper than any furrow.

"What is it? What's wrong?" Mr. Collier is on his feet, reaching for me, but his voice seems far off, and I back away, the hurt too fresh to think straight.

"How would *you* know what my dad wants? You never even met him."

"Paige—"

Stupid tears blur my eyes, and I bolt from the room faster than any thoroughbred horse ever ran.

He can keep his stupid manure books, his slick sports jacket, and his fancy posters. If we had met a year ago, I'd have liked his class, maybe even loved it. But things change.

He doesn't understand what it means to be up before dawn and to bed after dark. To be twelve and dead tired but still working because there's no one else to get the job done.

He doesn't know that the last words I spoke to my dad were a promise, and I'll keep that promise or die trying.

CHAPTER EIGHT

No Spark, No Fire

By the time the bus gets to our street on the Sho-Ban Reservation, most of the kids have already gotten off.

"I'm telling you, it was awesome." I sling my backpack over one shoulder as the bus stops in front of Kimana's house. I slip past two boys, heads together, watching a phone. One of them has three braids; the other has his hair cut short.

"The owl flew right over your head? Were you nervous?" Kimana pats the shoulder of a girl in a gray hoodie—one of her brother's friends—and glances at Mateo behind me as she exits the bus.

"No. It was sort of magical. Like the veil between here and heaven stretched thin enough to cross over if I could fly." I grab the hand rail and hop down the steps to the road.

Mateo passes us and turns to walk backwards, his hands palm out. "Maybe you should change your mind, rejoin Lego

League, and build yourself some wings so Kimana can program them for you."

"Not you too! No ganging up on me about robotics." I wag a finger at Kimana. "Your evil plan to guilt me into joining the league won't work."

"It wasn't her," Mateo says. "I was looking at the team list on Mr. Shelmen's door, and he practically made me promise to talk to you. He wants you to join the team really bad. Like really, really, really bad."

"Right." I laugh. "Whatever."

We all look to the bus driver and wait for her to wave us across the road.

"Maybe next time he should send gifts," Kimana says. "Are there any bribes that would work?"

"Probably not, but it would be fun to try. He should send chocolate."

We step across the yellow dotted line.

The bus horn blasts, and Mateo yanks us out of the other lane as a blue minivan screeches to a stop. It's so close, I could touch it.

The bus driver lays on the horn again and gestures, furious, but I can barely hear anything over my heart pounding louder than a drum inside my skull. Each beat shakes me, as memories of past and present slip free and collide inside me.

I stare at the teenage girl inside the minivan. Her left hand grips the steering wheel, but her right hand holds a phone, screen bright, against her heaving chest.

She had been texting.

My breath hitches again and again, and I tremble as Mateo steps closer to the minivan and yells, "What's wrong with you? Put your phone away! You could have killed us!"

Images of a mangled ten-wheeler wrapped around and over the remains of a tractor flood my mind. I blink, but I still see it all again with my eyes open or closed. Bent irrigation pipe scattered across the road. The truck driver searching for his phone instead of trying to help the man hanging from the tractor seat.

Looking for his phone, because he had been *on* his phone when he hit the pipe wagon and the tractor.

My *dad's* tractor.

The pipe never made it to the field. And Dad never made it home.

I let Kimana pull me across the road and down her driveway, her arm around my shoulders. She knows I hate talking about it, and Mateo and she purposely talk of other things— anything other than cars and trucks, tractors and texts.

Kimana tells us about this kid she likes—Dante—who does the Fancy Feather Dance with two bustles splayed with feathers—one secured behind his hips and another between his shoulder blades—and I tilt my head up, letting her words and the sun wash over me.

Here with my besties, there's no judgment, no expectation, and no pushing. If I don't want to talk, I don't. My chest eases a little, and I remember how to breathe.

They don't give me pitying looks either—not like I get from teachers. Mr. Collier apologized all over the place—apparently he didn't get the memo about my dad when they hired him—but he still says the extra credit is my only chance of passing, and that's only if I do *all* my homework for the rest of the year.

Halfway down the lane, nanny goats bleat a happy welcome, pressing their horned heads through the fence, their ears waggling. They have perfected the art of begging for food by looking adorable.

"Don't believe them," Kimana advises. "My brothers fed them this morning before school."

"Where's your bike?" I ask, feeling calmer the closer we get to my friend's house.

"In the shed behind the arena." Kimana leads us down her dirt driveway beside the split-rail fence that surrounds the training paddock where her brothers train their horses for Relay racing.

As we pass her ranch-style house, Kimana's Hutsi steps out onto the porch with a watering can in hand, silver and stone rings reflecting the afternoon sun. She nods at us as she lifts the plastic mini-greenhouse off a workbench and pours water over tiny green seedlings. "What are you three troublemakers up to today?"

"Troublemakers?" Mateo looks behind us, eyes wide in mock horror. "Where?"

"Hi, Hutsi," I wave. "What'cha growin'?"

"Basil, sage, chives, dill." A breeze teases a wisp of gray against her soft brown cheek. "Plus tomatoes and chili peppers. A little of everything."

I give her a double thumbs-up. "Nice."

"You gonna have some sweet corn for me this year?" she asks.

"Of course!" I answer as if it's not even a question. As if I know for a fact that I'll be here to harvest sweet corn come August. I mean, I *will* be here. I have to believe it's true.

"Good. I used the last of our freezer corn a couple days ago." She covers her plants and pulls open the screen door. "You let me know when it's ready, okay?"

"You bet."

"Oh." Hutsi sets down the watering can. "Kimana, did you hear Little Man is hosting a powwow for his senior project? He called to invite you to compete. Oh! And Feather's doctor says she's due any day."

"But I don't have my jingles yet. When is it?"

"Next month."

"I guess I'll have to up my game on beads or something. Thanks, Hutsi." She leads us around the corner of the house. "Bike's over here."

"Who's Feather?" Mateo asks.

"My cousin. I'll babysit for a couple days when she has her baby."

Tucked like a chick nestled under a wing, the lean-to cozies up to the side of the barn. A dirt bike rests on its kickstand in the center of the floor. Globs of dried mud speckle its fenders and wheels, but the engine shines where Kimana cleaned it all out.

Mateo taps the spare half-shell helmet clipped to the rack over the back tire. "I still say you should bolt some great big

Viking-style horns onto this. Can you imagine Paige rocking that with her braids?"

Kimana doesn't bother looking at him. "My dad's a police officer, remember? Safety first. He might let me paint it, but that's it. But *you* could always wear a helmet and glue buffalo horns on it to go with that big head of yours."

"Hey, my head's not that big."

I sneak a glance at Kimana, who mouths the words "real big" and spreads her hands apart like she's showing me a big fish.

I grin and take a knee, my worn jeans sinking into the dust. "You said it makes noise when you try to start it, but nothing happens?"

"Yeah." She sweeps her long black hair over her shoulder and hunches down beside me. "When I stomp down on the starter, it coughs like it wants to go, but it never catches. Nothing happens. I'd have my dad look at it, but they're training new Fort Hall officers, so he's pulling double shifts this week."

"Have you tried kicking it?" Mateo asks, and we both look at him. "What? It works."

"No, and I didn't poke it with a stick either, but thanks for the advice." Kimana fake-whispers to me, "This is why I didn't ask *him* to fix it."

Mateo sniffs. "No one appreciates my genius."

He's actually pretty good at fixing things, and I know they're both still trying to distract me. If the engine isn't starting, it's either no spark or no fire. I just gotta figure out which it is. Maybe it's just a loose wire, or some other easy fix.

When we were little, our moms drove us back and forth to each other's houses. But after Kimana's mom died, her dad dropped out of the rodeo and became a police officer so he could work closer to home, and Hutsi moved in with them to care for the kids. But these days, if Kimana is going to help at my place, she needs her wheels back. Without a running engine, this little Honda 50CC of hers might as well be a pile of rocks.

"Show me what it does." I stand up and step back to give her room.

She throws a leg over the bike, sets her foot on the starter, and stomps it down. A growl starts but chokes off each time she kicks it.

"Okay, wait." I raise my hand and stare at the bike for a minute.

"You want me to ask my dad?" Mateo offers, but I shush him.

As far as puzzles go, this one is easy. There are only so many ways an engine can fail to catch, and I certainly didn't need anybody's help to figure it out. I tap the fuel tank. "You sure it's got gas?"

"Oh, come on. I checked that first thing." Kimana folds her arms. "I checked the oil too."

"Chill. I'm just checking off the list. Any chance you've got water in the tank?"

"We never leave the gas cap off." She checks the tightness of the cap.

I touch the spark plug at the top of the cylinder, but it's snug and secure. No loose wires.

I scan the head, jug, crankcase, and exhaust. Nothing seems wrong from the outside. "When's the last time anyone cleaned the carburetor?"

"Um . . ."

Snatching a nearby screwdriver from off an upside-down bucket, I unscrew the hockey-puck-shaped metal tin to take it apart, but it's pretty clean inside, and the float seems okay. As I put it all back together, I peer at the engine and try to think of what I'm missing. It's just like any other engine I've worked on a hundred times. The answer is here somewhere. I can almost hear my dad teasing, *You want a hint?* And I blink a few times and shake my head.

Mistaking my motion for defeat, Mateo says, "I bet my dad would come right over. He should be done with the cows—"

"Just give me a minute. I got this." I know I do. I just need to figure out the right angle.

Giving up after you fail once is like abandoning a calf 'cause it didn't stand up the first time it ever tried. I touch a chunk of hard-caked mud on the fender, an idea sparking in my head. Sometimes the simplest answer's the best one. I grin at the muddy handlebars. "Who went mud racing?"

"Dakota took it up in the hills with some friends last

week," Kimana says. "I think he said he slid down a hill on his side with it."

Scratching with the screwdriver, I gently tease clumps of mud off the handle grip and run the blade around the creases until, all at once, the red kill-switch button pops up, little flakes of dirt falling away.

"Is that it?" Mateo steps closer.

"Try it now." I stand back as Kimana gets on the bike again.

She slams her heel down on the kick-starter.

The engine roars to life, and I laugh as Mateo raises his hands in victory. "All hail Paige, queen of fixing things!"

CHAPTER NINE

A Little Lost

A moth flutters in and out of the rafters over our heads as I lie on top of the straw stack inside the barn. Dust-coated spiderwebs crisscross the open spaces between the wood, and I can't decide if the moth is avoiding the threaded snares with skill or by luck. There's a good-sized hole in the metal roof above us, but his little mothy brain can't find it.

Curled into a scruffy orange donut, Scuzbag sleeps on my belly, his rumbling purr vibrating through my chest as I stroke his fur. When I was five or so, Dad walked into the house to find a scrawny, filthy kitten sitting right in the middle of the kitchen table, licking the last of the butter off our dish. Butter smeared his whiskers and nose—some even hung off his ears, though how he managed that I don't know. Quick as a horsefly, Dad plucked the half-starved ball of fluff up by the scruff of his neck, looked him up and down, and said, "Hey, you little scuzbag. That's *my* butter."

The kitten got fatter, but the name stuck.

My eyelids droop with Scuzbag's vibrations, but I force them open again. I already moved pipe for Grandpa after school, carrying them clear of the mower. Normal three-inch pipe's not so bad when it's empty, but these were four-inch, and some of them had ends full of dried mud. I had to drag those.

It doesn't matter if my arms feel all stretched out and full of jelly, or if that minivan by the bus got my insides all shaky. I gotta stay awake. If I fall asleep now, I'll never get the chores done before dark. As is, I should be doing them now, but I needed to check on Royal—and Scuzbag used a sneak attack of cuteness. That ball of fluff sure knows how to work those adorable eyeballs of his.

Beside me, Scotty sits crisscross-applesauce, analyzing my pheasant book as he compares each fact to Royal and the encyclopedia he's got stuffed inside his brain. "But peacocks and pheasants are nothing alike!" Scotty touches his fingers to his thumb one after the other. One, two, three, four, one. "They don't even have the same nutritional requirements."

Royal bobs his head like he agrees, but I roll my eyes. "It's all they had at the library. They both have feathers, beaks, feet—what more do you want?"

"I want to know where he came from. Why did he pick our farm? What happened to his old home?"

"Maybe someone sold it." I toss another handful of straw over the edge.

The pages flip under his clever fingers. "Maybe. Or maybe something tried to hurt him and he escaped."

Royal tilts his head and blinks at me, and I still wish he could talk. Where has he been? What has he seen? Did he have to fight for his home too?

"Maybe that's how he got hurt," I say. "Something attacked, and he barely escaped. Oh! And that's why he's in the barn. He's hiding."

"Maybe. But it's all guesses, not facts." He turns a page. "I need facts."

I curl my fingers behind Scuzbag's ears, and the purring kicks up a few gears. "Speaking of facts—Kimana and I were talking."

He closes the book and leaves it on the straw. "Yeah?"

"What if Miss Dolly's really a hypnotist and she's got Mom and Grandpa brainwashed?"

"Hypnotist? Like at the fair?"

"Exactly. What if that's what's going on? Sort of like a spell, but it's all inside their heads?"

Scotty shakes his head before I even finish talking. "No hypnotist could make them sell the farm if they didn't want to. They can only make you do stuff you're already willing to do. Don't you remember? The people at the fair explained the whole process."

"That was just a show. How do you even know what a real hypnotist can do?"

But before he can answer, T-Rex barks right outside the barn, and I pull Scotty down beside me. If anyone finds us up here, our Royal secret will be blown worse than a broken mainline.

"Bring them over here, Dad." Mom's voice fills the barn, and we flatten against the straw. "Set that box down by the stack. I'll sort it out later."

Scotty's wide eyes meet mine, and I shake my head real slow. *Don't make a sound.*

"How many more boxes do you need?" Grandpa's shuffling steps pass right under the straw stack, and I hold my breath, but Mom is a long time answering.

"I don't know. What do we really need from here? We can't take all this with us. I don't even know where to start." She sighs. "If Steve were here, he'd know what to do. I keep feeling like I'm missing something. It's like there are these sinkholes hidden all over, and I never know when I'll fall in another."

Holes.

Holes in the roof.

Holes in Scotty's jeans.

Dad's name attached to a hole where my dad used to be.

This would all be so easy if he were here.

Beside us, Royal fluffs his tail and stretches his neck like he wants to see over the edge too.

Scotty waves a hand at the bird, trying to shush him as if he were a cat, but Royal spooks at all that waving, jumps up and turns away, his long feathers sliding along the wire and making all sorts of racket.

"What was that?" Mom asks from below, and Scotty's eyes open even wider, his fingers fluttering.

Grandpa clears his throat. "I didn't hear anything."

Royal completes his turn, but there's no hiding the rattle his tail makes as he shudders and settles down. It might sound as soft as falling sand, but Mom's ears are sharp.

"There's something up there. Have you seen any skunks or raccoons today?" A plastic lid scrapes against a container, and we lie real still, but she's already coming to look. My heart speeds up with every footstep we hear.

"Mew!" Scuzbag sits up and arches his back, yawning.

I lift him off and scoot him up almost to the edge so Mom can see him from down below.

With his fur all mussed up, and his legs spread wide, Scuzbag glares at me over his shoulder for spoiling his nap, before settling down into a long stretch with another yawn.

"Oh, kitty. Was that you? I knew there was something up there." Mom's steps stop and retreat.

"Look at that yawn. He's got a rough life, that one." Grandpa chuckles.

"Sleeping sixteen hours a day and eating all the cat food and mice he can dream of? Yeah, real rough."

"Oh, come on. You know that one doesn't dream of mice. He dreams of butter." Grandpa chuckles again.

My chest caves in a few inches at the same time that Mom makes a little half-laugh, half-cough. "He would, wouldn't he?"

Mom sniffs like she's got a cold, and the lid clatters against the container again. "Maybe we can make a list or . . . I don't know. It's . . . it's . . . ." She sniffs again, and Grandpa clears his throat.

"Well, I don't know about you, but I find things always seem a little brighter when I have some grub in me. How about we go back to the house and make something other than potatoes?"

Mom's voice is a little watery. "Sounds like a plan. Come on, T-Rex. Let's go find the kids."

As their footsteps fade away, Scotty and I slowly raise up and peer over the straw. Mom and Grandpa are gone, but T-Rex only goes as far as the middle of the road before looking back at us and flopping onto the ground. He might be old, but he's no dummy. He doesn't need to follow Mom to find us; he already knows where we are.

Scuzbag grooms himself, licking a paw and wiping it down his head over and over.

"Good save, Scuz!" I reach to pet him, but he slides out of reach.

"He's offended." Scotty grabs his book again.

I laugh. "Sorry, Scuz."

Scotty double-checks that Royal is secure and moves his food dishes to the other side so he can reach them without having to turn around again, then we crawl to the wall and climb down.

"I think he needs a bigger enclosure," Scotty says. "He can't turn around very well in there."

T-Rex ambles over to greet his boy, tail wagging, and I scratch his head. "He only turned around because you scared him. He needs to rest."

"But still. A peacock needs—"

"We'll make a bigger spot as soon as we can. A couple days maybe. And then he'll be even more healed up, okay?"

"Okay."

We stop beside two pink plastic totes at the foot of the straw stack, the bright color more out of place than shoes on a bull.

We stare at them for a few heartbeats before I drop to one knee and lift the lid. The smell hits me first. Horse, sweat, dust, and Dad. His gloves rest in one corner of the box, the leather fingers curled toward the palm as if they remember what it was like to be worn. Beside them, Dad's favorite lasso sits wound up and tied off, the fibers stained from countless hours spent chasing after lost calves and cows.

Framed pictures fill the rest of the box, and Scotty crouches beside me to pull one out. It's Dad and his first horse, Pia, riding herd beside Grandpa, a giant grin on Dad's face.

I pull out the next frame, and it's Dad and five-year-old me riding together inside the cab of a Deere 4850 tractor, with my hands on the wheel but his feet on the pedals. With me as his right-hand man, we could do anything.

The bus horn blares inside my head, and I try to lock the memories away where they belong. I shoulda been there, watching his back. He asked me to come with him, to help him move pipe from one field to the next, like we always do, but I was making him a surprise—a little robot that I designed myself, to help on the farm. I was gonna show him when he got back.

So I told him no.

Since then, I've dreamed that moment a thousand times, saying yes, yes, of course I'll go. But I always wake up, and remember I said no.

I told him I'd look after things till he came back. I promised I would. Sure, he only meant to be gone for the afternoon, but that doesn't make my promise mean any less. If anything, my promise means more now, because I gotta pull enough weight for both of us.

Reverently, I slide the pictures back inside and close the lid. My fingers curl around Dad's wishstone in my pocket, and I try for the hundredth time to think of what his last wish might have been. "You think Dad would be glad we're fighting for the farm, or mad that we're disobeying Mom?"

"Course he'd be glad. Why else would I get a whole jar of grasshoppers? Dad would want us to save our family, right?"

Save the family. That sounds about right. Dad was always saving things. Calves, chicks, me.

The hens cluck and coo from the coop at the back of the barn, and I struggle to put words to the jumble in my head. "Maybe it's like when calves get lost in the hills and need help gettin' back home. Except it's Miss Dolly leading Mom and Grandpa off somewhere inside their heads and we gotta bring them back." I take the pheasant book from him and brush straw off the cover. "I don't know. Maybe it's just me who's lost."

"You're not lost. You're right where you belong: with me." Scotty taps the tote, and the corner of his mouth curves up. "But that doesn't mean she's a hypnotist."

"Doesn't mean she's not either," I tease.

"Science says she's not." Scotty pries open the other tote.

"Then it should be easy to snap them out of this crazy talk, right?"

"Maybe. As long as we don't make things worse." With a gentle finger, Scotty nudges aside dried flowers to touch a sun-faded photo of Mom barrel racing from her rodeo queen days. Trophies, crowns, and silk banners fill the rest of the tote.

"Worse like how?" I glance at the chicken door and let my gaze slide across the barn.

T-Rex snoring softly beside Scotty.

A pair of doves roosting in the rafters.

Scuzbag blinking down at us from above.

The black magic cat beside him—where'd he come from?

I shrug. "If the farm sells, everything's gone anyway. What could be worse than that?"

CHAPTER TEN

Calling to Strangers

My friends at school sometimes talk like dawn and sunrise are the same thing, that when you work from sunup to sundown, you must be the hardest working person in the history of work. But when I hear someone got up at sunrise, I wonder why they slept in.

Dawn is that moment when darkness begins to fade. The dark doesn't give up easy, though. It clings to every shadow, hiding in nooks and crannies, clutching the cold night air tighter as the sky over the mountains fades from deep blue to gray and washes the stars away. Then, like a stone tossed in a pond, the sun pushes ripples of colors on ahead in all directions, lighting the bellies of clouds first, then filling the world with a strange half-light of red, pink, or orange. The brighter the sky, the colder the air, and thin crystals form on windshields and creep down blades of grass. The coldest time of the whole night is that last frozen moment just before the sun peeks over the mountains and breaks the spell.

The night might be gone, but my breath still hangs in wispy clouds of ice.

Flakes of frost sprinkle my stained leather gloves and melt against my cheek as I heft a sack of pig feed over my shoulder and trudge toward the pen. At dawn, everything sounds different, amplified. Gravel crunches under my boots, and a magpie chatters from branches high overhead as if to say, "Keep it down!" But by then, it's too late for quiet.

A long cry rises up over all other birdsongs, echoing a *"Ha, ha, heyo, heyo!"*

And the world goes quiet to listen as Royal breaks his silence. More piercing than a goose's honk, the first two sounds cry out a question: *Are you there? Can you hear me?* Then he answers, *I'm here. I'm here.*

"Ha, ha, heyo, heyo!"

I'm part thrilled to hear it, because that's gotta mean he's feeling better, but sound can travel for miles around here. Who else is up early enough to hear?

I wait for more, but he must've said all he wanted to say, so I turn back to the pigs.

Excited squeals and snorts greet me as sows push and shove for the best spots by the trough. A flock of mourning doves settles behind them, pecking and cooing where sharp hooves and leathery snouts have turned up the soil.

I pull the string on the sack, opening up one corner, and pour a long line of feed down the metal trough, the mash swishing like sand against the metal sides. The second bag fills the rest of the feeder, and the squeals quiet into happy grunts. Too much in one spot, and they hurt themselves all bunching up at once, but spread out, there's room for all.

Cupping my mouth, I call, "Here pig, pig. *Sooey!*"

I don't know what "sooey" means. I should know. Shoulda asked Dad when I had the chance, but it was just one of those things he did, and I never thought to ask why. His voice was deep, wasn't it? I keep trying to remember, but it plays at the edge of my mind, and I can't quite catch it—fragments of a tune where I can't remember the words.

My heart aches where the memory of his voice used to be, another piece of the puzzle erased, the leftover edges raw and bleeding.

Enough. There's no time for hanging out at the trough all mopey—not when there are more chores to do. Every minute that slips by splashes more golden rays of sunlight against the barn walls and frosted leaves. Scotty and Grandpa ought to be about done checking irrigation lines, and I can't keep them waiting.

Empty feed sacks in hand, I hurry to the cows and try to ignore Dolly's brand-new sign at the end of the driveway, where it sits all bright and awful like a maggot perched at the edge of a pie. Her workers came by late last night to put it up again. She's determined, I'll give her that, but oh, just knowing it's there chafes something terrible.

The whole thing's as welcome as a blister.

Sawing it down twice in a row would make for too many

questions, so I gotta think of some other way to get it down. I could burn it, but fire's tricky-dangerous, and it's not in a good open spot like the wishfire.

A robin lands in a clump of daffodils beside the path, pecks at something, and flits off. Wild daffodils are Mom's favorite flower, 'cause they keep coming back no matter what.

They're not as pretty as Mateo's hanging basket, but . . .

I stop. I totally forgot about Mateo's flowers. Did it frost last night? Did I leave the fans on? I jog to the greenhouse.

"Please be alive. Please, please!"

Pushing the blue tarp aside, I step inside the plastic dome. Empty seed trays lie in a jumble on one side of the wall, and a few scruffs of grass grow where our garden ought to be, but the hanging basket is alive. Long ivy vines hang from the sides like green tentacles from a jellyfish, and flowers bubble up from the middle and trail down like pink frosting. Pink ribbons spiral down from the hook overhead, and a smattering of baby's breath dots the center with tiny explosions of white.

Mateo's mom had a scare a few years ago with breast cancer and survived. Now they celebrate her birthday with something extra special. This year, they must've spent a fortune on these flowers.

It's a little wilted and thirsty maybe, but alive, so I grab the watering can and give it a good drink. I'll have to remember to refill the watering can and turn on the fans later.

The blue tarp crinkles as I slip back outside and start jogging toward the cows. Every minute, the sun creeps higher, and my time gets shorter.

When I cross the canal, three ducks quack like mad and explode off the water way down the ditch. Squinting to catch sight of whatever critter mighta startled them, I peer upstream, but steam rises from the water, making a line of fog down the bank. Something moves out there—a quarter mile or so down the way. Mateo's fox, maybe?

No.

A man-shaped silhouette walks down the canal—headed *away* from the farm as sneaky as a viper slithering away from our beds.

Someone has been here.

I bite my lip and watch the tiny form walk away as I try to talk myself out of worrying. But how can I not worry? Sometimes bad folks walk through just to make trouble. What if the stranger bothered my animals, or lit the haystacks on fire? That happened once before. A whole year's worth of hard-earned feed gone in one awful night of fire that smoldered and smoked for weeks afterward.

"Please don't let him be a firebug," I whisper as I break into a jog. With one eye on the haystacks, watching for smoke, I rush from pen to pen, checking for open gates, tampered feed, damaged equipment, or anything else amiss. The pasture gates seem okay, but what about the barns? Could he have gone after the tools? I check the doors on the shop, the toolshed, the animal barns. I poke my head inside each one just to be sure, but I don't see anything.

I'm still scowling in the direction the man disappeared

when Grandpa and Scotty rumble up in the truck and step out, T-Rex ambling up beside them.

"What's the matter?" Scotty follows my gaze.

"Someone was here. I saw a man on the ditch."

Grandpa slams his door. "Unless something's missing, I wouldn't worry too much. People walk by sometimes."

"What if it's a firebug?"

T-Rex nudges my hand for a scratch, and Grandpa surveys the haystacks. "If he had started a fire, we'd have seen smoke by now. You know how fast they go up. It's probably just someone out for some morning air. Folks don't always know ditches are private property."

"Well, he should." He wouldn't think it was okay to run around in someone's backyard in town, would he? Maybe I should have marched right up to see who it was and showed him the "no trespassing" sign, but walking up to a stranger without Grandpa or Dad feels like poking a rattlesnake.

"No use worrying about it now. It's over and done." Grandpa gathers irrigation valves out of the truck and carries them by the long handles, two dangling from each hand so they hang past his knees like oversized aluminum bells. "You two check the chickens and that cow of yours."

"On it," I say.

As we near the barn, Scotty bumps my arm. "Did you hear Royal? Wasn't it awesome? It's like our farm has a tiny piece of the *Jungle Book*."

"Did Grandpa hear it?"

"I don't think so. He didn't stop working. Mom says he

doesn't always hear so good. Oh, and Dad's cat has a new friend. You see it?"

Tucked into a pile of loose straw by the doorway, Scuzbag's lean orange body curls protectively around the magic cat's black shadow.

Scuzbag's lazy green eyes watch us come, and his ears flick at the sound of Scotty's voice. But before I can say anything, the black cat's yellow eyes open wide, and it streaks into the barn and out of sight.

Scuzbag arches up as I stop to stroke his head. "I've seen him twice before. The same day you found Royal."

"You think it's a female?" Scotty starts to climb up the straw stack. "Maybe we'll have kittens."

"Maybe." Dad was always real good about catching and fixing any strays, so most of the cats we have are all grown up, but a feral cat that skittish is harder to catch.

I pass food and water up for Royal and check the feeder levels for the chickens, then pour a few more buckets of grain in. "It looks good down here. How's Royal?"

"Great! Did you give him the oyster shells for grit?"

"Yep."

"I wish we had some worms to give him. That's what we need: Lumbricus terrestris." Scotty slips down the stack, and we trek to Milkshake's barn. "Peacocks are omnivores—not herbivores. He needs more than grain to eat."

"I know. That's why we gave him cat food too. He'll be alright."

"Carnivorous cats. Felis catus." He skips ahead of me, his

fingertips tapping his thumbs one after another—pointer, middle, ring, pinkie—on repeat. "Lumbricus terrestris. Did you know worms have gizzards same as chickens and other birds?"

"I think I remember that." I grab hay for Milkshake and break up the flakes into her trough.

"That's 'cause worms don't have teeth. They gather tiny rocks into their gizzards, and the muscles squeeze all the food they eat right through all those rocks. Like a garbage disposal for leaves and stuff. The rocks chew the food—but worms use smaller rocks than chickens do. A worm couldn't eat pieces of oyster shell. I think it's more like sand. Tiny sand-sized pieces of rock."

"Did you just read that?

"No. I knew that forever ago." He sighs. "Library day isn't till Friday, and I've read everything already."

"Why don't you ask if you can check out more books?"

"We get five. Mrs. Foster says five new books every week." He dumps a measure of grain in with Milkshake's hay.

I reach through the wood slats and scratch the short, thick fur on her forehead. "You should ask for more books. I bet the librarian would let you. She's nice."

"The other kids only get fi—Hey! Who else was in here besides Grandpa?" He crouches beside the stall and touches the shallow heel of a footprint in the dust. It's not crescent-shaped like Grandpa's boots, and the toe is far too round.

I peer over his shoulder. "That's from a dress shoe."

"Does Grandpa have dress shoes?" Scotty stands and looks up at me.

"No. He wears nice boots to church, not dress shoes." Who would wear dress shoes to a barn? That doesn't even make sense. Tennis shoes, sure, or maybe work boots, but dress shoes? "C'mon. I want to check something."

We run back toward the pigs and stop at the canal, where I scan the ground for a moment before spying the same shoeprint pressed into the soft dirt, leading away in the same direction the man went. My heart hiccups at the thought of a stranger in the barn with Milkshake.

"The man on the ditch was in our barn."

"Are you sure?"

"Definitely." I may have to look twice at letters and things, but shapes are just big puzzle pieces. And this one fits perfectly.

The hum of tractors on the road grumbles, and we glance over to see Mr. Rivas in his Deere 4850, the plow raised high and proud behind him like a shiny green rooster tail. A couple hundred feet behind him, Mateo motors along in a yellow front-end loader with a wide blade across the whole front and the long excavator bucket arm curled up behind him. Mr. Rivas cruises right on by toward their farm 'round the bend, but when Mateo nears our driveway, he pivots a bit from right to left, like he's having trouble controlling the loader.

I take a step forward. Did something break? My brain clicks through the different parts that might have failed—the steering column, maybe the front axles, or the ball joints?

Mateo fights with the controls, his whole posture proof of his struggle to get things back in line as the tractor slows down, angles to the side . . . and catches Miss Dolly's sign head-on.

I never knew how beautiful the sound of wood splintering could be in the morning air.

Black diesel smoke billows up from the exhaust stack as the blade jerks up and rolls right over the sign. Plywood breaks into smithereens and dirt flies as the stakes topple over and smash to the ground. Wood chunks soar over the cab and bounce across the road—and in the middle of it all, Mateo raises an arm as if to apologize for being so careless.

"Oh!" Scotty gasps. "Poor Mateo. I bet that was scary— accidentally running off the road like that. Noisy too."

Mateo swerves back onto the road, a few pieces of the sign clinging to the blade for a yard or two before falling away as he guns the engine and disappears around the bend after his dad.

A slow smile starts deep in my chest and wriggles all the way up to my face. "You know, Scotty, I think he went exactly where he wanted to."

CHAPTER ELEVEN

Baby Spider Hotel

After school, Mom worries on everything like a cow on a salt lick. We help her move stuff around like she wants, but a shed with twenty boxes in it looks an awful lot like a shed with fifteen boxes in it.

Finally, T-Rex raises his head, and I expect to see Miss Dolly's black Cadillac, except it's not her car coming down the driveway. It's the Dodge Ram with the driver's window rolled halfway down.

Scotty squeezes my arm. "It's him. The guy from the road when we were—"

"Shh," I hiss, glancing at Mom, but she's on the far side of the van, watching the truck come up the lane.

As the shiny red Dodge pulls in next to Patches, the two vehicles seem as different as a peacock and a pigeon. Where the truck sparkles in the sun, we have rust spots. And Patches's faded blue might qualify as a color, but the mirror finish on the truck is so flashy it's like the van isn't there at all.

I squint at the guy inside the truck, but the man with the sunglasses isn't alone. Miss Dolly sits tall in the passenger seat with her own pair of movie star sunglasses and waves her taloned fingers at us.

"You think he was spying for her?" Scotty whispers.

"Seeing as how they came together, I'd say chances are pretty much a hundred percent."

The driver-side door opens, and the man steps out. He's wearing fancy leather shoes, gray slacks, a dark-blue suit jacket, and a white button-down shirt with tiny dark-blue stripes. He's spiffy enough to wear a tie, but the collar's unbuttoned, and he traded a tie for a city hat—the kind you see on TV that doesn't actually shade anything but lets people pretend they're wearing a real hat.

Miss Dolly slips out her door and glides around the truck, her lacy silver scarf trailing partway down the front and back of her black dress, a clipboard under her arm. She walks real graceful too until her high heels sink into the soft grass and lock her steps up. She gives me a little wave when she passes me and asks Mom, "Do you know what happened to my sign?"

"We thought you were bringing it this week." Mom glances at Grandpa. "Right?"

"I brought it *last* time. After my original sign and poles were gone."

"Well, if'n you did, it didn't last the day." Grandpa hitches a thumb on his belt. "We looked for it at supper, and there was nothing there."

Miss Dolly's lips pucker like she's trying to decide whether to call Grandpa a liar or not, then covers it with a plastic smile. "No matter. It appears there may have been an accident that knocked the second sign down. I'll have another put up this afternoon." She lifts her chin. "It's just a little hiccup. Now, Hope, have you gotten those barns cleared out yet?"

"We've started, but it's only been a few days," Mom says. "We'll get there, but we need more time."

I watch Mom's nervous, shy smile as she apologizes to strangers on her own farm, and I wonder who this little mouse is. Nine months ago, she was unstoppable.

Miss Dolly glances up at Sunglasses Man. "Well, it's not ideal, but I suppose you can use your imagination. At any rate, introductions . . ."

He waves it off and steps forward with a smile, hand outstretched toward Mom. "I'm Asher—Asher Ferro. Miss Dolly told me all about your place here."

Mom shakes his hand. "Mr. Ferro. I'm Hope McBride. Nice to meet you." Mom raises an eyebrow at me, and I know she wants me to say something sappy, but the thought makes me want to barf, so I pretend not to notice.

"The pleasure's mine."

"Are you in the market for a farm?"

The spy chuckles. "No, no. I'm researching farms for a story."

Miss Dolly leans toward Mom as if telling a secret. "Mr.

Ferro is a freelance journalist. You've probably seen his human interest articles in national magazines and periodicals? I'm such a fan."

Peri-whats? I run down the list of "peri" words in my head. Periodontal. Paramedic. Paradox. I dunno. Sounds an awful lot like *parasite* to me. Besides, if it isn't in the almanac, on Dad's calendar, or in a manual, then what good is it?

"What would a reporter want with our farm?" Grandpa's gravelly voice drops. "We don't want no trouble."

"No, no. This isn't that sort of story," Sunglasses Man says. "I'm interested in the personal side of your farm. Dolly tells me that your family has lived here for generations. I'm interested in your legacy."

"He's here to help," says Miss Dolly. "Trust me. We want allies in order to find the right buyer."

"Well, I suppose that'd be alright," Grandpa allows.

Mom nods toward the porch. "Did you need me to show you around? I've got dinner on the stove, but I can turn off the burners."

"I wouldn't want to inconvenience you." He tips his tiny hat as if it were a real cowboy hat, but it's as awkward as a horse with a shorn tail trying to flick a fly.

"Oh, no, Hope, you've got enough on your plate. Leave this to me. We'll be fine." Miss Dolly spies me standing there and stretches that plastic smile even wider. "And if we have questions, I'm sure our sweet Paige here can answer them for us. Isn't that right?"

Our sweet Paige? I'm not *her* anything. I open my mouth

to say so, but Mom beats me to it. "That's a wonderful idea. Paige, could you show Miss Dolly and Mr. Ferro around?"

I sigh. Well, I suppose it's better to keep an eye on them. "Sure."

Mom opens her mouth like she wants to say more, but Miss Dolly's already leading Mr. Ferro off across the yard toward to toolshed. Then Miss Dolly calls over her shoulder, "Come along, Paige. Let's start over here."

As soon as they leave, Mom shrinks in on herself, her thin arms folded tight against her chest as if that could shield her from whatever changes Miss Dolly has planned. When Dad was here, she lit up a room—the sun to his moon—but now she almost hides in plain sight.

I glare at the shed where Miss Dolly's voice titters on about this and that, each of her words cheerfully snipping away at the strings that keep Mom upright.

With a sigh, Mom starts for the house, and Scotty turns to follow, but I touch his shoulder. "I think we need to give that guy a *real* welcome to the farm. Don't you think?"

"Welcome him? Why would . . ."

With a hard stare, I pretend to dump out a jar, then point a finger at the Dodge's open window.

Scotty's mouth forms a little O, and he grins. "I'll get them!"

"Don't let Mom see you. I'll stall Dolly and the spy."

He hares up the porch steps, and I catch up to the intruders just as the breeze picks up like it does almost every afternoon.

"Are all these tools still in use?" The spy gazes at Dad's tool wall.

"Heavens, no." Dolly laughs. "These relics? Look how old they are."

"We *do* use them." I ease into the doorway. "Grandpa uses every one of them, and Dad showed us how. They're not relics; they're useful."

"All of them?" Miss Dolly steps back and scans the wall.

Mr. Ferro watches me from under his silly hat and points to a pair of sheers on the wall. "You know how to use this?"

Was he serious? "Course I do. It's for sheering sheep."

"What about this one?" He taps a metal spike with a wooden handle at the top.

"It's a punch, an awl—you know, for poking holes in wood or leather." Was this a test?

"Ah, I see." His gaze travels down the length of the wall. "And you know how to use them all?"

"Sure. Don't you?"

"Actually, no." He shrugs. "I wish I did. I grew up in the city. If we needed repairs, we called maintenance. How old are you?"

"Twelve."

"The twelve-year-old kids I know wouldn't know what to do with all this any more than I do. Now cell phones and apps, on the other hand . . ."

"Then maybe they should spend more time on a farm and learn." What good are workin' hands if you don't know how to use them?

"Maybe."

"Trust me, a new owner could call a repairman out here whenever they wanted. It's nothing to worry about. Excuse me, dear." Miss Dolly wiggles her fingers to shoo me out of the toolshed. "To each their own, I suppose. Heavens, I thought all those belonged in a museum."

"A person should know how to fix things on their own farm." I back out of the way.

"I agree," Mr. Ferro says at the same time Miss Dolly says, "If it's still a farm."

I stand as tall as I can. "It *is* a farm. It's *our* farm."

Miss Dolly smiles. "Oh, don't worry. I've got your family's best interest at heart. Trust me. I didn't mean to upset you. If you need a break, I can show Asher around."

Her voice is so sweet, I half expect honey to start dripping out of thin air between us, but she's not foolin' me. She just wants to get rid of me so she can sneak around doing who knows what to our place.

"I'm stayin'."

"Wonderful. Lead on." Dark stubble frames Mr. Ferro's white-toothed grin, and I'm pretty sure I detect a little smolder mixed up in that smile of his, but a fox can ooze charm all day long and it still won't make him a rabbit.

I lead them to a small outbuilding and slide the wooden bolt on the door before shoving it open. A single unlit bulb dangles in the center of the dusty cement room. As Dolly and her spy darken the doorframe, I lead the way inside to a raised wooden platform and heave open a trapdoor.

"This here's the pump house, where all the well water comes from. Every time the water has a problem, we gotta climb down there to shut off the water valve before we can fix it." I jab my thumb at the black hole. "Just gotta get past the spiders first."

"You have to climb down there?" Miss Dolly peers over my shoulder at the trapdoor.

"You bet." I smile sweet as can be. "You can climb down if you want—you know, for the real personal tour."

"Ah, thank you, but I'm not dressed for it." Miss Dolly lifts one of her high heels. "I'll be better prepared next time. I ran straight here from the office today."

"Do you have trouble with the water often?" Mr. Ferro asks me.

"Oh, yes. Loads." At least twice that I can remember. That counts, right? "And the only way to turn off the valve is down there. It's not so bad if you brush the spiderwebs out of the way before you crawl through them. Course, there might be black widows. You never know. But their webs feel different—kinda stickier."

"Black widows?" Dolly squeaks, and I fight to keep the smile off my face.

"Sometimes. Mostly other spiders though. There's not too many, only a few dozen—Oh! Look at the size of that one crawling up here now. Don't know if I've ever seen one that big before."

I point to a cat-faced spider spinning threads in the center of the hole. "That one's so fat, I bet she's just bursting with eggs. Another couple weeks and we'll have hundreds of tiny spiders. Maybe thousands. It'll be like a spider hotel in here with little eight-legged babies running everywhere."

"Thousands?" The color drains out of Dolly's face so quick, it's like she's sprung a leak.

"Yep." I spy a knot of webbing overhead in the rafters and point. "There's gobs of spiders in those webs, and probably loads more wandering around without webs, like jumping spiders—they're my favorite. You know, the real hairy spiders that follow you with their beady little eyes whenever you walk by."

Dolly ducks and covers her hair like there's a whole swarm of bats overhead. "I'm really not good with spiders. I think maybe—"

"You might not be good with 'em, but I am." I grab a stick and reach toward the cat-faced spider. "If you want a closer look, I can get it for you. She'll have her web rebuilt in no time if I just—"

Dolly drops her clipboard, bolts for the door, and stops in the middle of the grass, shivering like a spooked colt.

"Let's not disturb it." Mr. Ferro touches my shoulder. "I think we can see well enough from here."

He flicks on his phone's flashlight and shines it into the hole.

Past the shimmering spider threads, pipes with shut-off valves sprout from large blue holding tanks in the bottom of the cement room. The light hovers right over the spider resting with her banded legs sprawled out in the middle of the web.

Her tan, enormous butt curves up into two little points on ei-ther side like little ears on a kitty's head. Scotty likes to remind me that it's not actually a butt, it's an abdomen, but whatever.

"He doesn't look hairy." Mr. Nosey-Spy-Man inspects my spider.

"She." I gently close the trapdoor so I don't hurt her. "Boys are smaller. It's the girls that are huge. And cat faces aren't hairy."

"I see." He picks up Miss Dolly's clipboard and hands it to her when we join her outside.

Her voice squeaks, so she clears her throat and tries again. "Ah, I think we've seen enough of the pump house for one day. Shall we move on?"

"You bet." I almost skip as we leave the building. "Follow me."

Maybe running these intruders off won't be near as hard as I thought. Mr. Ferro kept his cool, but fancy Miss Dolly doesn't seem to like my pump house spiders very much at all. Fact is, I bet she never wants to step foot in there again.

A sharp edge tugs on my smile.

Perfect!

CHAPTER TWELVE

Trained Attack-Grasshoppers

It's a little weird to be walking across my barnyard with two city ducklings on my heels, but Scotty's depending on me to stall, so I'll be the best dang tour guide ever.

"Do you use the well water for the fields?" Mr. Ferro asks.

"Some farms do, but we got canals for that." I lead them around the barn and up a slope, where a soft hiss teases our ears, rising from a *shhhhhh* to a roar as we near the culvert junction. Falling water breaks the canal's mirror surface, spilling over the top of a concrete wall into white, churning froth below. Headgates jut up from the start of three new canals like underwater sliding doors guarding their tunnel entrances.

Tapping one of the tall, threaded rods rising up from the center of each headgate wheel, I touch the square metal frame with a toe as I explain. "When it's our water turn, we come out here in the middle of the night, step out over the dark water onto the frame like this, and grab the wheel to crank open the headgates."

"In the dark?" Dolly asks. "Why so late?"

"'Cause when there's frost, we gotta turn on the pump and run the sprinklers to keep the garden from freezing. It's real spooky at night. Can't see hardly anything. Real easy to fall in if you're not careful."

"Where's the water from?" Mr. Ferro leans against a head-gate and peers back along the ribbon of water.

"Somewhere way upstream this connects to the Snake River. That's where our water comes from." I *could* say that Kimana's dad told me the river's *real* Shoshone name is Biagaweit, that the river begins in Yellowstone National Park, and that all these water skippers coulda floated by herds of buffalo on their way here.

But I don't.

The only thing *I* want him to know is how much people like him don't belong here.

Miss Dolly and Mr. Ferro talk about water rights and whatever while I watch a water skipper row its little heart out at the crest of the waterfall, trying not to go over. Ten bucks says he's drop-dead tired, but he keeps swimming, because what else is there for him to do but try?

I know what that's like.

Mr. Ferro leans over the pit of roiling water, peeking down inside the culverts. "I've been to farms in countries where they barely get rain. They'd think water like this is a miracle."

"Shouldn't lean out like that. One slip and you'd be down

in the junction. Get stuck against one of them headgates un-derwater with all that suction, and you're a goner. A whole tractor couldn't pull you loose before you drown."

"Right." Mr. Ferro pats the square metal frame and backs away.

"Yep. It'd be just you and the leeches till they shut the wa-ter off somewhere up there."

"Leeches?" Miss Dolly eyes the canal.

"Sure! Have you ever seen a leech? They're all slimy and dark. If you lie on your belly and put your arm in the water, you might could catch one. I could hold your clipboard for you, if you wanna try." Not that I've ever actually seen leeches in the canals—usually just crawdads and water skippers—but the water's all murky today, so who knows? There might even be piranhas and alligators in there.

Not really, but the idea makes me smile anyway.

Miss Dolly's phone buzzes. "I'm afraid I need to take this, but please, continue."

While she talks, I lead them over to the silo. "Stuff out here is real dangerous. If you climb up into one of these and the grain shifts, it's a death trap."

"Trap like trapdoor, or . . . ?" he asks.

"Like quicksand. One second you're standing on top, and then something gives inside and *woosh!* A thousand pounds of grain's over your head with no space for breathing."

"Sounds dangerous." He looks the silo up and down, but doesn't seem near worried enough.

"It is. You should stay away from silos. Like, *way* away.

Better just stay off the farm altogether to make sure you're safe."

He's still as calm as a dandelion seed floating on the breeze, so I push a bit more. "All this stuff is dangerous. You could get stepped on by a thousand-pound bull, or squished by a tractor, or get caught in machinery—especially if you're wearing some floofy loose thing around your neck." I stab a thumb at Dolly's frilly scarf. "You'd lose your head farming with somethin' like that on."

"I doubt she'd wear that to actually farm here."

Miss Dolly sets her phone on her clipboard and smooths her dress with her other hand. "Very true. As I said, I came straight from the office—*in* my office clothes. I'm a professional."

"So am I." I might not look like much in my jeans and shirt next to her pretty black dress, but my clothes were made for workin'. Hers belong behind glass.

"Do you know what all this equipment is?" Mr. Ferro asks.

"Sure." I stuck to Dad tighter than his own shadow. "I know every machine, what it's for, and when we use it." It was kind of a game: to puzzle out the next tool Dad needed and have it in hand before he could ask for it. Sometimes doctor shows on TV are like that, with the nurse handing the doctor one tool after another, but instead of wounds, we have repairs—with grease instead of blood.

"Let's keep going, shall we?" Miss Dolly strides toward Milkshake's barn, but I run ahead and spread my arms wide in front of them both.

"My cow is getting ready to calve in there."

"Oh, we're not interested in the cow. Just the building. Right, Asher?"

"If it's part of her family's life, I'm interested."

The last thing Milkshake needs is a bunch of people gawking at her. "It's better if you don't. You could stress her."

"Alright, how about in there?" She points at the chicken barn, but I shake my head. I don't want these guys anywhere near Royal.

"Better not. The chickens stir up a bunch of dust and feathers that would wreck your dress. Besides, it's just a building same as the others."

The spy peers into the gloom of the chicken barn but stays put. "What sorts of birds do you see around here? Any pheasants or quail?"

"Loads." I inch toward the house, hoping with all my heart that Scotty's got the job done.

Mr. Ferro scans the barns and equipment again, eyes lingering on rooflines and treetops. "What about peacocks?"

My body zings like I touched a hot wire. Why would he even ask that? The only way he could know about Royal is if he really, truly was a spy. I clear my throat and think hard and fast. "Um, peacocks are not native to this area."

"But have you seen any? Maybe one flying by?"

I hate being cornered into a lie, so I sidestep it all together. "I'm pretty sure I'd know the difference between a peacock and a chicken. And chickens don't fly."

"That's not what I meant." He looks like he's gonna say more, but Miss Dolly beats him to it.

"I've been told the interior of the chicken barn is in excellent condition. It'll be better once the animals are gone, of course. A picturesque example of country living."

They take a step forward, but I slide into their path again and mash a fake smile on. "If you really want to, I can show you, but skunks love it in there. There's probably one in there right now. They eat eggs, you know, and young chickens. Even bees, sometimes. Skunks are murder on Mom's hives. I usually stay away from 'em, but if you really want to go see, we can."

"Wait, you have skunks inside?" Dolly stops.

"Oh, yes. Loads and loads of skunks have been in here."

"You're pulling our leg." Mr. Ferro gives me a sideways look, but I lift my chin.

"Am not. We got a huge ninja-skunk who springs live traps and eats the bait eggs without getting caught. He's super sneaky, but he stinks bad enough to make your eyes water. We call him Reeker."

"But he's not a pet." Dolly's fingers tighten around her silver scarf.

"Nope. He's wild. Liable to spray at anything that comes close." I wave my hand back and forth in front of my face. "Oh boy, does he smell. It lingers forever. Just walking into a building that's been skunked is enough to make your clothes stink. Half the time we can hardly breathe out here because the smell's so bad. Fresh skunk smells worse than burnt rubber."

I look Mr. Ferro straight in the eye. "You ever smelled something so bad, it makes burnt rubber smell good?"

"Uhh . . ." He hesitates.

"That cloud of stink oil? It'll never come out of those fancy clothes of yours. Skunk lasts forever."

"Maybe you can show us the corrals instead?" Dolly asks.

"You bet." I make sure to point out every smelly, dirty thing we pass all the way to the house.

Mr. Ferro crouches down to look at something in the grass, but is up again quick, one hand in his pocket, the other on the rim of his worthless hat. "Are you sure there's not another reason you don't want us in there?"

What kind of a question is that? "Sure, I'm sure."

"Well, Miss Paige. It's been enlightening. I look forward to our next visit."

Next visit? No thank you. "I've got loads more spots full of skunks, poop, and compost to show you. *Real* smelly."

They keep to the path on their way to the cars, so I slip around the other side of the house to beat them to the front. I look for Scotty, but he's nowhere.

Dolly and her spy almost make it to the front yard when Mom comes out onto the porch, a tray of glasses in hand. "Would you like some water?"

"I'd love some." Mr. Ferro steps up beside her and takes a glass. "Thank you."

Scotty slips out the screen door behind them, and I raise my eyebrows and give him *the look*, but he hops down the steps and doesn't meet my eyes. I keep watching while Mom, Dolly, and Mr. Ferro make small talk.

The truck seems the same as always. Window partway down. No jar anywhere. Maybe Scotty did, or maybe he didn't. I can't tell. I bite my lip and watch.

Next time, we'll have some kinda plan to really get them good.

"Thank you for the water, but we really need to get back." Dolly leans her head toward the truck. "Well, *I* need to anyway. Meetings, you know."

"Well, it was nice to meet you anyway." Mom takes the empty glasses from Mr. Ferro and Dolly. "Please come back and visit anytime."

"I believe I'll take you up on that," Mr. Ferro says. "I think sometimes I get a better feel for a story if I can work alongside my subjects and get my hands dirty, so to speak." The spy smiles with that smolder thing again, and I scowl at him.

"Oh, we'll be back." Miss Dolly presses a hand to her chest. "I'm making you my top priority."

They step off the porch and walk to the truck, and my heart skips worse than a zippy baby goat kicking its heels.

Scotty's focused on petting T-Rex and giving no hints at what he's done, or not.

Mr. Ferro opens the door for Miss Dolly, who waves at Mom like some kinda beauty queen, and a tiny bit of guilt worms its way inside my head. I try to squash it flat, but it niggles at me. Somehow I didn't expect *her* to sit in the truck first, and she's all done up pretty . . .

Dolly calls, "Don't you worry. I'll have this place sold in no time! I've found several charming houses and a duplex in town that would suit your family size and budget. I'll show you pictures next time I come by."

Sold in no time? Duplex? Well, consider that guilt smushed. I narrow my eyes. I gotta remember: this is war.

Mr. Ferro slams the passenger door shut . . . and the screaming begins.

A blur of tiny bodies and wings ricochets everywhere inside the truck. Papers fly across the cab, smack the steering wheel, and fall out of sight as Dolly flails her arms and beats her scarf, a crazed whirlwind in a one-sided cat fight.

Scotty's eyes go wide, and he claps his hands over both ears as Dolly's squeals become high-pitched screeches.

Mr. Ferro, who had been halfway around to the other side of the truck, dashes back. "What is it? Are there bees in there?"

"Bees in the truck? Heavens!" Mom rushes to help as a white-faced Mr. Ferro wrenches the door open and reaches for Dolly—but she's already tumbling out, falling to one knee as she howls, rips the scarf off her neck, and slaps at her hair.

Like a miniature, flying stampede, the insect horde launches in a hundred different directions.

"Attack of the arthropods!" Scotty giggles, and I cover his mouth.

Like a blizzard of antennae and tiny legs, grasshoppers bounce off the windshield, smack into the doorframe, and whir overhead with wings of bright red, orange, and green.

"Where did they all come from?" Mom ducks as a grasshopper launches off Dolly's head.

A big one creeps along the brim of Mr. Ferro's little hat, and he brushes away another one snuggling up to his shirt collar.

"Get them off!" Dolly screams, then clamps her mouth shut as a grasshopper bounces off her lips.

Grandpa shuffles over quick as Dolly smashes her clipboard against the ground, whips it through the air, and beats it against the truck.

His grease-stained hands catch the board mid-swing before it hits Mr. Ferro's leg. Grandpa drops the clipboard to the ground and helps Miss Dolly to her feet. The frilly scarf lies forgotten on the ground, and her hair sticks dang near straight up like one of those heavy metal guys on Dad's old CDs.

Mom and Mr. Ferro gather close, and everyone stands in the yard, watching the last of the grasshoppers crawl, hop, and fly away.

Scotty and I take big breaths, trying to avoid the giggles. If Mom catches us smiling, we'll be dead meat.

Grandpa clears his throat, or at least tries to. "Scotty, how about you and Paige give this fella's truck a once-over—get rid of any leftover hoppers."

"Sure thing, Grandpa." Scotty snatches a paper bag from the porch, sidesteps Miss Dolly, and skips to the truck like there was ice cream inside. I hold the bag for him while he crawls all over inside the cab, searching every nook and cranny.

Inside the truck, grasshoppers crawl under seats, sunbathe

on the dashboard, and skitter across the headrests. He finds, them under the pedals, on top of the steering wheel, and—somehow—inside the center console. Each time he hands me one, I shake the bag so the others fall down inside and I can stuff the new one in.

On the lawn, Mr. Ferro soothes Miss Dolly. "Maybe it's like those butterfly migrations you see on the internet."

"Where are they migrating to?" she shrills. "The glove box?"

Grandpa eyes the bug-filled bag. "Could be you got a female stuck in the truck when you pulled in and all those males followed her in."

"Oh! Moths can do that." Scotty shifts from one foot to the other. "Female lepidoptera secrete hormones that tell potential mates how to find them."

"These aren't moths." Dolly runs a hand over her hair. "I feel like they're still on me. Are they on me?"

"No, I think you got them all off." Mom pats her on the back. "Would you like to go inside and freshen up? The bathroom's right down the hall."

"I would. Thank you." Dolly sniffs and limps toward the house, mumbling under her breath. "Never in all my life . . . Grasshoppers attacked me. My dress! I need a dry cleaner."

The screen door slams behind her, and Grandpa drawls, "I've seen a lot of things in my time, but trained attack-grasshoppers ain't one of them."

"Attack of the grasshoppers—modern plague or biowarfare?" Mr. Ferro muses. "Sounds like an excellent tabloid headline."

Mom shakes her head and smiles. "I'd pay to read that story."

"It'd fit right in with all those aliens making crop circles and abducting cows." Grandpa winks at Mom. "Pesky aliens."

Mom laughs—*really* laughs—and it's like when the sun breaks after days of endless fog. Fits of laughter bubble up inside her, and just when she pulls it back in, she looks at Grandpa and it starts all over again.

It's the first I've seen a lick of Mom—the real Mom—in months. Maybe Kimana is right, and all we really need is time.

Something inside me throbs like the first shovel of fill-dirt smacking the bottom of a great empty hole.

She laughs again.

Basking in the warmth of that beautiful sound, Scotty and I watch her, and we laugh too.

CHAPTER THIRTEEN

Stuck

Miss Dolly took forever to come out of the bathroom, but seeing Mom smile again was worth the wait. Course, then Mr. Ferro got to talking with Mom and Grandpa about all sorts of things, like the countries he's been to and places he's lived. Seems like he spends so much time gone, he only owns an apartment for fun. His kids are plenty busy too, always on the go, and never without their phones. I suppose he might be a reporter like he says he is, but I still think he's got more of a spy sneak going on. I mean, he says he used to own a plane. Why would anyone need one of their own when there's perfectly good airplanes flying overhead all the time? Unless they wanted to sneak stuff around right past security with no one the wiser. I left when he asked Mom about where she thought we might move.

Finally, he left and Dolly left and everything was better,

until Miss Dolly's workers came and put up a new sign—this time with metal posts.

I admit I might have thought about putting a dead fish in their truck when the sign guys pulled in, but no amount of bug hormones could explain that away. Besides, they drove off too quick for me to do anything except think about it.

ᥱ ᥒ

The next morning, Mom got up before chores and made us hash browns out of the baked potatoes I left in the fridge. She must've been feeling pretty good after all that laughing yesterday.

Sure does make choring better to start the day with real food. We got everyone fed in no time at all—I even filled the watering can again for Mateo's basket. All in all, it's a great morning. I'm not even that tired.

With the mower deck on the red ol' Massey Ferguson, the engine rumbling underneath me, and the tractor wheel in my hands, I'm mowing down the rest of last year's sweet corn. It's one of my favorite jobs, 'cause running things over with a tractor is just plain cool. Sometimes, I imagine the cornstalks trying to flee.

No! The tractor is coming. Run! Aaaah!

But I mow them all anyway like I'm Godzilla of the corn.

It's fun, and way less boring.

Don't judge.

After a few hours of me running the Massey and Grandpa

discing the next field over in the Deere, Grandpa heads back to the house, and I finish my field and follow.

Scotty and T-Rex are waiting beside Mom when I hop down off the tractor.

"Good timing, hon," Mom says. "Grandpa and I are running errands after we meet with Miss Dolly. We'll be back around four. Can you think of anything we need from town?"

"Milk?" I wipe the sweat off my forehead with the back of my arm. "And we're out of apples."

"Pizza," Scotty says. "We're definitely out of pizza."

"We'll see," Mom says as she walks to Patches and opens the door. "Be good."

After Mom and Grandpa head out, Scotty and I make the rounds and check the animals. The pigs are fed already, but they keep nosing the fence by us instead of digging into the mash like they should.

"I think they want strawberries." Scotty rubs his fingers against his thumbs, then squats down to give T-Rex a good rub. "Do you think we should give them some? I could get a few jars of Mom's homemade jelly."

"Only if we want Mom to kill us." He's not wrong though; the pigs would love strawberry jelly.

"Miss Dolly didn't like the grasshoppers."

"I think you're right." I grin.

"You think she hates us?"

I chew on that as we near the front yard. "I don't think so."

Scotty's already halfway up the stairs when we hear a low

moan from the barn. Deep and low, laced with pain, a moan like that could only come from one place.

"Milkshake!" And I'm running.

"Wait!" Scotty calls, but I'm already across the yard, my feet flying over the dust to the barn. I skid to a stop at Milkshake's stall, and my already thundering heart lurches at the sight of her. A *lot* has changed since last night.

Her sides are slick with sweat, her head hangs down as she sways from side to side, and her tail is stuck straight out behind her. This calf is coming right now, and it's coming fast.

"Is she calving?" Scotty runs in with T-Rex as I round the side of the stall to get a better look at Milkshake's tail.

"Yeah." I duck under the rail.

Milkshake's water sack hangs out the back under her tail like a giant pink bubble about the size of a basketball. A low moan rolls out of her throat as another contraction hits, and her spine arches, her straight tail quivering as her whole belly lifts, flexing hard.

I hold my breath as she strains, and I sag against the rail when the contraction finally ends.

With panting breaths, Milkshake shudders, her sweating legs and head shaking from stress and pain. She's had calves before without any trouble, but I don't remember her ever shivering like this.

"Is she okay?"

I try to ignore the quaver in Scotty's voice and choke down my own panic. "I don't know. Sometimes it takes a while. She might be alright."

But after just a few minutes, I'm sure something's not right. "I'm gonna check her. We can winch the calf out if we need to. I've helped Dad do it loads of times. This is no different."

Except everything is different. Helping Dad at calving time was always exciting and wonderful—one of the best times of the year. Even when we lost one, we knew we'd done our best because Dad said so. And when we brought one back from the brink of death, it was better than winning a million trophies.

Without him, life and death is all on me—and the whole thing is terrifying.

"Easy, Milkshake. I won't hurt you," I murmur, rubbing her side gently as I ease around to her shivering tail. Still encased in a pink bubble, a single pale hoof hangs out the back.

I bite my lip. There should be two hooves, not one. I prod, trying to see if maybe it's just hung up on the side, and jump back when the water sack bursts, drenching my whole arm. Where there should be two hooves coming out together with the calf's nose resting on top—sort of like the calf is diving into a pool—there's only one hoof, with no head in sight.

"It's not coming out right." I try to think. Maybe it's just folded over. I'd helped pull other hooves down before, right? Right. I can do this.

Milkshake moans and pants, and I wait for the contraction to pass before I reach to feel inside her. Up to my elbow, I feel what might be a hoof, but then she sidesteps and the leg slips out further—and I see what I should have noticed before. This isn't a front hoof. It's the back leg.

The calf is breach.

"Oh no," Scotty whispers.

My lungs pinch like I'm caught between cogs and a chain, but I chant inside my head: *We've done this. I can do this.*

I feel around, trying to find the other leg, but Milkshake backs up, and I barely have time to get out of the way before she slams into the side of the stall so hard that dust falls from the rafters.

Her moans rise in volume, and she bellows so loud that Scotty covers his ears. "Get out, Paige! She's gonna stomp you!"

I climb the rail and sit with one leg on either side as Milkshake turns in the stall, hunching and straining, sweat running down her sides in rivers.

I start to hop off the rail, but Scotty grabs my pant leg with both fists. "Don't go back in. Please. Don't go."

"It's fine, Scotty. That was my fault. I forgot to tie her halter up. I'll get the lead, tie her up, and everything will be fine. You'll see."

"No. If she hits you, you'll die. Crushed people die. We need Grandpa."

"Grandpa's gone to town, and Milkshake's not going to crush me."

Another contraction hits and Milkshake kicks out, her hoof hammering into the stall wall as she bawls.

Scotty clamps his hands over his ears and bares his teeth. "You don't know that. Nobody knows that. Nobody gets dead on purpose!"

T-Rex whines and nudges his boy's side, but Scotty's too wound up to notice.

I swing my other leg inside the stall. "Dad already showed me what to do. He said it's *my* job to take care of things."

"It doesn't matter what he said," Scotty wails. "Dad couldn't save himself from getting dead either!"

I grip the rail as the world rocks beneath me, and I blink like my life depends on it, because it does. What happened to Dad was not his fault. And it sure as heck doesn't make what he taught me any less real. My world stands on the building blocks he taught me, and I will not let anyone—not even Scotty—take that from me. "I said I've got this. You don't have to be scared of every little thing!" I don't mean to yell, but I do.

Scotty goes still. "Dad also said we gotta do what we think is right."

"Then I guess we'll both do what we have to do." I pretend not to care as Scotty runs out of the barn, T-Rex behind him.

I slide off the stall, grab the lead rope, and clip it to her halter before tying it to the rail. "C'mon, girl. Let's get this done."

It takes me a minute to grab the calf-puller off its hooks on a beam, hoist the curved part over my shoulder, and drag it to the side of Milkshake's stall. Straw bunches up as I shove it under the bottom rail and then climb over to pull it the rest of the way in.

With a gentle voice, I coo to her, "It's okay, Milkshake. Just let me find that other leg and we'll get this calf right out. You don't need to be scared."

As I ease over to her rump to try for that other leg, I tell myself I'm not scared, but my heart keeps trying to jump straight out of my chest.

The tiny, new hoof is more whitish-gray than black, and the wet leg hangs out past the first joint, almost to the hock. I slide my hand up the dark red fur to the flank inside, but before I can grab the other hoof, Milkshake swivels again and kicks out from the pain.

The wallboard beside my foot cracks in two.

She shudders so hard, I'm scared she'll fall, but she keeps her feet and lets out a whine that ends in a grunt of pain as another contraction takes her.

This time, I go around front and look her straight in the eye, talking to her all the while and stroking her head. "C'mon, girl. Let me help. You can't do this on your own. Dad taught me what to do. Don't be scared. I'm here. Okay?"

Her beautiful brown eyes blink slowly, and she takes a big breath as if to say, "Let's do this."

Letting my hand trail over her damp hide so she knows where I am, I walk alongside and behind her again. With my arm up almost to my shoulder, I catch the other hoof and pull it through, careful not to tear her.

Milkshake strains, but the calf won't budge.

Right. Time for the calf-puller.

The whole thing is shaped like a giant slingshot. I push the Y part up against her thighs and strap the rubber band part over the top of her hips to keep it all from falling down. This part is so familiar, I can almost hear Dad's voice guiding me.

"Okay, Paige, now make a loop and half hitch above the ankle and then do it again just above the hooves. Don't forget to keep the chain right over the toes, so you don't hurt the joints."

When both feet are chained, I hook the loose ends up to the handle of the puller, but before I can crank the lever, Mr. Rivas's Chevy pulls up with Mateo riding shotgun.

The doors fly open, and Scotty jumps out, chattering all the way from the truck to the barn, as if his brain is stuck on overdrive. " . . . and Paige said not to call, but complications are more probable with a breach calf, and an eighteen-hundred-pound cow has got to be at least as dangerous as a horse, which can kick with two thousand pounds of force per square inch, so . . ."

Mr. Rivas and Mateo step up onto the stall rail, watching me work.

"I got this." I grip the long handle with one hand and pump the lever carefully back and forth with the other.

Mr. Rivas climbs in, eyes the chains, and braces the handle on my calf-puller. "Ándale, sure. You do it. Go on."

I don't want him in my stall. This is my place; just me and my dad come in here.

"Do you need help?" Mateo asks, and I shake my head.

"I can do it!" Gripping with both hands, I slowly pump the lever up and down, the chain dragging the tiny hooves further out into the world.

I breathe deep and block Mateo out. His dad out. Scotty out. I have to focus. I have to remember everything Dad taught me.

Every inch forward pulls me back in time, to the hundred times I've done this with Dad. Spring births are always a miracle, but when you have to fight for them, pull them into the world, it's different. Dad always says it's like shaking hands with God—*I'll do my best, and you do the rest.*

His voice echoes inside my head. *Easy, easy. A little more pressure.*

With every contraction, I push the lever, cranking back and forth. Hope flutters in my chest as the legs emerge bit by bit. When Milkshake rests, I slip my hand up the calf's legs as far as I can reach and rub around, keeping it all slippery.

Don't let her tear, Dad would say. *Gentle now. Focus.*

Milkshake bellows and grunts, her breath coming in gasps, then her sides lift and strain. Quickly, I pump the lever, keeping tension on the feet, but letting her do most of the work. The calf comes faster and faster. First the thighs, then hips, and tail.

Stay in the moment, Dad says. *She's counting on you. Don't give up on her.*

The bottom of the rib cage peeks out, and Scotty cries, "It's coming!"

Let it come on its own if you can. Watch her close. Help as much as she needs and no more. Dad stands beside me, close, just in case.

"Wait." His hand darts forward, helping make space for the newborn. "Okay. Go ahead."

Almost done. Everything is exactly as it should be: just me and my dad guiding a new life into the world.

Shaking hands with God.

I smile up at my dad . . . but Mr. Rivas smiles back.

Mr. Rivas.

Not my dad. Never my dad.

"Oh!" I choke, my eyes darting to the side and back. "Where—"

"Ándale, Paige. You're doing so well." He touches my hand on the lever, gently urging me to crank it again. My hand shakes under his, and it's all wrong, but I pull because I must.

The calf doesn't move.

I pull the lever again, but Milkshake bellows, and everything stops.

The calf is stuck.

CHAPTER FOURTEEN

Milkshake

Mateo's head pops up. "Is she stuck?"

"Oh gosh, oh gosh." Scotty twists the collar of his shirt hard enough to leave a rash.

I push up inside, trying to feel if maybe a leg or something is hung up against the cow's hip bones, but it's all so tight I can't hardly reach anything. Think, *think!* What would Dad do?

He was here with me, but he wasn't. And now everything is too fast, too bright, too loud. It's supposed to be my dad standing here, not someone else.

But Milkshake needs me. She pants and grunts, a soft groan of pain and fear.

"I can do this. I can do this." But in that moment, my brain is stuck harder than the calf. I know what to do—if I could just think—but with Mateo and Mr. Rivas right there watching and Scotty twisting his hands all together, the next step teeters on the edge of my brain, and all I can think of is how much I wish Dad really was here.

My voice shakes, "Uh, we need to . . . need to . . ."

Without a word, Mr. Rivas angles the handle down to the ground and the calf shifts, sliding forward another inch. He reaches past me and cranks the lever, then drops the handle to the ground once more, and this time, the calf rotates just enough. I've seen Dad do it before. I *could* have done it. But it all happened so fast, I hadn't had time to think, and now it's over and done.

"That's it." Mateo smacks the top rail. "It's free."

"I know." As the handle comes back up the second time, I crank the lever fast to take up the slack.

With one long desperate bellow, Milkshake's front knees buckle, and the limp calf slides to the ground with a wet slurp.

A heartbeat later, I'm on my knees, and Mateo jumps in beside me to wipe the slime away from the calf's nose and mouth, helping me rub it down with fresh straw.

Mr. Rivas pulls the quick-release knot to free Milkshake's head, and I bite my lip. I shoulda done that as soon as she fell. I knew that too. He's rushing me; that's all. Nothing else is gonna slip by me. I rub the calf harder.

Finally, the calf lets out a pitiful bawl and rolls its head, its legs flailing as it struggles to right itself.

"Woo!" Scotty's fists pump. "He's okay!"

A knot wedges tight in my throat as relief wars with shame inside me. I'm so glad they're both okay, but I could have done it alone—*should* have done it alone.

135

"You've got a little bull." Mateo nudges my shoulder, and I nod, 'cause no words can squeak out anyway.

Patting the wobbly little guy one more time, I go to Milkshake, my hands smoothing her quivering hide. "You did good, momma. It's a boy. You've got a boy."

Sweat stains her forehead and runs down her jawline. Flecks of foam cling to her mouth, and her nostrils flare wide with every deep breath. Hot air washes over my forearms as she rests her chin on my hands. When her eyes meet mine, there's no panic. No pain. Only trust.

She doesn't know I almost failed her. She only knows I tried and that all is well.

When her breathing evens, we help her to her feet, and back away as she cleans her calf, her long tongue rasping over the little one till his hair sticks out in a dozen bad cowlicks going every which way.

T-Rex's tail wags a steady beat while he leans against Scotty, watching through the rails as a tiny bawling voice is answered by Milkshake's deep rumbling moo.

Mr. Rivas ducks between the rails and pats Mateo's back. "She is good now, eh?"

"She sure is!" Scotty beams at him as if Mr. Rivas was the one who pulled the calf. "Thanks for coming."

"*No pasa nada.*" Mr. Rivas waves off Scotty's praise and walks to his truck.

Mateo stays beside me and tries to catch my eye. "On the way here, I saw some dogs out by the juniper grove."

"Are you sure they weren't Kimana's dogs?"

"No. These were new. A pack of four or five." His eyes go soft when he looks at my calf. "Just keep an eye out."

"Thanks. I will."

Beyond him, Mr. Rivas waits in the driver's seat, one elbow out the window, the other hand resting on the wheel. He catches me looking and nods.

After a few steps, Mateo turns back to me. "Oh, and Paige?"

"Yes?"

Looking me straight in the eye, he touches his heart. "You did good. You should be proud."

"Thanks." I give a half-hearted wave as he leaves. I turn to watch my cows. Even though I know they're both alright, I don't really let myself believe it until the wobbly calf finally gets to his feet, latches on, and suckles with greedy little slurps. Only then do I slip outside to the spigot and wash my hands and arms down with well water cold enough to sting.

"I'm gonna check on Royal." Scotty tugs my shirt, telling me to follow him, then skips on ahead.

"I'll come later. I want to watch the calf a while."

"Okay. It's a good thing Mr. Rivas came, don't you think?"

"I didn't need his help!" I holler after him, but he's already halfway to the chicken barn. From the doorway of Milkshake's barn, I watch him run away, and I let the breeze play with my hair and tug at my shirt.

I kick a dirt clod across the road and watch as it soars, bounces, and breaks apart, skittering in a dozen different directions.

The whole calf-pulling spins in my head like blades on a windmill, repeating 'round and 'round. One second I was there, in the perfect moment, with Dad right by my side, and the next he was gone, and it was just me and Mr. Rivas, and I didn't know what to do. I might have been able to help Milkshake on my own—I've seen it done a hundred times—but I couldn't think, and now I don't know for sure. I'll *never* know. I only know I hesitated when it mattered most.

I close my eyes and try to focus on the facts.

Milkshake's okay. The calf is okay. Scotty and me are both okay. Everything is fine. Dad would understand.

I repeat it in my head until I almost believe it.

An hour later, after the calf settled down for a nap, Scotty and I lie propped up on our elbows, watching Royal eat a piece of bread. His sleek blue neck shimmers each time he bobs down, pecking with his black shiny beak. So far, we've discovered he loves bread, berries, ants, beetles, grasshoppers, worms, flower petals, leaves, and fruit—especially melons. He eats melon rinds right down till the outer skin curls inward because every bit of the flesh has been pecked away.

"You think he's got a family nearby?" Scotty's freckled cheek rests against his fist and a half-chewed straw dangles from his lips.

"Maybe. He sure made a ruckus the other day."

"They're *supposed* to make noise." He lifts a finger for each point. "They honk when danger is near, they cry for mating and other reasons, they rattle their tail feathers, they—"

"I know, but most of the time he's so quiet. Maybe he's just hiding, you know, so he won't attract predators while he's hurt."

Royal watches us as we talk, his head cocked one way to focus his shiny black eye at me, then the other way for Scotty.

"You think he'd help run Miss Dolly off if he was better?" asks Scotty.

I raise my eyebrow. "Well, you did say peacocks kill any snakes and spiders they find in their territory . . ."

T-Rex swivels his head and wags his tail as Mom and Grandpa pull up in the truck, the bed filled with plastic totes and boxes.

"Come on." I tug Scotty's jeans and motion for him to follow me.

We crawl off the back of the stack and slide around the back wall by the coop. By the time Mom and Grandpa unload some totes and spot us, we're dumping a sack of chicken scratch into the feed bins.

Scotty raises an eyebrow at me, and I nod. It should be safe to say hello from here.

"Mom! Guess what?" Scotty says, running up and taking a tote from her. "Milkshake had her calf today."

"I heard," Mom says.

Grandpa clears his throat. "Javier Rivas said you did a right fine job, Paige. Kept a cool head and pulled that calf right on out."

"What I want to know is why we had to hear it from Javier." Mom gives me *the look*. "Why didn't you call us? Where's your phone?"

I shrug. "It's at the house, in the kitchen maybe. You guys were in town, and Mr. Rivas is right next door, so Scotty called him."

"You could have texted." She brushes past me.

I sigh. There's only so many times a person can say the same thing without being heard before it becomes pointless. "I don't text."

"Mateo texts," Scotty pipes up. "And Kimana texts."

"Yay for them. Doesn't anyone want to know about the calf?"

"A healthy young bull, I hear." Grandpa pats me on the back.

Finally! My shoulders relax. "Wait till you see him. He's got the cutest, curliest red coat ever, and he eats like his belly button's rubbing a blister on his backbone. He's great."

"I'm glad he's healthy, but my point is you shouldn't have had to do it at all." Mom sets Scotty's tote on top of hers. "Anything could have happened—you could have been hurt."

"It was fine, Mom. Really." *Drop it already.*

"Well, at least you won't have to worry about the cows much longer." She sidesteps as Grandpa puts another tote next to the others.

"What does that mean?" Milkshake isn't a worry to me. No more than T-Rex or Scotty. I raised her myself. If anything, she's my friend.

"I asked Javier to help get the pigs to the sale. He can do it tomorrow, but then he'll be busy for several days after that, so we've been talking about having a sale right here for the cattle and horses. We've had plenty of offers; that's for sure."

"You can't let him take the pigs. They've got piglets. It's not even time yet—the price won't be good until July. That's three months away!"

"Paige, I know." Mom keeps talking like it's all done already. "It has to happen, and I expect you to help."

"But we'll lose—"

"No buts. I know you think you know best, but you don't. Sometimes we have to make hard decisions. I need to know I can count on you."

I stare at her. She can't be serious.

"Well?" Mom prods.

"I keep my promises." But my oldest promise always comes first. Take care of the farm; take care of the family.

"Can I count on you or not?"

Woodenly, I nod. But inside, my brain is on fire. Every night she locks herself in her room and checks out like she's a hen sitting in the dark, shut off to everything—to us—until dawn. But dawn feels so far off, I've almost given up waiting for it. She's *always* been able to count on me. I'm the one that does chores and looks after everything when she's here but still gone.

I'm the one. Me.

While she sews and studies and hides, I'm the reason why

the animals are fed and happy, why everything is running like it should be.

I did that. Me.

It's not anything out of the ordinary either. Farm girls do this day in, day out. Dad did this every day of his life. I did it the week of his funeral and every day since. It's as natural as breathing. But Mom talks like it's something to run away from, or to let go. You don't let go of family. I promised I'd take care of them, and I am.

I try hard to let Mom's words splash and slide off me, raindrops on glass. She's just worried, like Scotty was. I know that.

"Do you see what I mean?" Mom murmurs to Grandpa. "We can't do this on our own. She could have been killed. We have to sell."

I'm her example for why we can't farm.

Me.

It's so unfair it makes me want to scream.

CHAPTER FIFTEEN

Count on Me

Stars cling to the sky when I wake the next morning, but I don't wait for the dawn. All night my dreams were full of stuck calves, Milkshake's pained bellows, Mom's voice saying, "We can't do this on our own," and Dad saying, "Don't give up on her. She's counting on you."

No more sleep for me tonight.

I get everyone fed and watered long before the sun breaks over the mountains, but I save Milkshake for last.

She lies on her side, her rusty-brown hide shadowed next to her calf's soft red curls. With bright eyes and perked ears, she tracks me as I walk to her empty feed trough.

"Hey, momma. Did you sleep better than me?" Fresh hay flakes crackle as I toss them in, filling her trough, then sprinkle a measure of grain on top.

Milkshake heaves herself to her feet, and the calf raises his head, blinking with long lashes.

With his momma rooting for grain, he tries out one leg and then another until he gains his feet and stands there all knobby knees and scrawny legs.

Milkshake moos, her mouth full of grain and hay. He answers with a tiny, "Mah!" and kicks up his feet in a little sideways hop.

Quivering, he flings his tail around as if to see what it does, then nuzzles her udder to nurse. Hard and fast, he thrusts his tiny muzzle up against her like quick punches, his pink tongue peeking out as he swallows.

"Oh, you're adorable."

At the corner of the stall, I slip between the rails and pull a manure fork in with me. It's sorta like a plastic pitchfork but for poop. Scooping and dumping into a wheelbarrow outside the stall, I clear all the soiled straw and spread fresh down.

The rake slides through the bars, and I prop it against the rail, then follow it through. All is well here. My cows are clean, fed, and safe.

I palm Dad's stone as I watch Milkshake and her calf. I rub my thumb over the bump-bump of the heart, then swirl into the groove in the middle. How many wishes did he make on this stone before he threw it in the wishfire with all of them attached?

I bring it to my lips and whisper my first wish. "Let him grow up healthy and strong."

The calf's tail waggles, and he bobs his head with happy smacking and sucking sounds.

I tuck my stone in my pocket and pat the rail once before

leaving. Tomorrow I'll probably move them out with the herd, but today, they get to be together, just the two of them. Safe and sound.

When I get back to the house, it's almost time to leave for school, but Mom's still in bed with the lights off.

"Mom?" I gently shake her shoulder. "Are you taking us to school?"

"Mmm-no," she mumbles but won't wake up. She curls in on herself, hugging Dad's pillow to her chest.

It's one of her dark days. Best let her be.

I tiptoe back out and ease the door shut before tapping on Grandpa's door. "Grandpa? Can we get a ride?"

Ten minutes later, Grandpa drives us to school in the truck, with me riding shotgun and Scotty riding cowboy-middle-hump-chump between us, his knees knocking the gearshift every time Grandpa shifts.

Country music teases my fingers into tapping against the doorframe, my elbow resting out the window, as we coast over gravel, then paved roads. The side mirror reflects bright morning sun, and the wind beats whatever red strands escape my braid against my face while we drive past wheel-lines kicking misty rainbows over the first crop of alfalfa. There was dew this morning, but no frost, and the world smells rich and earthy.

Every spring, it's a guessing game to see which crops are rotated to which fields. Potato fields are easy to tell, with baby seed potatoes hiding under long lines of dirt mounds. Sometimes when we drive past, the lines whisk by so fast they seem to stall and rush backwards like spokes on a wheel. Fall wheat is easy too, since it sprouts a few inches before winter and hibernates that way, waiting until spring to finish growing.

I spy corn peeking from a field Scotty swore we'd see in beans, but everyone's too tired to tease much this morning.

Used to be, Mom would have loads of dark days, and Grandpa took us to school all the time, but back around Christmas, she got a little better and took over the driving. Still, I'm glad Grandpa's our backup plan. He's like our old oak tree, rooted deep and steady. Always there.

Except—Dad was our rock, and it only took a tap on a phone screen to shatter stone and wrench him out of our lives. I shove that thought out of my head and rub my wishstone harder than I need to. *Make Grandpa safe, safe, safe.*

Grandpa catches me staring, and his caterpillar-eyebrows inch up. "What's going on in that head of yours, sweet pea?"

What I think is, *Are you going to leave us too?* But what I say is, "Um, I was wondering, in my class, we have to do a report on someone who made an impact on history and on our lives—and it can't be someone everybody knows, like Einstein. Can you think of anyone whose life affected yours?"

"Someone not well known?" He sucks his teeth. "Well, I'd normally say John Deere, but everyone knows his name, so I'd have to say Henry Blair. He invented and patented the first seed planter so farmers didn't have to plant each seed by hand anymore. I believe he was the second black man ever to own a patent. Had another one for something with cotton—another planter, I think."

"Why him?"

146

"Well, while everyone else had their noses rooting in the dirt, planting seeds one at a time because they didn't know any different, he went and raised his eyes long enough to see the problem and find a solution."

"So he was an inventor?"

"Yes, but more than that, he was practical. A man can only do so much dropping a seed into every hole. But automate that, and suddenly whole fields can be planted in a fraction of the time. He had the mind of an engineer. A real problem solver." He taps his forehead, then signals to turn off Yellowstone onto Tyhee Road. "I suppose he reminds me to stop and examine the problem."

"But wouldn't someone else have figured it out? Planting it all by hand would take forever."

"Maybe, but it's mighty hard to see the horizon with your face pressed to the ground."

"You don't have to have a planter to plant seeds," Scotty says, moving his knee out of Grandpa's way as he shifts again. "Formicidae spread seeds too."

"Formi-whats?" The gears grind as Grandpa coaxes the truck into first and eases into the drop-off loop at Tyhee Elementary.

"Formicidae—ants—can carry fifty times their own body weight and run almost three hundred meters an hour."

"That so?" Grandpa taps the wheel.

"And an average hundred-and-ten-pound human can carry almost a hundred and sixty pounds."

"Good to know," I say. I open the door and jump out so Scotty can scooch over.

Grandpa laughs. "Boy, if those forms-ants of yours start carrying humans around, I'm moving to the North Pole."

Scotty's mouth is stuck in fifth gear. "Oh no. Ants can't carry humans, but in a crisis, people sometimes gain unexpected strength and can lift extreme loads like cars, trucks, and tractors. Humans can be stronger than they ever imagined when there's no other choice." He drops to the asphalt and adjusts his backpack, but turns back for one more fact. "But on a regular basis, ants are always stronger. Also, the North Pole is a bad place to farm."

"Thanks for the lesson, buddy." I climb back in and shut the door, and Scotty marches off to the playground.

Grandpa and I drive in comfy silence, both of us listening to guitars strumming on the radio.

"So, you asked me, but who did you pick for your report?" Grandpa asks.

"Oh, I haven't decided." We stop at a light, and I scowl at a man in the car beside us with a phone pressed up against his ear. "I thought about Annie Oakley or maybe Malala Yousafzai. Mateo thinks I should do Dolores Huerta, and she's cool, but Mr. Collier says he wants us to write about someone that speaks to us. I don't know if I've found the right one yet. I'm still looking."

"Seems to me plenty of folks are speaking. Maybe you need to open those ears of yours and listen."

"My ears work just fine, but thanks." I rummage through my bag as we make the last few turns before Hawthorne Middle School.

"Your mother's a good one to consider," he offers.

I sigh. "Mom's wrong about me, you know. It's not fair that she thinks of me as being in danger on the farm. I got the calf out, and nobody got hurt. That should prove I *can* do this, not that I shouldn't."

"Aw, she just worries about you. You know that."

"Sometimes it feels like she can't hear a word I say."

"If ever there was a woman who could speak to the soul of things, it was your grandma." Grandpa sighs. "She held her peace and thought things through long and hard before she ever said a word—doled them out like precious gems, so I valued every one. Hard worker too, like you. I see her in you sometimes—when you're not dumping grasshoppers on folks."

I'd just arched my back, elbows up in a nice stretch as I yawn, but I dang near choke to death at that last part. How could he know? He wasn't anywhere near us. "Hey! I didn't—"

"I didn't say you personally did anything, but when cows trample a garden, who's responsible? The cows? Or the one who turned 'em loose?"

"Um." I squirm. "I . . ."

Mercifully, we arrive at school, and I grab the door handle as if it were the reins of a runaway horse. "Gotta go, Grandpa. See you!"

He tips his hat as I slam the door and jog toward the school entrance with the clay totem poles standing guard out front.

Grandpa is too quick for his own good sometimes, which

149

makes it all the more weird that he ever fell under Miss Dolly's spell.

At the steps of the school, I turn to watch Grandpa's old truck pull out, and I touch the wishstone through my pocket. "Don't worry, Grandpa. I'm gonna break her hold on you no matter what. I promise."

CHAPTER SIXTEEN

Many Hands Make Light Work

With the open house coming tomorrow, concentrating at school is about as impossible as a mouse ignoring a rattler. Kimana and Mateo promise to come by right after school so we can work on our plan.

I think better when I'm moving, so I walk while I wait: from barn to barn, over the canals, and back. At each spot, I try to think like a city person. What would they hate? Smells, obviously. And bugs—gotta have lots of those. Spiders for sure.

Mr. Ferro didn't seem scared at all when I told him how dangerous machinery can be on the farm, but what if I we set up something really scary? Probably Mateo can help me think of something to plant on—

I stop. *Plant.*

Mateo's plant.

I didn't open the greenhouse this morning.

Suddenly the warm day seems a lot more dangerous. I run

to the greenhouse, and I can feel the heat even before I touch the tarp door. All day long, the sun heated the air inside the greenhouse like an oven, which is usually great *if* I have the fans on. But I don't.

I forgot.

The greenhouses were never my job before. Mom always did them. I mean, I helped, but only when she asked.

The C-clamp clatters to the cement as I push the tarp aside, hot air billowing out around me.

His beautiful plant hangs limp and droopy.

I lift it off the hanger, lug it outside, and set it down so the vines trail to the side but not under the pot.

"Let's give you a drink." I grab the watering can, but the metal almost burns my hand, and the water inside is warm enough to bathe in.

Dumping it out, I run and get fresh, cool water and hurry back to pour it over the thirsty flowers.

Plants can do amazing things when they have what they need.

Probably this will perk up.

I frown at the way the wilted white geranium bends almost upside down.

Probably?

I'll check it later.

If the worst happens and the plant doesn't make it, I'll ask Mom or Grandpa to take me to the store and get him another one.

I squat beside the sad little plant and touch a withered leaf. "Live, buddy. You can do it. Please? Mateo is gonna kill me."

I'll give it a day or two before I decide what to do. No need to worry him if it's gonna be okay, right?

A dirt bike growls in the distance, so I leave the plant outside the sauna and jog toward the house.

Kimana's the first to arrive, and I wave her over to the chicken barn. "In here!"

With a backpack slung over her shoulder, Kimana flicks her kickstand down on the hard-packed dirt, takes off her helmet, and shakes her hair free of the straps. A beaded rose barrette clipped to the top of her long black braid catches the sunlight and sparkles with her every movement. She hangs the helmet on her handlebar. "We're meeting in there?"

"Yeah. My mom's probably still in bed, but just in case she wakes up, it's better to be out here. I like your barrette. Is it new?"

She reaches up to touch it. "Yeah. And guess what? There was no way I was gonna trade enough or make enough to get my jingles and the rest of my stuff the way I was selling my work before, so my dad said I should sell them online."

"Online, like your own store?"

"I know, it's crazy, right? But I've already got orders for everything I have. I still don't think it'll be enough, but I'm trying. I'll get there eventually."

"After the powwow's over, can you make me something with a peacock on it? It doesn't have to be very big." I mostly leave my hair in braids, but if I had a barrette with a peacock on it, I'd feel fancier than a queen.

"With the feathers? They might not last very long."

"No, just with colored beads, if you can."

"If I think of something cool to do with it, I will."

"Deal."

Mateo's bike rumbles up the driveway and skids to a stop beside the barn. He jumps off and brushes his hair out of his face, but when he sees me looking, he smirks and purposely messes it up enough to make any porcupine proud. "Sorry I'm late. The Pruitts asked my dad if we could help them move their piano."

"They're moving?" I ask.

"Yeah. Mr. Pruitt's brother is there helping, but the piano needed a couple extra hands."

With all the crazy stuff going on, I'd forgotten all about Mrs. Pruitt. "I haven't seen her since the day Dolly put that sign up—the first time."

"The bank took their farm." He glances at Kimana. "Have you heard where they're going?"

"I think she's got a kid living in Bountiful, Utah."

"What would a bank do with a farm?" I try to imagine a banker driving a tractor in his suit, and it just doesn't fit.

"They'll sell it in parts, for houses or whatever," says Mateo.

Nosey or not, the Pruitt family has been farming here forever. But then their kids moved away, and now their farm's going away. Seems like every year, another farm disappears, and there's not many of us left.

If the Pruitt family can lose their farm, what chance do we have of keeping ours?

Mateo scoops up a stick and strides into the barn, tapping the wall and straw stack as he goes. "So, how are we going to fight—"

"Honk!" Royal's warning call fills the barn. *"Honk!"*

"Is that the peacock?" Mateo scans the top of the stack.

"Yeah. I think you scared him." I climb up the side and check over the top to be sure there's not a real danger like a fox or skunk up there giving him trouble.

Royal's alone, but he's also standing. He swivels his head to look at me and blinks. If he's back on his feet, he needs a better place to be.

"Hey, can you guys help me make him a bigger enclosure? I think he's starting to feel better."

"Sure," Kimana says at the same time as Mateo says, "Let's do it."

It takes a good hour of stacking straw bales, moving chain-link panels, and getting lawn tractors out of the way. Each of us brings different parts to help—twine, fencing, rabbit hutch panels, straw, and wire—but it takes all of our pieces to make the whole and build his home. By the time we're finished, a new ten-by-ten space is ready with feed, water, and a sawhorse to perch on.

"How should we move him?" Kimana asks.

"Maybe we can lure him with food?" Mateo taps a wheat barrel.

"No, he might try to jump down. I don't think he's ready

for that yet." I grab the fishnet we use for catching roosters. "Can you pass me your hoodie? I've got an idea."

Royal honks one more time when I slide the net over him, but he settles down quick when I cover his head with the hoodie. Getting him down off the stack is a whole lot trickier.

I hug him gently, but firmly, so he can't flap around, and Kimana keeps his hoodie in place so he doesn't panic. He's too big to hold with one arm, so I wrap both of mine around his middle, holding the wings closed. Heavy as three big pop bottles and just as awkward to carry, he pants real quiet under the hoodie as I shuffle forward on my knees, his long feathers dragging across the straw bales behind us.

"Pass him to me." Mateo rolls a bale onto its side, stands on it, and reaches up.

Kneeling at the edge of the stack, I lean over as far as I dare and ease Royal into his arms. The hoodie slips, and Royal kicks out, his claws raking down Mateo's side, but Kimana slides down and drapes his head again, and he quiets.

"Did he get you?" I ask Mateo.

He sucks air through his teeth, but laughs it off. "Just a scratch. It's not like he's got horns or anything."

We hold the door to the new pen open while Mateo slips inside and carefully sets Royal on the floor. Backing out, he leaves the hoodie in place until he's as far from Royal as he can be, then tugs it off and slips out the door so we can shut it.

Royal's blue head pops up and swivels this way and that, eyeing his new digs: the tall straw-bale walls, the fence-panel roof, and the chain-link door at the front.

"You like your new house?" I drape an arm around Mateo's shoulder as we watch Royal stand, ruffle his tail, and take a limping step forward.

"He's still hurt?" Kimana squats beside the door, her fingers hooked through the chain-link.

"I think he might have sprained something in his hip. I'm just glad he can stand." I like to think maybe the extra bread and fruit helped, but probably time and rest did most of the work.

Feet pound the dirt outside the barn, and I drape a tarp over the door, hiding Royal from any nosey spies.

Scotty pops into the barn and cups his mouth. "Grandpa wants you!"

"All of us? Or just me?" I ask, but he's already running out the door.

Mateo, Kimana, and I glance at each other, shrug, and follow, through the yard, up the porch steps, and into the house.

Grandpa and Mr. Ferro sit in the rocking chairs, visiting like old friends.

No good can come of this.

"Come in, darlin'." Grandpa's grease-stained hand beckons, and Mom walks in from the kitchen, her arms folded across her middle and her hair done up in a clippy.

She nods to us but doesn't say anything. If she's up this fast, she'll probably be almost better by tomorrow.

"You gonna help your dad move all them pigs tomorrow?" Grandpa asks Mateo.

"Uh, yes, sir. Probably."

I eye Mateo sideways. If we can get things to work right, he won't have to load those pigs at all.

Grandpa nods. "Good. Many hands make light work. Anyhow, Mr. Ferro here thought it was high time we cleared the air."

Mr. Ferro stands, his little hat in hand. "When we were here two days ago—"

I brace for him to scold me for all them grasshoppers. If Grandpa figured it out, a reporter probably did too.

"—Scotty mentioned something about me being a spy for Miss Dolly."

The little snitch. I hear boots scuffle behind me, but before I can give Scotty the dirty look he deserves, Mr. Ferro continues, "I don't work for, or with, Miss Dolly. I think you've misunderstood why I'm here."

Grandpa nods like this makes complete sense, and it roasts my insides to see him taken in again by smooth-talking city folk.

I fold my arms. "But you came here *with* her. And I saw you sneaking around on the ditch. Seems an awful lot like spying to me." I wait for him to deny being the man on the ditch that morning, but he doesn't. *I knew it!*

"Okay, those are fair points. I can see how it would appear that something untoward might be happening, but as I said, I'm not an employee or even a coworker of Miss Dolly. I'm here for a story."

Scotty pipes up. "Grandpa tells great stories—even if most of them are made up."

"Hey now," Grandpa winks. "You leave my stories be."

"My job is to find human interest stories," Mr. Ferro says. When we don't answer, he tries again. "I'm not here to sell your land. I'm here to tell the world your story. I want people to see what it's like to walk in your shoes."

"Boots," Scotty says.

"What?" Mr. Ferro leans to look around me and address Scotty, but I save Scotty the trouble.

"He's saying we wear boots, not shoes."

"See? That's what I'm talking about. I want to know the things you know."

A phone rings, and Mom checks her cell, grimaces at the screen, and turns the ringer off. "Not again."

A few days ago, she unplugged the house phone too—pinched the cord where it disappears into the phone and plucked it out, leaving it hanging unattached like a little white tail wagging below the dead phone. Someone wants to talk to her real bad, but she doesn't want to talk back.

"Sorry about that. Go on," Mom says.

"I'm a journalist." Mr. Ferro spreads his arms, hat and all. "I'm doing a series right now on the disappearing American family farm. I saw your sign and called the number on the board. Dolly was happy to bring me along."

The disappearing American family farm? "Our farm is not disappearing," I say.

"You're researching!" Scotty slides up beside me, his fingers tapping each other. "To support your theory, you need facts and information."

"Precisely. And I would love to talk to you about your life here, maybe even spend a few days working with you all."

"Grandpa says many hands make light work." Scotty nods.

I eye Mr. Ferro's dress shoes—probably the same ones that made the marks in the barn the other day. "You gonna farm in those clothes?"

"No, I'll come back tomorrow in proper attire."

"It's settled then." Grandpa slaps the arm of his rocking chair. "Hope's feeling a mite under the weather, so if we can take some load off her, all the better."

"Sounds good. One more thing." Mr. Ferro looks to Mateo. "You have a paper route, right?"

"Yeah."

"I know this is a long shot, but a few mornings ago I was walking the canal to get a feel for this area and heard what I thought was a peacock cry. Did you happen to hear anything that morning?"

"Peacocks?" Mateo glances at me. "Ah, I did not hear a peacock a few days ago. No."

"I see." Mr. Ferro deflates a little and turns to Grandpa. "Will you keep an eye out for me?"

"For peacocks? Around here?" Grandpa clears his throat. "Whatever for?"

"I know it seems like a silly request." Mr. Ferro gives a soft chuckle. "But you see, I'm looking for one."

CHAPTER SEVENTEEN

Too Late

The next morning, Mateo, Kimana, and I gather in the barn extra early to get a little planning in before Mr. Ferro arrives. The tricky part is gonna be keeping Mr. Ferro away. Not like it's booby traps or anything, we just don't want him to trigger whatever we set up too early.

I think about that for a minute.

Okay, they're totally going to be booby traps, but still. We don't want them to go off too soon.

"Did you know you've got balloons at the end of the drive-way?" Kimana unzips her bag.

"Balloons?" I scowl.

"Pink ones.

I brought the stuff you asked for." She pulls out Vaseline and some tape. "This will make for some excellent slime, don't you think?"

"For sure." I cut rows of twine into two-foot sections. "I'm thinking that would work great on the cows. Nobody wants slimy cows, right?"

"I wouldn't." She grimaces.

"Maybe we can make them look like zombies. Doesn't that sound great? Zombie burgers?" Mateo plunks a sack onto a straw bale, and Scuzbag hops up beside it, sniffing. "One soup bone, old jeans, a T-shirt, and three jars of strawberry jam. Check." He leans toward Scotty. "Mamá would kill me if she knew about the jam."

"What about me?" Scotty tugs his collar. "I have four jars of arachnids, various arthropodas, and some Schistocerca americanas. That's *muy bien*, right?" He grins at Mateo.

Mateo raises an eyebrow at me, but I shrug. Don't ask me what those long words mean.

"Great job, Scotty." Mateo pats him on the back. "*Que chido*! For sure."

Scotty beams under his praise.

"Where are your jars?" I ask Scotty.

"They're in the pump house behind the door, where nobody will find them."

"How long do we have before the lady comes with all the people?" Kimana asks.

"Maybe three hours? But they might come sooner. Miss Dolly didn't say if they were coming together or separately. I'm not sure."

"If we had more time, I was thinking I could program a robot to dump Scotty's spiders on command so we wouldn't have to be there ourselves."

"That would be so cool." Mateo picks up a roll of electrical tape and some wire. "You think they'll scream? I bet they do. Everybody screams if spiders fall on them."

A sliver of guilt worms its way into my head. If Grandpa figured out about the grasshoppers, he'll know for sure that this was me. But if I don't do something, we'll end up like the Pruitts, with a lifetime of work, and no farm to show for it.

This will either be the best thing I've ever done, or the worst.

I set red spray paint on the straw bale next to a can of fart spray and a bucket of manure. "Here's the deal. We're doing the cows first, then the horses, and then anything else we can get to before they come.

"Scotty, you tie your pieces of twine all down the calf fence and paint them with honey and oats. You decide where the best place for your jars might be. Tell me when you're done." As he gets up, I touch his shoulder. "But don't let Mom see you—not Grandpa or Mr. Ferro either."

"I won't! Come on, T-Rex."

T-Rex's droopy-eyed gaze follows Scotty as he races out of the barn, then sighs and heaves himself to his feet. He'll follow his boy to the ends of the earth, but sometimes I think he waits a bit, to see if maybe Scotty might change his mind and come back so T-Rex doesn't have to go quite as far.

"Kimana, there are sugared carrots in the bucket behind you. You think you can get them to the horses?"

"No problem."

"Okay." I take a breath and look at my two best friends. "We're burning daylight. Let's get this done."

Mateo peers into the last bucket. "What did you have in mind for this?"

"There are rubber gloves under the bucket, and a garden shovel over there. I don't know—be creative."

"Got it." Mateo lifts the bucket and pockets the gloves. "My dad will come soon for the pigs, though."

"That's fine. Just do as much as you can and stop when you have to."

"Hello?" Mr. Ferro calls from outside the barn, and we all look at each other with wide eyes before tucking bags and spray cans behind straw bales, out of sight.

"Oh gosh." I hop up and run to meet him. "Hey, hi. Can I help you?"

"Is your mother with you? I thought she'd be out here, working with you." He tilts his head to look past me, but I grab his arm and tug him around.

"No, she's probably in the house. Let's go find her."

Without waiting for his reply, I set off for the house. By the porch, I glance at Mr. Ferro's truck, but must've slowed down too much, because he pulls the key fob from his pocket, glances at me, and then presses a button.

Lights flash with a *chirrup!*

"Never can be too careful," he says, and winks.

Mom steps out onto the porch. "Asher, good to see you again. Are you ready for this?"

"I'm at your service. Are you feeling better today?" He

spreads his hands, and for the first time, I notice he's not in dress pants and fancy shoes. He's got jeans and tennis shoes on. If it weren't for the tiny hat, I might not know he was a city boy at all.

"Much. Thank you." She nudges a stack of totes on the porch. "These need to go to the barn, and the garden tools by the fence need to go to the toolshed. Paige can show you."

We tromp up the stairs, and I lift one tote, but when he picks up two, I drop mine on top of the last one and heave them both up.

"You got that?" Mr. Ferro asks. "We can come back for it."

"I'm good." Even with my arms all the way down, I can just barely see over the top. I slide my toe forward, searching for the edge of the porch. "I got this."

He hurries down and waits for me at the bottom—the show-off.

"That's right. Step. And another one right there. Step. Two more. Step. Last one . . . and you're down. Good job."

By the time I hit the bottom, I'm thinking picking up both totes wasn't the smartest choice—not that I'd ever admit that to him. He'd probably put it in his paper somewhere.

Walking beside me, he matches my pace. "I hear your neighbors down the road sold their farm back to the bank. What do you think of that?"

"It's sad." I grunt, trying to ignore the way my fingers are going numb.

"Sad because they're leaving or because it's being developed?"

I lean against the pump house, propping my totes up against the wall long enough to shake out my hands before we walk on. "Sad because it won't be a farm anymore."

"But why do you care if it's developed or farmed? If the family's not going to be there, what does it matter what happens?"

"Gimme a sec." I hurry the last few yards to the barn, check to make sure it's empty, and set the totes down against the wall. Red indents score my fingers, and they're kind of stuck curled in. I rub them against my jeans, stretching out my fingers.

Behind Mr. Ferro, Kimana scurries into the horse barn with the bucket of sugar carrots in tow.

He starts to turn to follow my gaze, and I blurt, "Okay! It's like . . ." I bend my fingers with my other hand, back and forth, thinking fast. "Imagine your family had the best place in the whole world to look at the stars, and every night you watch them twinkle and light up the sky. You know the names, the stories of every constellation—and you know exactly where to find them because they're like family to you, the way they come back year after year."

"Okay." He watches me, and I head for the garden tools.

"Now imagine someone comes in and builds a parking lot with those bright lights all around your house—right on top of your stargazing place. What would your night sky look like then?"

"In the middle of a parking lot?" He matches my stride.

"Like nothing. The lights would be too bright to see much past them."

"Exactly, and your stargazing spot is gone forever. You can't use it, but no one else can use it either. Farming's like that—except worse because you can't just cut the power and get it back. Once they pave over fields, it's done. There's no going back."

We round the corner, and T-Rex stands beside Scotty, who ducks behind a bale of hay by the calf corrals. A hundred feet away, Mateo stands frozen with the soup bone in one hand and a can of spray paint in the other.

"So!" I tug Mr. Ferro's sleeve so he's looking at me and not to his right. "How long have you been a journalist?"

"About twenty years. Worked for about ten of those with my ex-wife—she's a photographer back East."

"You're married?"

"I was."

I wait to see if he's gonna say more, but he doesn't.

When we get back to the yard for the garden tools, Miss Dolly's standing on the front porch, talking to Mom. With jeans new enough to still have the sticker mark up the side, and boots sparkly enough to decorate a Christmas tree, Dolly waves from the porch. "Paige! Are you ready for the big day?"

I grimace. "Not yet." But I will be.

The worn handles of the garden tools are smooth in my hands as I set them aside one after the other, but none of them are Dad's shovel. I'm starting to think maybe I'll never find it.

Mr. Ferro takes a little more than half of the tools from me and carries them over one shoulder like a fishing pole. "What do you do for fun?"

"I farm." The hoes and rakes over my shoulder clink together with every step I take.

"No, for fun. Do you play basketball? Softball? Soccer? Are you in dance? What do you do in your spare time?"

Spare time? I barely have time to sleep. "I told you. I farm. If I have spare time, I spend it fixing things. There's loads to do and only one of me."

"But you're not doing this alone, right? Your mom and grandpa farm with you."

I shrug. "Sometimes."

"What about cell phones? Kids these days are usually glued to their phones, but I haven't seen you pull yours out once."

"It's in the kitchen. I don't like carrying it."

"My kids would probably have theirs surgically implanted if they could." He rubs the back of his neck. "At the kitchen table, in the bathroom, you name it—they gotta have their phones."

"Where are your kids?" I set the tools inside the toolshed.

"With their mother in Boston." His tools plunk beside mine, and he laughs softly. "We video chat a few times a month, but they like it better where they are. What's next?"

Hmm. What will take him the longest time? "We could put the garden tractors away. I'll show you how to start them."

As far as tractors go, the two garden tractors aren't much bigger than a riding lawn mower, so they seem a safe bet to keep him busy. "These are good for all sorts of things. We

rototill with them, and plant peas, and they're great for mowing too." I pat the seat. "Jump on up here."

"You want me to drive?"

"Sure! You drive a pickup, right? This is way easier."

His long legs poke up from the sides like a grasshopper as
he folds himself into the seat.

"Push your left foot down on the clutch— like that, yeah—
then make sure it's in neutral." I wiggle the stick to be sure it's
out of gear. "Then start her up."

He cranks the key and grasps the steering wheel as the engine rumbles to life.

"See?" I lean closer, yelling over the engine noise. "Easy!
Now put it in first gear and go park it in the shop. Then come
back for the other."

"How do I stop it?" The way he's grinning, you'd think I
stuck him on a speed racer instead of a tractor with training
wheels.

"Just turn the key. It'll die."

He gives me a thumbs-up, and I run off to find Kimana.

I spy her in the horse barn, but before I can reach her,
Mr. Ferro motors right past—definitely *not* in first gear—and
cruises into the chicken barn.

"Hey! Wrong building!" I run after him. "Not in there!"

But he's already inside, the clanging engine noise bouncing
off the metal ceiling. If Royal sounded an alarm after Mateo
hit the wall with a little stick, what will he do when a whole
tractor roars inside his house?

"No, no, no," I chant, but even before Mr. Ferro cuts the engine, Royal's emergency calls ring out, *"Honk! Honk! Honk!"*

I'm only ten seconds behind him, but it's enough. I burst into the barn as Mr. Ferro pulls open the tarped door to Royal's cage.

"Honk! Honk!"

"No!" I yell, but it's too late.

An explosion of feathers launches at Mr. Ferro, and he ducks.

Using Mr. Ferro's back as a springboard, Royal leaps into flight.

Wings spread wide, his gold-tipped flight feathers catch rays of sunlight, and his blue-and-green tail flaring behind.

I raise my arms to stop him. "No! Wait. You're safe here!"

But his brilliant blue head angles and he banks out of reach, wings pumping, rising up and up, soaring over my head and out the door.

CHAPTER EIGHTEEN

Escape

The peacock rises over the toolshed and circles the silo. Magpies and swallows flee before him, as his enormous train and wingspan dwarf all other birds on the farm.

"Don't leave. Please don't leave." I grasp my wishstone and bring it to my lips. "Stay. Please stay."

"Did you know that peacock was in there?" Mr. Ferro jogs up beside me and shades his eyes with one hand. "I thought I heard it before, but I couldn't find where the cry had come from."

I rub the stone and slide it into my pocket, my eyes never leaving Royal's flight. He banks and dips, then settles into the top branches of our giant cottonwood tree. *"Ha, ha, heyo!"*

"That's it exactly! That's what I heard." His hand squeezes my shoulder, and he grins like a kid seeing fireworks for the very first time. "I thought he was long gone."

"Gone from where?"

"My grandfather raised them, but this one got loose weeks ago. I thought I'd never see him again. What luck!" He glances at me, then at Royal, and back again, his smile fading. "You knew, didn't you?"

I take a step back. "I better go help with the open house."

"You knew I was looking for a peacock, but you didn't tell me he was here. Why would you lie?"

"He came to us for help. And I didn't lie, not technically. He was hurt, like he escaped from something. He ran away, and we were protecting him."

Laughter gone, his gaze becomes sharper, like he could peel back my brain and peek right inside. "That's quite the loophole you've painted for yourself. Lying by not lying. Keeping it all a secret."

I want to say he's got it all wrong, that we were helping Royal, but I know what Dad would say, *"What's done is done; all that's left is to move on,"* and my protests die on my lips.

"It seems you've spun yourself a very long tail of not-lies," Mr. Ferro says. "Be careful not to trip on it."

"Paige!" Scotty runs to the barn, a jar under each arm and another one hugged to his chest. "Did you see Royal? He flew! Our Royal can fly!"

"I saw." I wave a hand down low at him. "Go back. Go!"

"Wait." Mr. Ferro walks past me and plucks a jar from Scotty's arms. Beetles cling by the dozens to little sticks propped up inside the jar. The bottom is a wash of churning black bodies. "I see."

Scotty's eyes are wide, and he steps back quick as Mr. Ferro plucks the other jar from his arms and lifts it to the light.

Spiders crawl over each other and scale the sides on webs.

"Scotty? Paige? Are you alright? What was that noise?" In a pale-yellow sundress, Mom hurries to us. "I heard an engine revving and then some kind of animal."

Her steps slow as she sees Mr. Ferro with the jars of beetles and spiders.

He passes them to her. "I think we found our grasshopper problem."

"Scotty? What is this?" The beetles tumble from their sticks as she tilts the jar one way and then the other. "Can you explain?"

Fingers twisting in his collar, he looks to me.

"Paige?" Mom turns to me. "What's going on?"

"Ha! Ha! Heyo! Heyo!"

"Is that a peacock? What in the world?" She presses the jars into Scotty's hands. "Get rid of these. Right now."

Rocking from foot to foot, he whispers to me, "Where should I put them? For you-know-what." Except his whisper isn't very quiet, and Mom hears every word.

"What? Give them to the girls. They'll eat them." She jabs a thumb at the chicken barn, then points a finger at me. "Paige Elizabeth McBride, he didn't think of that on his own. You *will* tell me what's going on. Right now."

Scotty disappears into the barn, but I'm too mixed up to say anything at all. If I tell her, what's to stop the open house

173

people from walking all over the farm? But Dad would never let me disobey my mom.

She clucks her tongue and takes my hand, dragging me along. "Come with me."

Our march slows as we near the calf corral, where dozens of calves lick and slurp at blue pieces of twine tied to the fence rail.

"What is this?" She touches a string, and a long drooping bow of slobber clings to her fingers. "Was something on these?"

"Looks like honey and some oats, I think." Mr. Ferro examines the top of a twine without touching it.

Mom folds her arms. "Out with it. You're trying to ruin the open house, aren't you?"

I sigh. "It doesn't count as ruining if it saves the farm."

"What else did you do?" Mr. Ferro asks.

"What else?" Mom squeaks. "There's more?"

"Why stop with some string and some bugs when you've got a whole farm to protect? Am I right?" He leans closer. "What did that devious little mind of yours dream up?"

"Show me," Mom orders.

Slowly, I walk toward the cow corral, where several cows munch happily on hay, their cheeks, ears, and necks dripping with Vaseline.

"Wow." Mr. Ferro raises a brow. "Were you going for sickly?"

I nod.

"Mission accomplished."

"Is this all?" Mom asks.

I shake my head and walk on.

In the horse barn, Queenie and the others knicker with joy at seeing my Mom, but thick foam drips from their lips and puddles on the floor.

"Queenie!" Rushing to cradle Queenie's jaw in her hands, Mom examines her eyes and nostrils before smoothing her hand down Queenie's neck. "What did you do? Feed them all sugar cubes?"

"Sugared carrots," I admit.

"Will that hurt them?" Mr. Ferro asks.

"Not unless she gave them a lot of them. Did you?" She eyes the chunks of half-chewed carrots on the floor.

"They each got two."

"Okay, okay." She rubs Queenie's forehead and spears me with a look. "What else?"

We walk past the flock of roosters Mateo let out, then past the mess of farm cats rolling and yowling by the toolshed, where Kimana hid the catnip.

Scuzbag races toward us at full steam, then flops over and rolls from side to side, purring.

"Catnip?" Mom asks.

"Yep."

"Paige . . ."

"I know."

Halfway to the pigs, I spy Mateo's bucket and put out a hand to stop Mom from walking on straw piles scattered across the road. "I don't think you should step on those."

"My gosh, you didn't set actual traps, did you?" Mom scans the road and all the new piles of straw.

"Just land mines . . . of poop."

"You really went all out." Was that approval in Mr. Ferro's voice?

"Is this all of it?" Mom asks.

"One more." I lead the way to the pigs.

A red handprint stains the fence rail, then trails down into the pigpens. Other, more hurried prints glisten on the wood, the red drops leading to a churned-up section of deep crimson soil, where torn jeans surround a large soup bone jutting up from the mud. Two sows play tug-of-war with what's left of a blotchy red T-shirt. It tears into long strips as the pigs shake their heads.

"What did you do?" Mom gasps. "Their mouths! My gosh, look at their faces!"

The pigs grunt, squeal, and nose the fence, thrusting their red-stained snouts through the rails, toothy mouths open.

"Ha! That's brilliant." Mr. Ferro laughs. "What's the red stuff?"

"Strawberry jam," I say quietly.

He squats beside the pen. "What were the spiders and beetles for?"

"Well, we thought maybe when people walked into the barn, under the loft . . ."

"Paige, how horrible." Mom touches the paint, still fresh enough to come away wet on her fingers.

I give up. "Well, I *tried* to talk to you, but you wouldn't listen. I'm supposed to look after the farm, but you're selling everything! How am I supposed to do my job if all you want to do is get rid of it?"

"Is that what you were doing with the peacock?" Mr. Ferro asks. "Looking after it?"

"Scotty found it hiding in our barn. *Our* barn. On *our* farm. Because it needed help. And we couldn't ask Mom for help because she keeps listening to Dolly about getting rid of the animals."

"We're selling them because we have to," Mom says.

I fold my arms. "No, we don't! You don't have to listen to her."

Cars pull up the driveway, and Mom runs a hand over her face. "What do we do? We can't show them the farm." She points at the pigs ripping Mateo's T-shirt to bits. "There's a murder scene, for heaven's sake." She strides toward the house, murmuring under her breath. "For the life of me—I can't believe . . ."

When we reach the yard, Miss Dolly is on the porch in front of a small crowd of men and women in business suits. "Ladies and gentleman, I'm pleased to welcome you to this golden opportunity. The new Siphon I-15 on-ramp and Northgate Project—combined with the construction of housing developments, a children's museum, and dozens of new businesses—has this city ready to explode in growth to the north, right where we are now! A new interstate exchange means new gas stations, shopping malls, and offices—all of which need somewhere to build . . . and developers to seize the opportunity." She spreads her hands. "That's where you come in."

The suits scan the farm and the surrounding fields, but their eyes don't linger on the buildings. It's like our house and barns are invisible.

Grandpa clears his throat. "There's no reason they couldn't buy it and keep farming the land, is there?" His sun-squinted eyes shift from face to face, though no one seems inclined to listen. "It's right good ground. Rich soil. Good moisture. We always cut a good crop of hay."

"What can you tell us about water rights?" a burly man asks.

"They're excellent—both ground water and canal rights through the Fort Hall irrigation project. I've printed up growth projections and figures for you." Dolly passes out fliers from her clipboard.

I scowl at all of them. They don't even care about the rest of the farm. They just want to pave the whole thing over.

"If you've got kids, the neighbors are wonderful. You couldn't ask for better . . ." They all ignore Mom's soft voice, and she trails off.

We stand to the side while Dolly chats with the suits, shakes a bunch of hands, then waves them a cheery goodbye as they pile into their fancy cars and drive off.

"They didn't even *see* the farm," I mumble. "What was the point of cleaning at all?"

Miss Dolly shines her bright smile on us, her face flushed. "I think that went really well!"

CHAPTER NINETEEN

Sounders and Squealers

Mr. Rivas's diesel truck pulls up the lane with a livestock trailer behind it, and Mateo appears behind me. "My dad's here for the pigs. I need to help load. You okay?"

He glances from me to my mom and back, and I know what he means. *Are you in big trouble? Did anything help at all?*

I shrug, not really sure how much trouble I'm in yet.

The porch door swings open, and Scotty and Kimana step out onto the porch and walk down the steps.

Mr. Rivas pulls in beside the pigs, and Mom turns to Mr. Ferro. "Asher, can you help Mr. Rivas? He'll probably need extra hands."

"Of course." Mr. Ferro touches that tiny hat brim of his and follows Mateo toward the pigpens, while Mom, Dolly, and Grandpa visit on the far side of the yard. Before Mr. Ferro clears the fence, his phone rings. He taps the screen and stays on the lawn. "Hey, Vanessa. I was hoping you'd call back to-day."

"S'up, Dad? What did you need?" A girl with dark eye shadow and big, shiny earphones peers up from the screen. "How's Idaho?"

"Good, good." Mr. Ferro holds the phone up so the girl can see the fields behind him. "I thought since next weekend was mine, I could fly you out to see your great-grandparents' place before it sells. What do you say?"

"Oh, I would but, um . . ." She wrinkles her nose. "I promised my friends I'd go to a concert with them this week-end. And Mom's going to Paris again for a shoot in a couple weeks for some new clients, so we'll probably go there in-stead."

He walks to his truck. "What about the week after? No? Next month . . . ?"

"Why does he keep coming around?" I whisper to Scotty. "Why not just write his report and leave? What more does he want from us?"

Scotty scratches T-Rex's ears. "Humans require neural mir-roring."

"Mirror what?"

"Texting and talking on the phone can't stimulate human brains like face-to-face talking does—the endorphins don't re-lease."

Kimana glances from Scotty to Mr. Ferro, who is now leaning against his truck. "So people can talk on the phone all day and still be lonely?"

"Yep."

"Video chats don't count?" I ask.

"Two-dimensional images—even moving ones—are not the same. And you can't trick your brain into thinking the person is really there. His brain is missing connection."

Well, if texting doesn't count as talking, why does it matter if I text or not? At least when I talk to people, I know it counts.

"Your Mr. Rivas is here to sell the whole herd of pigs?" Miss Dolly says, walking toward the house. "That's wonderful. One more step in the right direction."

"Sounder." Scotty worries at his shirt collar.

Dolly stops beside him. "Beg your pardon?"

"A family of pigs is called a sounder, not a herd." Nervous or not, he'll spout facts till his dying breath.

"What does that have to do with anything?"

I tug Scotty toward the stairs. "You said the wrong word," I tell Dolly. "He's giving you the right one."

"Is that what you're doing? That's adorable." She ruffles Scotty's hair, and he flinches, curling inward. He's very particular about who touches him, and Dolly is definitely not on the list of can-touch-me's.

"Ask first." I step between them. "Don't touch people without asking first."

"I only meant to say—" she sputters.

"I know what you meant. But next time, ask. That's all."

"Let's go inside." Mom walks up the steps and opens the door. "I think we've had a misunderstanding."

We file into the house, and Dolly prances over to the table, pulls out Dad's chair, and sits, as if that's the most normal thing in the world.

For a moment, time freezes. Mom, Grandpa, Scotty, and I all stare.

"Get off—" Angry words boil up my throat, but Grandpa rests a hand on my shoulder and murmurs, "It's just a chair, darlin'. It's okay."

But it's not just a chair. It's *his* chair. And no one sits there. Not any of us. We *have* to keep it open for him. What if he needs it? I try to jerk my shoulder away, but Grandpa's hand stays, rooting me to the floor.

"Dolly," Mom asks, "who did you invite to the open house? Weren't there any farmers interested?"

"Yes, I had some calls, but I thought it better to keep this one small. Let the guests know they had an exclusive invitation." Her smile falters as she looks from Mom to Grandpa and back. "It's okay. If it doesn't work out, we can always try again."

Grandpa clears his throat. "Not one farmer in the bunch, was there? Only developers."

The chair creaks as Dolly leans back. "I'm getting you ten times what your land is worth. Maybe twenty. This land is a gold mine if we play it right. You could be set for life."

Mom glances at Grandpa. "We know that—we do. But you said you'd try to find someone who wanted to keep this as farmland. That was part of our agreement."

"I did say that was a possibility, but . . ." She taps the table with her electric-green nails. "You do understand I'm trying to help you, right? The more money I can get for you, the better. Think college funds and retirement." She points at the door and offers a smile. "You could replace that old van with a new one that's all one color."

"Patches runs just fine." Scotty stares at the floor. "It's got a good motor."

The chair creaks again as she leans forward. "It looks like it's been patched together."

"That's because it has been." I glare at her, but she seems more confused than hurt. "Dad built it."

"Please let us know when you've contacted those other folks you turned away this time." Grandpa opens the door and holds it for Miss Dolly.

"What?" Dolly asks. When she stands, Scotty sidesteps her and slides Dad's chair back into place.

Mom sighs. "We told you what it meant for us to keep it as a working farm. All you brought was developers."

Dolly walks to the door but faces Mom. "That's because they're the ones with the finances to make the purchase. As I understand it, you've only got a few weeks before foreclosure. I could have this place sold like that"—she snaps her fingers—"to one of the people who came today, and you'd never have to work a day in your life again. Are you sure you want to take this risk?"

"This land has been in our family for a hundred years. What's a legacy worth to you?" Grandpa asks.

"Alright. I'll try again. But keep this in mind: if I don't find a buyer you accept, and the property forecloses, the bank *will* sell to developers. It will happen either way. I just think it's better to make the sale and get the payoff." She smooths her shirt over her jeans. "There's a reason why Asher Ferro is here to do a story on family farms. They're an endangered species. Every year more go under."

"Seems to me," Grandpa says, "if farms are endangered, the need to protect them is greater, not less."

"Think about it. I'll be in touch." She steps out the door, and we follow her onto the porch as she walks to her car, waves, and drives away.

We're still watching her dust trail when a high-pitched squeal cuts through the air.

A midsized piglet bolts through the yard, little legs churning.

Twenty feet behind it, Mr. Ferro runs full-out, his hat gone, sweat glistening on his forehead, and grass stains and dust on his jeans.

Mateo dashes over from the other side of the house. "Help us corner it!"

The pig spins in front of Mateo and runs back to the corner of the yard between the two, snorting and squealing all the way.

We line up to make a human wall between the pig and the rest of the yard, our hands stretched low and to the side.

"Alright now," Grandpa says, "everyone stay real calm and close in slow. Don't let him past you."

We take one step and another, the pig watching us warily.

"Paige," Mateo murmurs, "if you can get him to look at you, I think I can grab him."

I pucker my lips and make kissy sounds. "Here, pig. Here, pig, pig."

The pig's big ears focus on me, its nose raised and sniffing.

Mateo lunges, arms reaching, but the pig jumps straight up, tiny hooves kicking grass in Mateo's face as it bolts toward Mr. Ferro.

I groan. It'll take forever to catch it now.

But Mr. Ferro dives, tackling the pig to the ground and holding on for dear life as its whole body wiggles back and forth, legs kicking.

"You got it!" Mom laughs, and me and Mateo pounce on the struggle, me grabbing the back legs and Mateo the front.

Mud smeared up one side of his face, and hair sticking up all over, Mr. Ferro pants from holding on so tight.

"Alright now," Grandpa says, "stand up real easy, and don't let go."

It takes some doing, but we get Mr. Ferro up—without losing the pig. We carry it to the truck, where Mr. Rivas and Kimana wait with the others. After bolting the door shut, Mr. Rivas looks Mr. Ferro up and down: his stained pants, and the mud and grass smeared across his face and shirt. "Looks good."

Mr. Ferro chuckles and wipes his dirty hands down his shirt, which only makes it worse. "I did say I wanted to get my hands dirty. I like to be thorough in my research."

"That was a good catch." Mateo pats him on the shoulder and grins. "Couldn't have done it better myself."

I never thought I'd see a city guy tackle a pig, but I think the dirt stains on his knees suit him better than any fancy clothes.

"Mateo, *ya nos vamos*," Mr. Rivas calls, and they walk to the truck.

The truck engine growls to life and fills my ears.

"Honk!" Royal's warning call sounds from the tree high overhead. *"Honk!"*

The tires start to rotate, and I want to run ahead and put my hands out to stop it—a boulder teetering at the edge of a cliff, and there's no going back.

I glance at the pigpens: gates open, pasture empty.

Grunts and squeals echo from inside the metal box trailer instead of from their home where they belong. I see only bits of them peeking through the trailer holes.

A nose sniffing, an ear, a tail wagging.

Usually we keep sows and a boar, Dad's handpicked stock, to make a new start for the next year, but *all* the pens are empty.

None are left.

The truck rolls forward with all of Dad's pigs, and I stumble after it, an invisible force pulling me along, stretching between us like saltwater taffy. It pulls and stretches until it hits the road—and snaps.

Another piece torn out of me.

Mr. Rivas swings the truck wide to make the corner, and

the trailer snags Dolly's bundle of pink balloons at the end of our driveway.

Freed from their tethers, the balloons rise up and away like wishes blown from a dandelion puff.

CHAPTER TWENTY

Hoe to the End of the Row

I think I'm probably grounded till I'm dead.

As far as prisons go, my room is pretty comfy, but still, it's *inside*. The gabled windows on the south side of my room tease me with blue sky and open fields, but I'm stuck in here till Mom decides I can come out. In the meantime, Mom's list of "things I'm not allowed to do" is pretty long. For instance:

1. No messing with the livestock at all—no paint, no new foods, nothing.
2. No spiders, beetles, or grasshoppers of any kind.
3. No changing the electric fence.
4. No moving poop around to anywhere it shouldn't be.
5. No leading city folk into destruction.

You get the idea. She's not real happy with me.

When Grandpa asked for my help this morning, Mom let

me out for an hour to get animals fed and watered, and, if I
ignored the pigpens, it wasn't so bad. Then I remembered to
check the greenhouse again.

It frosted last night . . . and I never put Mateo's plant back
inside.

The plant had perked up after I almost cooked it, but
there's no coming back from being frozen to death. I'll have to
buy him another.

After chores, I got sent right back to my room.

I rub my face, flop my hands to the side, and stare at the
puzzles on my bedroom walls: framed pictures of farms, mountains, trees, and horses.

All the things Dad loved.

Sometimes Royal calls from the trees overhead. *"Ha! Ha!
Heyo! Heyo!"* And I smile to know he's still here, somewhere,
even if I can't see him. Once, I think I hear an owl too, but it's
too soft to be sure.

Lying across my bed on my quilted comforter, I tap the
dream catcher Kimana hung on my brass bed frame when
we were eight years old and watch the feathers rock back and
forth. Dream catchers are supposed to guard against night-
mares, but when the worst has already happened, what else is
there to be afraid of?

My social studies book lies upside down at the foot of the
bed, where I dumped it after wasting an hour trying to find
someone from history whose life has anything to do with mine.
Mr. Collier claims our lives are threaded together, each of us

tethered to the contributions of people who came before us, but all I keep finding are loose ends.

Something taps against a window, and I sit up.

The short hallway between my room and Scotty's room is empty, his room dark except for what light slips past the solar system stickers on his window.

What was it? Did a cat get in?

The tapping comes again, and a quick shadow flits across the south gable window as Mateo waves from his perch on the roof, his finger against the glass.

Floorboards squeak under my feet as I rush to lift the window open. "What are you doing?"

"You weren't doing chores. Are you still grounded?"

"Is the sun still shining?"

He laughs as I close my social studies book and set it on my old wood desk.

I sink onto the head of my bed. "Mom had me do chores early so I would be"—my fingers crook into air quotes—"'out of the way,' and back where she can keep an eye on me. Except she's in her room, so what does it matter?"

"So what do you think? Did our plan help at all?"

I shake my head. "They didn't even see what we did. Only Mom and Mr. Ferro. Those other guys? We could have covered the whole farm in spiders and they wouldn't have cared. All they wanted was the land to build on."

"I'm sorry it didn't work like you wanted." He stares at the only poster on my wall, a silhouette of a girl and her horse, and rubs the back of his neck.

I almost tell him about the plant, but I know how disappointed he'll be. Better to get a replacement first, then tell him. Sorry about the old one, but here's a new one. Ta-da! My bad.

"So, I found something." He sits at the foot of the bed.

"Really?"

"Yeah, we were digging a fence post, and it turned up." He pulls something out of his pocket and cradles it in his hand for me to see.

An arrowhead.

"Oh, that's cool." Plucking it up, I hold it to the light. "Can I keep it?"

He tugs on my fingertips. "No. You have to give it back—even though you've collected things like this your whole life. It's *totally* normal that I'd climb up the tree, jump onto your roof, and crawl through your window to show you the thing that I'm *not* giving you."

"Jerk." I laugh and stand up to place the arrowhead on my shelf beside the row of other arrowheads, unique stones, feathers, shells, and a tiny sugar skull that Mateo gave me. I still remember where he found each one. In fact, there's nothing in my collection that he *didn't* give me. So does that make it *my* collection, or Mateo's?

The shelf below it holds solved Rubik's Cubes, wooden and metal 3-D brain twisters, and a few boxes of my favorite jigsaw puzzles from when Dad and me used to solve them on my desk. Some of my old robots sit there too. I haven't decided if I'm going to keep them or not. Mostly I pretend not to see them.

"You didn't have to climb in the window." I lean against my doorjamb. "Mom would've let you in."

"And you didn't have to ignore my texts this morning."

I shrug. "The phone is downstairs."

"So is your mom." He gets up from the bed and waves me closer to the window. "Come see this."

The yard seems the same. Grass, trees, a half-fallen-down wood fence. "What am I looking for?"

"Look right there." He points to a high branch of a pine tree, where a slice of blue stands out against the forest green.

"Royal! He stayed!"

"Look behind him and up a branch."

I squint, but can't see anything until a barn owl swivels its head.

"They're so close," I say. "Both of them together."

"I thought you'd like that. Owls are one thing, but how often do you see a peacock from your bedroom window?"

"Thank you for showing me."

He waves that off. "Have you put food and water back in his cage?"

"Yeah. We filled it right before he got away."

"Keep it filled. If he's hanging around, maybe he'll remember where to go when he's hungry."

Below us, Mr. Ferro walks across the yard, a long fishnet over his shoulder. He gazes up at the cottonwood where Royal was yesterday and stares for a long time. At last, he sinks to the ground, drops his pole in the grass, and sits with his legs stretched out in front of him.

Mateo nudges my elbow as an orange furball creeps onto the lawn. "Looks like he's been spotted."

"Get him, Scuzbag," I whisper. "Attack of the kitty!"

Scuzbag winds through the grass, ears pricked and tail straight.

"Collision in five, four, three," Mateo counts down, "two, and . . . boom!"

Scuzbag slides under Mr. Ferro's arm and crawls onto his lap.

With a quick glance down, Mr. Ferro runs a hand down Scuzbag's back, petting him from the hollow between his ears to the tip of his tail.

"Well, Scuzbag likes him," Mateo says. "He must not be all bad."

"Scuzbag likes everybody. Doesn't Mr. Ferro have a job or something?"

"I think this *is* his job. Research and experience and writing the story."

"I don't want to be his story." I walk to my desk and pull out Dad's calendar. His handwritten notes fill every square.

Today's square says: *Cut asparagus. Lay pipe to north field, east pasture, garden, and corn.*

"Have you seen Grandpa today?" I check which week we're in. The dates always change, but it's easy to tell what needs to be done by counting which week of the month we're in.

"No." His phone buzzes, and he glances at the screen. "My dad needs me. I gotta go. Don't do anything stupid without me."

I laugh and pull him away from the window. "It's a deal. C'mon, you can go down the stairs."

We traipse down the stairs and out the door.

"See ya." Mateo waves and goes to his bike.

"Bye." I walk from one side of the porch to the other, scanning the fields for a tractor or anything moving.

A lone man stands in the wheat field to the east. He's too far to see clearly, but even tiny, I'd know that old cowboy hat and overalls anywhere. I trot down the stairs and start after him.

"Paige?" Mr. Ferro calls. "Have you seen Royal today?"

"Up there!" I point to the top of the pine, but don't slow down.

In the pasture beside the grain, Milkshake munches grass while her calf sprints with the others, in spurts and stops, his little red tail flying straight up like the antennae on a dune buggy. They probably don't even remember the scary parts of the birth, though I don't think I'll ever forget.

The grain is past my ankles, the ground rich and thawed. Water runs in the canals. Everything's ready for us to put pipe out on the field. All I need is Grandpa's go-ahead and we'll be good to go.

"Grandpa, can we lay pipe out today?"

"I thought you were grounded."

"I am, but I'm sure Mom would let me work with you."

"It may be best if we hold off and see how the next few weeks go." He scratches the wire-brush whiskers on his chin as we start to walk through the wheat field. "No sense laying pipe if'n we have to pick it right back up again."

Grandpa was born to farming like a horse was born to run. Watching him hesitate and second-guess himself is as alien as a horse shying from pasture for fear of squishing the grass.

Since when do we farm based on what ifs? Farming is full of them. It's the greatest gamble there is. What if the sun don't shine? What if a killing frost wipes us out, or a hailstorm pounds our crops into dust? None of that matters. When there's work to do, we do it.

"Sometimes you get the job you want to do, and other times you get the job you have to do. This is a *have*-to-do kind of job. It needs to be done," I say.

"Who told you that?"

"You did! Same as 'Hoe to the end of the row' and 'Put your shoulder to the wheel' and all that." I think he'll laugh, 'cause he always does when I give his advice back to him, but he doesn't.

"Maybe tomorrow."

Real gentle, I try reasoning. "You don't have to help if you don't want to. I can have Scotty drive the pipe wagon and lay it down myself. I know what to do, and I can help him corner if he has trouble."

"Let it rest, Paige. I said not today."

"No sense in waiting." I keep my voice all cheerful, like it's no big deal, even though it is. I promised I'd take care of things, and no pipe means plants will thirst to death. "You can go do whatever you need to. I can take care of this."

"Don't worry about it."

Well, isn't that like choking down a hot poker? Don't

worry about it? I *have* to worry about it. No one else is. "I can do it. I really can. You don't have to listen to Miss Dolly. You can change your mind if you want to."

Fight it. I will the words to him. *Pull Miss Dolly's lies out by the root.*

His face softens, and I almost hope, but then he shakes his head. "No dice."

The words are quiet, but final, and ring with an emptiness that slices straight through me.

What else is there to say? I drop my gaze to the scuffed toes and stains on Grandpa's leather boots, because it's easier than looking him in the eye when all he wants to do is give up. It's rooted so deep I can't even touch it.

Grandpa pats my back and kisses the top of my head, and I almost drown in all the words I don't dare say. I should know by now that I can't count on anyone—especially grown-ups.

I walk away a few steps, and the wishstone bumps against my thigh. I pull it out and roll the smooth stone in my palm, flipping it end over end.

This is not how this is supposed to end.

Holding my wishstone tight in my fist, I stand in front of him where he can't help but see me. "Grandpa?"

His gaze flicks to mine.

"I need this."

"You heard Miss Dolly. If she doesn't sell to them developers, like as not, the bank will take our land and turn it into houses or a mall or something anyway."

"But they don't have it yet."

"I'm tired, Paige. A man can work a lifetime, and what do we have in the end?"

I tug his sleeve. "But that's just it, Grandpa. This isn't the end. Dad always said there was no quit in you, but all I hear is quit. I already lost my Dad. Don't make me lose you too."

He drops to a knee and takes my chin in his hand. "I'm not lost. I'm right here."

"But *I'm* lost." I wipe my sleeve across my nose. "If we leave, *you* can say you grew crops all on your own, that you did your best all the time. What can I say if I never even get the chance to try? My whole life I'm gonna remember this. That I coulda tried to grow things and make Dad proud, but I didn't."

"Darlin', I—"

"Please, Grandpa? Please? If you don't want to, that's okay, but I need to try. I can do it on my own. Let me try, please."

He pulls me in close and oil, dust, sweat, and peppermint fill my nose.

"Hush. Sweet pea, your daddy is already proud of you. And so am I."

⤫ ⤬

For the rest of the evening, we lay out three-inch pipe.

Grandpa drives the tractor with the spare pipe wagon behind it real slow, so I can lift each forty-foot section off the trailer, carry it to the row, and slide the ends together, one inside the other, always making sure they latch. Hollow, aluminum lines stretch out behind me in silver ribbons.

They don't fit together as good as Legos, or tractor parts,

but when the water pressure comes up, the seals close, and water soars out of the Rain Bird sprinklers.

We don't get all the fields done, but we finish one and get a good start on another. All the while, Grandpa sits sideways, driving with one hand on the wheel and an elbow on the seat back behind him, so he can look ahead to watch where he's going, but never lose track of me and where we've been.

When we come in for the night, the stars are just starting to show, but I still check on Milkshake, her calf, and the herd. When I check the chickens, a soft rattle comes from Royal's open cage, and I smile to see him perched on his sawhorse with his head pillowed against his chest.

Scotty will be beside himself when I tell him Royal came home.

Carefully, I close our peacock's door and promise to let him out again soon.

CHAPTER TWENTY-ONE

Don't Say He's Gone

On our afternoon bus ride home, Mateo, Kimana, and I each sit on individual seats with our backs to the windows and our legs stretched out. Like always, we're almost the last ones home.

I flip through a biography about Henry Ford and half-listen while Kimana drills Mateo with study cards for their English test.

"Okay." Kimana flips a note card. "What was the quote about fear?"

Mateo grins at me. "'Though she be but little, she is fierce.' William Shakespeare, *A Midsummer Night's Dream*."

I smack his seat. "Hey! I'm not little."

"So why'd you think I was talking about you?" He smirks. "Sound familiar?"

"Beep! Wrong." She wiggles a card. "That was *fierce*, not fear. Try again."

Closing his eyes, he softly bonks his head against the window. "Um . . . some kind of warning, I think." His eyes fly open. "Oh yeah! 'Beware! For I am fearless and therefore powerful.' Mary Shelley, *Frankenstein*. Right?"

"Right."

"Okay. My turn. Hand 'em over." He reaches for the cards and starts flipping through them. "Do . . . the dream one."

After a deep breath, Kimana says, "'It does not do to dwell on dreams and forget to live.' J.K. Rowling, *Harry Potter and the Sorcerer's Stone*."

"Ah, that was too easy." He slips card after card behind each other.

"How many do you need?" I ask.

"The class picked twenty at the beginning of the trimester, and we'll be tested on ten, but we don't know which ten, so we have to memorize them all," Kimana says.

"The teacher is cruel, I tell you. This takes up too much brain space." Mateo curls his fingers against his forehead. "Aaaah, my brain's melting! Okay, name the quote about yesterday."

"'It's no use going back to yesterday, because I was a different person then.' Lewis Carroll, from *Alice's Adventures in Wonderland*. Give me the cards."

We pull up to my stop, and I swing my backpack over my shoulder on my way to the door. "Don't hurt your brains too much."

"Too late!" Mateo waits till I look back, then opens his mouth in a wide grimace. "Aaagghh! Brains!"

"See you, Paige." Kimana waves. "Mateo! Pay attention. Say the 'don't cry' one."

"Um . . . Dr. Seuss. 'Don't cry because it's over; smile because it happened.'"

I'm smiling when the bus pulls away—until I spy Scotty.

He waits at the end of our driveway, his collar stretched to the side where he's been worrying at it.

"What's happened?" I glance at our little island of trees at the end of the lane, though I don't know what for. Smoke? Fire? "What's going on?"

"He's gone. He's gone!" He taps thumb to fingers over and over.

Images of Grandpa fill my head, and I grab Scotty's arms, holding him even as his fingers flutter like wounded moths. "Who? Scotty, who is gone? Is it Grandpa?"

"No. No, no." He shakes his head. "It's Royal."

He must've forgot Royal wasn't in the trees anymore. "No, I just put him away last night. I told you."

He shakes his head. "No, no, no. Inside the barn. Dogs came inside the barn."

"Wait—what do you mean *gone*? Like dead?"

His face crumples. "I don't know. I don't know!"

I don't wait for Scotty. His lighter footfalls fade behind me, a distant echo to my boots pounding the dust.

The words "He's gone" repeat in my head, but in Mom's voice, not Scotty's, and I don't want to believe it. *He's gone.*

He can't be. Not this time. Not again.

My backpack hits the dirt somewhere by the yard, but I

don't stop till I reach the chicken barn and clutch the rough-hewn beam framing the door, my hand pressed to my side.

It takes me a moment to understand what I'm seeing. Splintered rabbit hutch panels lie beside what used to be a wall of straw bales. An overturned feed dish rests by the barn door with ground oyster shells strewn across the floor. The chain-link fence tilts, collapsed on top of the sawhorse, and claw marks rake the ground around the cage.

Almost nothing is left of our peacock cage. The dogs tore it all apart.

Gaping holes mar the edge of the straw stack where frenzied animals ripped down the straw. Broken and ruined bales sprawl at the base of the cage amidst feed barrels tipped on their sides, precious grain spilled into the dust.

In the center of it all, Mom's rodeo tote lies on its side, with silk sashes torn and soiled, trophies scattered and broken, and shattered rose petals lost to dirt and straw.

"Oh gosh." My breath comes in quick little gasps. How many would it take to do this? We'd had dog problems before—people always dump them out here—but Dad was always here to run them off.

Stupid. *Stupid!* It's *my* job to protect the farm now. I should have been here. I let school get in the way.

Unnatural silence presses on my ears. Why can't I hear the chickens?

The hens! I'm halfway to the chickens at the back, when something moves inside the hushed coop and my steps stall.

Are the dogs still in here? I know better than to come

empty-handed. I glance to the side for a hammer—something, anything to fight with—but no, it's only the chickens moving behind the coop's thick wire door, their heads bobbing, watching with bright black eyes, their silence an eerie witness to the violence of the day.

Scotty runs up to the doorway. I want to hold him back, but he's already seen it all. Every spike of fear and anxiety I hide is laid bare in him with every twitch of his fingers.

Maybe Royal took shelter at the top of the stack?

I climb up and almost fall from relief when no blue body greets me. A few downy blue feathers and one broken tail quill are all that's left of our Royal. Cradled in my hands, the broken feather feels light and fragile, and I know I failed him.

It was my responsibility to keep him safe. I should have been there.

"He's not there." Scotty rocks from side to side. "I looked before I got you. And he's not in his cage, or in the tree."

"That's a good thing." Wasn't it? A body would be worse. But my brain is churning like an engine stuck in high gear. The tracks below tell the story plain enough. A half dozen big dogs tore the place apart, and somehow, they knew our Royal was here.

The few loose blue feathers here are more akin to what's left behind when a pheasant bursts into flight. If they'd gotten hold of him, feathers would be everywhere.

"They didn't kill him." My certainty grows with every word.

"You sure?" Scotty stills, his whole body focused.

"Positive—at least not in here. I think he got away."

"But he's hurt. What if they follow him?"

"I don't know." I climb down, trying to make sense of it all. What sent them into such a frenzy to start with? Did they hear him? Seems like those dogs had to be chasing something already to be so worked up by the time they hit the barn.

I study the rooflines of every building and stare at every tree, but as far as I can tell, Royal isn't anywhere. I grab a pitchfork by the wall. Whatever happens, it's my job to find him and take care of what's left. I owe him that.

"Come on. Let's see where the tracks go."

It's hard to tell direction, with paw prints everywhere, but after a couple false starts, I find tracks heading toward the copse of trees along the canal. "This way."

Scotty scrambles beside me. "This would work better if we had bloodhounds on the trail. Their olfactory centers are highly specialized, you know."

Even a bloodhound mix like T-Rex might help. He probably had a fit with all these strange dogs on his turf.

I skid to a stop. "Where's T-Rex?"

"What?"

"T-Rex? Where is he?" He would've chased the pack off or died trying. I cup my hands to my mouth. "Rex! T-Rex!"

"He's gone," Scotty says, and my knees almost buckle.

He's gone.

Royal. T-Rex. Dad.

"How can he be gone?"

"I don't see him." Scotty's dirty blond head shakes.

"But *when* did you see him last? Was he here when you got home?"

"Not since this morning. Same as you."

"Didn't you notice?" There never was a dog more devoted to a boy, but Scotty doesn't bother to notice when he's gone?

"Yeah," he answers in that distracted way of his when his mind is three steps ahead and the "now" is unimportant.

"If you noticed, why didn't you say anything? What's wrong with you?" I know I'm spitting sparks from a fire he didn't start, but he notices everything, knows everything, and the one time I *need* him to know, he's as clueless as me.

"I did! I did notice, but then I saw the barn . . ." His shoulders hunch, but my worry is too big to stuff down with a sorry, and I run on.

"Rex? T-Rex!" Nothing moves ahead. No blood, no fur. There's nothing but tracks.

At the foot of the trees, grass and weeds hide fallen branches, and scrub is everywhere except for a bare hollow on the east side beside a downed log. Tufts of grass lie torn and discarded in careless piles, ripped away by sharp, digging claws, and eager muzzles.

"Rex?" My steps slow, eyes scouring every shadow and crevice. No sign of him. No blue feathers either.

I really don't want to look in the hollow. What if he's hurt down there, or dead?

Please don't be dead. Don't be gone.

But I have to look. It's *my* job to watch out for them. I set the pitchfork down.

Gingerly, I kneel beside the log and peer down a small hole framed between several logs. No way could T-Rex fit down there, but the tunnel is fresh dug.

Deep in the gloom, two bright disks blink at me, and I still. We stare at each other, the eyes and me. One heartbeat, two. A shadow shifts, revealing the outline of a head and shoulder. The ears flatten.

A growl rumbles in the darkness, rising until a snarl tears from the hole.

An electric jolt as sharp as a hot wire shoots right through me, and I scramble back, expecting the shadow to come after me. I back away, and grab my pitchfork from the grass, but he doesn't come out, and the growling dies.

A fox.

They were chasing a fox. Not my T-Rex.

Heart thundering, I jog a dozen yards down the path before realizing I should have looked to see where the dogs went from there, but I'm sure T-Rex never went that way. If he had, he'd still be standing sentry outside the fox's lair.

So fine, T-Rex isn't here. Where is he? And what about Royal? If the dogs chased the fox up to Royal's cage, where'd he go? Did he make it to a tree? Or did they pull him from the sky by his tail?

Jaw set, I stride to the nearest outbuilding and jerk the door open. Maybe T-Rex got closed inside, or maybe Royal is stuck in there somehow. It doesn't make any sense, but neither does anything else. I was supposed to watch out for them, take care of them, and I can't even *find* them.

I slam the door so hard, boards vibrate on the wall and a horseshoe falls from overhead, the nails rotted out.

Bad luck, but instead of worrying, it just makes me madder. Why is everything a fight? I have to fight to keep my farm, fight to do the work, fight just to keep what's left of my family together, and stupid Scotty is just standing there with his hands over his ears like I'm yelling at him—but I'm not!

I round on him. "He's not here, okay? Put your stupid hands down. I'm not even yelling!" Except I am now, and I don't even know why. I try to dampen the heat inside me, but hiding underneath it is a fear so strong, I think I might die if I face it straight on.

T-Rex. Royal. Dad.

Things I've loved and lost are all mixed together in a mishmash of pain so great, I cling to my anger like a lifeline.

Set free, rage bubbles up like a fryer spitting hot grease on everything. But the more I erupt, the more anger there is to throw. The fury loops inside me till I can't hardly see straight, my hands in tight fists.

"Why does everything get taken away?"

The back door to the house slams shut, and I know Scotty's run up to his room, but I can't care about that yet. I've got more searching to do. I march off, cursing everything and everyone under my breath.

Barns, outbuilding, toolshed, pump house . . . All of them are empty.

No feathers, no T-Rex.

They're just gone.

He's gone.

I stomp into the house past T-Rex's pile of old sleeping bags, the hollow in the middle where he sleeps as cavernous and glaring as Dad's empty boots standing against the wall.

The darkened kitchen holds no welcoming smells, the counters wiped and sterile like I left them this morning. Only the stack of mail on the table tells me anyone's been here at all—and that's Grandpa's doing, not Mom's. I grab the stack and dump it into the basket—with all the other unopened mail—on top of the piano. The overflowing basket rankles me. It's one thing for *me* to ignore reading stuff if I can get away with it, but Dad would never have let the mail get that out of control.

Dad.

I stare at the phone on the counter. I hate it so much. It steals time. Steals people.

Snatching the phone, I unplug it to call Mom and Grandpa, but my finger hovers over the screen. What if they're driving? What if I call, and they answer, and—

I dial Kimana.

"Hey," she answers on the second ring. "What's up?"

"Have you seen T-Rex around?" I clear my throat, hating the wobble that squeaks out. "Or Royal—our peacock?"

"Not since I was at your place. Why? Is he missing?"

"There were dogs in the barn, and now they're both gone." I hate how weak I sound. "Let me know if you see them, okay?"

"Sure. You want me to come over?"

"Nah. I'll be okay. Call you later."

"Okay . . . ?" I pretend not to notice the question in her agreement, hang up, and dial Mateo.

"Bueno." Mr. Rivas answers.

I stutter, "Mateo—uh, I mean, *hola,* Señor Rivas, is Mateo there?"

"He's checking the herd. Left his phone inside charging. You want I have him call you?"

"That'd be great. Thanks."

Wood creaks from where Scotty eavesdrops on the landing, but I'm not ready to play nice, not when I'm left with nothing but a stupid phone. I start to dial Mom's number, but through the kitchen window, I see Grandpa's truck round the bend and turn onto our lane. I drop the phone and run out to meet him.

I'm flipping through all the things to say—and not say—about the barn and the peacock and T-Rex, when a droopy-eyed head pokes out the passenger window, jowls flapping in the wind.

T-Rex.

Not gone. Grandpa has him.

I brace my hands on my knees and let my head hang forward to keep from falling. I stay like that, eyes closed, as the truck pulls up to the house.

"T-Rex!" The screen door bangs open, and Scotty pounds down the porch steps. "Hello, boy."

I lift my chin to watch him as he runs—chattering all the while—and opens the passenger door, almost before Grandpa throws it into park. "There you are! You had me worried, you did. Where'd you take him, Grandpa? Did he go to the vet? Is he okay?"

Grandpa takes off his hat and wipes his brow. "Went for parts and didn't have anyone to ride shotgun, and when I opened the door, ol' Rex jumped right in."

"Is Royal in the truck too?"

"The peacock? No. Just the pup."

"He'll come back, right? We made him better." Scotty's small fingers scrub T-Rex's head and ears, his monologue only faltering for a moment when he passes me and flinches. "Did you go for a ride, Rexy? Rexy-boy, I missed you. I *knew* you were gone. I noticed and looked. I swear. Come on, pup."

I sigh. It'll take some doing to get on his good side again. The little squirt has a long memory.

As Grandpa shuffles through the gate, I take a few bags with the John Deere logo from his overfilled arms and follow him to the toolshed. "So, why didn't you tell me you were taking T-Rex?"

"Seeing as how your phone was on the counter like always, figured it wouldn't do a lick of good to call it."

Okay, so, point to Grandpa. "But where's Mom? Why didn't she go with you?"

He drops the armful of parts onto the workbench in the toolshed. "No time, not with her interview today and all."

One of the bags slips from my arms. "Interview? But what about the farm?"

"Things being tight as they are, she's lookin' to go back to work in town."

"If it's work she wants, we have more than enough here." I drop the bags beside Grandpa's on the workbench.

"Don't be too hard on her. She's doing the best she can, same as you."

Instead of soothing, his words stoke the fire that's still smoldering inside me, fear and anger all twisted and mashed up together.

I told Mom that Dad's calendar spells everything out simple, if we just follow it, but she won't listen. Our farm is falling. I can feel it teetering and going over, but with Mom, it's like I'm patching holes in a parachute as fast as I can, and she's following right behind, cutting new holes with a pocketknife.

"If she's doing the best she can, why is she hiding in her room all the time, and going to school, and now getting a town job? What about the farm? What about us? If she'd just work instead of doing all that other stuff, we'd be fine. She just needs to work *harder*. It's like she doesn't even care!"

The steel in Grandpa's eyes freezes my tongue.

"You best leave off your mom. You've got no idea what's going on."

CHAPTER TWENTY-TWO

Real Friends Know

Still stinging from Grandpa's tongue-lashing, I walk the ditch banks, searching for Royal. Like castle walls, our canals sit taller than the rest of the farm and make for good lookouts.

I knew I was out of line. I shouldn'ta been mean to Mom, and especially not to Scotty. I shoulda kept a lid on all that emotional stuff, but sometimes it builds up too fast, a pressure cooker of all the words I don't say superheated by all the feelings I bury. I think my steam valve must've overloaded.

I've barely walked a quarter mile when Kimana rides up, her long hair whipping from the back of her helmet, the beaded pouch bobbing low against her thigh. Two bucks says she jumped on her bike the minute I called—right after I said *not* to come.

Real friends know when to listen, when to help, and when to totally ignore everything you say and come save you anyway.

She slows beside me, her engine puttering. "What's going on?"

"T-Rex was with my grandpa, but I'm still looking for Royal. Can't find him anywhere."

"Where's your truck? You gonna walk all eighty acres on foot? Hop on. You look left and I'll look right, and we'll cover a bunch of ground really fast." She unstraps the half-shell helmet from the rack on the back and passes it to me, then tucks her hair into her gray hoodie to keep it out of my face.

"Okay." I swing a leg over, fold down the tiny footrests, and hold onto her waist. "Ready."

The bike wobbles a little when we start to roll, but evens out as we pick up speed along the canal, gray sky reflecting across the water beside us. I scour every branch, tree, and hollow in the fields. I lean with her into corners and hold tight when she flies down one bank and up another.

A pheasant struts through the wheat, and two hawks glide in lazy circles high overhead. Dogs stop to watch us from neighboring fields, but I can't tell if those were the dogs in my barn. Cows and calves graze, and Milkshake lies in the grass with her calf. Chickens scratch in the pasture, and horses' ears perk up as we drive by, but Royal is nowhere.

After circling the farm with no luck, we pull up behind the house.

"Have you checked our fort?" Kimana hangs her helmet on the handlebars and shakes out her hair while I clip the spare onto the rack.

"Not yet." I peer into the shadows of trees around the

house and barn, hoping against hope that *this* time, I'll see Royal perched on a branch somewhere. But he's not, and it hurts my heart to keep looking for someone I'm never going to find. I've done that for too long already.

At our tree, Kimana climbs the rungs nailed to the trunk and slips up through the trapdoor onto the platform of our tree fort.

"Do you see anything?" I call up.

"Just a minute." Kimana takes her time studying each tree all the way around. "Do you know you have an owl in your pine tree?"

"Hoo, hoo!" The owl calls out, but I can't see it from the ground.

"Yeah, he and Royal were kind of hanging out yesterday."

She stays another half minute, then starts down. "I can't see Royal, but your owl is creepy."

"I think it's the same one that used to be in the potato cellar. He flew right over my head when I opened the doors. Great big, powerful wings. Fast too. I used to think owls were the prettiest birds on the farm, but that was before Royal."

Kimana falls into step with me on the way to the chicken barn. "Their feathers are made for different things," she says. "One's built for speed and stealth in the dark, and the other's for looking pretty in the light."

"True."

Inside the barn, we clean up Mom's totes with the sashes and trophies, but when I pick up the roses Dad gave her, the petals crumble off the stems, raining down over my hand like ashes.

"Oh man." I pick up a couple petals, but they shatter at my touch.

This shouldn't be so hard. Just pick up the flowers and put them back. Maybe glue can fix it. I can do this. Gingerly, I pick up another petal, but it breaks in half.

"Dang it!" I throw the naked stem across the barn. "I can't fix anything. This is all so hard. Why does this have to be so hard?"

"Some things can't be fixed." Kimana brushes what's left of the roses off the plastic lid and tosses them outside. "And that's not your fault."

"But it was my job to look after things. I promised I would." We worked so good together—me and Dad. It was like I was the spark and he the fire, but with him gone, I'm sparking as hard as I can, but the engine just won't go. I'm stuck, and there's no way to make it better.

"Sit with me a minute." She sits on a straw bale, pulls her note cards out of her pouch, sets them between us, and then pulls out a long leather lanyard with blue-green beads vining a few inches up either side.

"Is that the peacock one I asked for? I thought you had a bunch of orders that needed to be done first."

She passes it to me. "Yeah, I do, and it's not done, but I'm working on it in between. Even if Royal never comes back, I'll still finish this, so you can remember him."

"Thank you." It's easy to see the bead pattern as feathers,

215

and it's beautiful, but it doesn't stop me from imagining Royal hurt or stuck somewhere.

"Do you really think that this farm is the only legacy your dad left behind? Seems to me, a person's legacy is more than what they own."

"The farm was his whole world—it was his dream." I slump down beside her and trace the beadwork draped across the callouses on my hands. "It's like trying to build a robot without the right parts, or coding when half the program disappears. I don't know how we'll make it without him."

"You *will* make it. I lost my mom, remember? I can't finish her work or do her job, but I can be the sort of person she wanted me to be. She was kind, she loved her family, and she cared about people. That's how I'm trying to be—how I carry on her legacy. Do you really think your dad's dream was for you to work yourself into the ground?"

A dirt bike growls up to the barn, and Mateo cuts the engine and jumps off. "Hey, my dad said you called, but I called back and you didn't answer . . ." His steps slow as he takes in the mess. "What happened?"

"Best I can tell, dogs chased a fox in here and they all went crazy and broke Royal's cage all to bits." I pass the lanyard to Kimana, and she tucks it into her pouch.

He whistles. "Did they get him?"

"I don't know. I can't find him."

"That stinks." He grabs a bale and tosses it on top of the stack, but it doesn't catch right, teeters, and falls back. With a grunt, he grabs the strings again. "Here, you climb up top, and I'll pass it to you."

"You don't have to. I can get it."

"Yeah, yeah, you can—but you don't have to."

I scramble up the stack, kneel down, and reach for the bale. One bale after the other, we wedge them back in place while Kimana cleans up the twine and broken pieces.

"Have you called Mr. Ferro yet?" He grunts and shoves another bale up.

I grasp the twine and heave it onto the stack. "Not yet."

"It's his peacock. You should tell him. He can help look."

"You call him."

He throws the last bale hard enough that it almost knocks me over. "Aw, come on! The one time you call me, I missed it."

"Mateo, will you put these away? Why are they in here, anyway?" Kimana picks up a stack of black planting trays and hands it to him. "You could call Mr. Ferro on the way."

"Sure." He grabs the trays and walks out.

Kimana stacks pieces of the rabbit hutch by the door while I pitchfork broken bales into the chicken coop. Ten minutes later, we've got the barn mostly put back to rights again.

A siren chirps outside—*whoop, whoop!*—and blue-and-red lights flash across the barn as a Fort Hall police cruiser pulls up.

Kimana drops some wood onto the pile and runs to meet the officer getting out of the car. "My dad's here!"

With more gadgets on his utility belt than Batman, Officer Charging Horse gives Kimana a one-armed hug.

"Officer Charging Horse." Mateo nods and slips past us into the barn.

Kimana grins and waves me over. "I told him you had dog trouble today."

Kimana's dad nods to me. "I already talked to your grandpa about bringing over some live traps, but I'm actually here to pick up Kimana."

"Me? What for?" she asks.

He smiles down at her. "Feather had her baby and needs you to come stay at the cabin with the cousins."

"Okay. Yeah. I'll come right now." She grabs her helmet and waves at me over her shoulder. "I gotta go. See you in a few days."

"Good luck!" I call, as she kicks the starter and rides away, Officer Charging Horse following behind in the cruiser.

"Wow. What do you think? Boy or girl?" I look for Mateo by the stack, but he stands by the coop door, his arms folded. "Hey! Boy or girl?"

He shrugs. "When were you going to tell me?"

"What do you mean? I heard about the baby just now, same as you."

"The flower basket. The one gift we had for my mom this weekend. It was supposed to be a surprise. If you didn't want to take care of it, you could have told me, and I would have figured something else out."

"Shoot." The trays. The trays he took back to the green-house—right next to the roasted and frozen flower basket. "I'm sorry. I was gonna buy you another one."

"You can't buy another one like that. Not here. My dad drove to Utah to get it. Asked them to make it special with the pink survivor ribbons for my mom."

Unsure how to fix it, or even *if* there's a way to fix it, I reach for him. "I wanted to tell you, but I thought I could make it better first."

"I know you didn't mean to." He walks past me. "I know you're stressed. I get it. I told you, I'm here to help." He touches his heart, his promise. "And I am. But if you didn't want to take care of it—or if it was too much to do—you should've said so. I coulda taken it back."

I hurry to catch up to him as he leaves the barn. "I can ask Grandpa to help. We can find something."

"There's no time to get another. It's for this weekend." He stops and looks at me. "You know what's dumb? I thought about checking on it before, but didn't because I trusted you."

My throat prickles like I've swallowed a cocklebur. "You can trust me. You know you can."

"I thought I did." He gets on his bike.

"I'm sorry. I didn't know how to tell you."

"All you got to do is talk." He pulls his phone from his pocket. "And if you can't say it out loud, at least you could text." He shakes his head. "But not you. Never a text from you. I bet you haven't even read my texts since the accident, have you?"

What am I supposed to say? He knows I don't text. I don't hide it.

"One call. That's all you had to do."

"Mateo, wait."

"I gotta go. Chores." He starts the engine and drives away. "Text you later."

Long after the sound of his dirt bike fades to nothing, I start moving again, putting new food and water on the floor and on top of the stack, in case Royal comes back to either spot. Kimana's note cards lay on the straw where she left them, and I put them inside the house on the kitchen table for safekeeping. I go through the motions, do all the chores as if someone else programed me to move, more robot than girl. I do pretty good at not thinking until I haul the broken bits of wood to the burn pile.

Seeing the broken pieces of Royal's cage left in a place that used to give us hope is almost more than I can stand.

Never has it seemed *less* magical for a wishfire than today, every piled scrap and splinter feeling more like shattered dreams than wood.

CHAPTER TWENTY-THREE

He's All Heart

Royal didn't come back that night. Or the next morning.

Mr. Ferro came over and looked all over the place with that little city hat of his and a net, but he didn't have any better luck than I did.

At school, Mr. Collier chewed on me for dozing off in class again, but all night, whenever I'd closed my eyes, I'd imagined new places for Royal to be stuck, or hurt, or both, and the not-knowing was frying my brain.

So I did the only thing I know how to do when thinking is too much: I worked.

Over the next three days, Grandpa really stepped up—working while I was at school, moving pipe with us, and fixing the tractors. He's a lot slower than he used to be, and he sometimes has to stop and catch his breath, but it feels a little like it used to when all of us were working together with Dad—except Scotty won't look at me, let alone talk to me.

Mr. Ferro keeps coming around to look for Royal, and ends up staying to help Grandpa or Mom. He messes up a lot, and doesn't know much, but he tries real hard. His new tennis shoes are even starting to look lived-in. He even brought us a couple things he found while cleaning out his grandparents' house, things he thought we'd like, as kind of a thank you for caring for Royal—which was probably nicer than we deserved. He gave Scotty a *National Geographic* magazine with a feature on peacocks, which Scotty read all the way to school.

And he gave me a little wooden plate with a peacock feather engraved around the outside and a quote in the middle. It said: "'The sparrow is sorry for the peacock at the burden of its tail.'—Tagore."

Seems to me, a sparrow only wishes it could have a peacock tail. But at least the feather around the outside is pretty.

I miss Mateo's morning drive-by stops on his paper route, and when I try to talk to him at school, he gives me short answers or says nothing at all.

Kimana says her cousin and the baby are doing great, but she doesn't know when she'll be back.

My heart adds both of my friends' names to my list of missing:

Royal, Dad, Kimana, Mateo.

By now my world has so many missing pieces, I don't even know what it's supposed to be a picture of.

This afternoon, Scotty and I are moving pipe while Mr. Ferro helps Grandpa with the tractor—or at least tries to help. Once we get the lines all hooked together in their new spot,

Scotty runs to the pump and flips it on while I wait in the field with wire in hand.

As pressure rises inside the lines, water scurries along the belly of the pipe, spilling out at each joint into tiny pools before rushing ahead to the next. I know it's close when air hisses from the Rain Bird sprinklers atop the risers, the *shhhh* sound growing more urgent until water chokes off the air and gurgles up into weak arcs of water dribbling out the spouts.

Some of the birds spin in lazy circles, the water looping the risers 'round and 'round, while others cough and sputter, spraying mist. Then comes the magic moment when the lines pressurize, and the birds come up all at once, rising from trickles to silver rainbows arcing over the field.

In my pipe-moving boots, I listen and watch for breaks in the lines, or clogged birds. We're lucky today. I only have to shove the wire down three birds to clear them out before they all work.

By the time I get back to the truck, Scotty's already there, watching the road and very definitely *not* looking at me. In fact, he's not-looking so hard, his little body is rigid. When I start the engine, he bumps a can of WD-40 with his foot, knocking it gently against a can of starting fluid. The *clink, clink* is better than silence, which is all Scotty's been giving me for days. Half the time when I do catch his gaze, he looks past me as if he's about to cry, so I don't push it, but I'm mighty tired of being invisible. All this silence is the pits.

With a sigh, I sneak a glance from the dirt road to Scotty. "Okay, I give."

Not even a flicker to show he heard me.

"Scotty, I'm sorry I yelled at you. Really, I am. I know better, and I was scared for Royal and then really scared for T-Rex, and I was mad."

He stirs a bit, and I nudge his shoulder.

"I'm not mad at you," I continue. "Never at you. I know it seemed that way. I mean, I acted like I was mad at you, but I was angry at a lot of things. And it's not your fault."

His eyes flick to my open hand and away.

Well, that's something. A start, at least. "Well, think about it. Okay? I'm tired of not talking. You hear?"

His shoulders curl up toward his ears, and I know he wants to plug them to block me out.

Fine. I'll try again later.

As we near the house, I crane my head to look for Grandpa, and find him hobbling behind the disc all stiff-legged and slower than a garden tractor in first low gear. Mr. Ferro follows behind, holding a toolbox under one arm and a big wrench in the other.

We pull in beside them. "Got the water done on one field. One more to go."

"Good." Grandpa grabs the handle by the tractor door, rocks back and forth, and heaves his leg up with a grunt, but his boot hits the metal step and goes back down. He adjusts his grip, lips mashed in a thin line under his whiskers, and tries again, but his boot doesn't quite make it past the guard. "Dangnabbit!"

"What's wrong with your leg?" Scotty beats me to the question.

"It's nothing," Grandpa grumbles. "Paige, get up in there and start 'er up."

Mr. Ferro waits till Grandpa turns his back, then mouths, *He fell off the tractor.*

Is he okay? I mouth back.

He shrugs and teeters his hand back and forth.

"Paige! Get up there."

"Sure thing, Grandpa!" I run up the steps and jump in the seat.

In park? Check.

Step on both brake and clutch pedals. Check and check.

Make sure everyone is clear of the tires. Check.

Okay. I pull the throttle down a little so it has some juice, turn the key, and press the start button.

The whole cab vibrates right down to my bones as the engine growls into a roar. Smoke bursts skyward from the exhaust pipe jutting up from the hood, black at first, then clear and hot. The tractor revs and shakes, then slows and settles into a nice, regular idle. Easy peasy.

"Alright now, back up a hair." With a hand extended to keep Mr. Ferro safely behind him, Grandpa curls his fingers to back me up.

I shift it into reverse, ease off the pedals, and the tractor starts to roll. Six inches later, Grandpa holds up a hand. "You got it! Hold there."

The tractor jerks when I throw it into park.

Mr. Ferro and Grandpa both step behind the cab and wrestle with getting the three-point hitch and pin off, then back out of the way, Grandpa red-faced and wiping his brow with his sleeve.

"Forward!"

At Grandpa's command, I shift into second and follow the men out of the field to the gravel by the house before turning off the key and shutting it down.

T-Rex moseys out of the yard to greet us, tail wagging.

"What's going on?" I hop down the steps.

"Tire change. We aired it up, but it'll be flat again quick if we don't change the tube." Grandpa leans against the front tire of the tractor and wheezes, then slaps his thigh and nods to Mr. Ferro. "Paige, get the jack out of the truck, and Asher, you grab the bead breaker. Let's get this done."

"On it." I start for the truck as, behind me, Mr. Ferro says, "What's a bead breaker?"

Maybe ten minutes later, we've got the tire lifted off the ground, and Mr. Ferro steadies the bead breaker—a metal wedge with a thin curve on the end—as Grandpa pounds it between the metal rim and the rubber tire with a sledgehammer.

"Let me do that. I'm strong enough." I reach for the sledge-hammer, but he pulls it away.

"Smart enough, yes. Strong enough? Tall enough? No."

T-Rex pads between Grandpa and the tire and lies down almost on his boots, but Grandpa shoos him away. "What makes ya think I want you napping underfoot? Go on, Rexy-boy. Give me some space."

Reluctantly, T-Rex slinks off a few yards, then sits and watches, his head tilted to the side.

With feet spread and hands tight on the handle, Grandpa swings the sledgehammer wide over his shoulder and slams it down onto the wedge with powerful, controlled blows. Devastating and dividing, the sledgehammer beats the wedge deeper, forcing the two apart.

"You kids—"

Boom!

"Get that—"

Boom!

"Other field done."

Boom!

He sets the hammer head on the ground and leans on the handle, gasping. "If you hurry, you can come help us after."

"Okay." I step toward the truck, but hesitate. "Do you want a drink? I could get you a drink first."

"Nah. I'm good. Go on."

He hefts up the hammer and swings again.

Boom!

The metal sings with the blow.

Boom!

"You coming, T-Rex?" Scotty pats his leg, but T-Rex lays his head on his paws and whines. "Aww, come on."

"Leave him be. He's tired." I open the truck door. "We'll be right back."

Scotty and me drive over to the field on the other side of the lane and get to moving pipe. This one's hook-and-latch, instead of ball-and-socket, so it's harder to get apart—especially when they're full of mud in the ends.

Once, I think I hear our peacock cry, but it's only once, and I can't be sure. Probably, I'm just wishing.

T-Rex's deep bark rolls across the field, a constant slow beat, and I look toward the house but can't see him from so far away.

Scotty darts ahead of me on each pipe and lifts the hook so I can pull it apart easier, then helps clip it all back together after I carry it to the new spot. He pauses to listen to T-Rex, but runs on once I get the pipe in place.

Mom putters up the road in Patches and waves to us as we work in the field.

I cradle the pipe in the crook of my elbow and wave back real quick before I lose my balance.

She cruises up the lane and disappears under the trees by our house.

I call over to Scotty, "Mom's home!"

He lifts the next hook and waits for me to pull, but doesn't look at me.

"You can't stay mad at me forever." Maybe so, but he's doin' his darnedest to try.

We make good time and finish the field, but right as Scotty flips the water pump on, a siren wails in the distance, and T-Rex howls.

The truck bed rocks as I climb up and stand with a hand shading my eyes. "Sounds like it's over by the Pruitts."

But no, it's too close for that.

The lights come first, bouncing off ditch banks and peeking through trees. Then the ambulance speeds into view.

I suck in a breath as it slows down near Kimana's house.

Not Hutsi. Please let Hutsi be okay.

But it accelerates again, swinging wide around the corner, siren wailing.

I jump onto the roof of the truck, the metal denting under my boots.

No. No. No.

Scotty comes running from the pump.

Flashing red lights sear my eyes until it's all I can see.

Don't stop. Don't . . .

Powerful, controlled, the ambulance cruises up the last rise—and turns down our lane.

I slide down the front of the cab to the hood and jump to the ground. "Get in! Get in right now!"

Scotty dives for his door as I wrench open mine. We jump in and slam them shut.

Boom!

Sprinklers sputter and cough, mist billowing from the Rain Birds as we fly down the dirt path. Tools bounce on the floor and fall from the dash.

Scotty braces himself with one hand on the seat, the other on the door.

First gear, second—my truck roars, and I shift into third.

Red lights blaze across our house, reflecting off bedroom windows, dripping crimson onto our porch.

WENDY S. SWORE

The birds come up, long arcs of life-giving water splatter across my window, and I twist the lever to wipe them away.

I don't have to ask who the ambulance came for. I know. I just don't know how bad.

We turn onto our lane and slow up before the house.

The ambulance blocks the front, so I pull to the side and park. I don't bother to close the door. I run.

A medic pushes the ambulance doors open wide, snatches something out of the back, and rushes around the side toward the tractor.

I follow right on his heels, but stop at the chaos on the other side.

Mom stands beside Asher, with her hands over her mouth.

Medics bark commands at each other, their hands a blur of blue gloves, wires, masks, and pads. They move so fast, try so hard, I can't see much of the man they work on.

I can't see the calloused hands, scruffy whiskers, gentle eyes, or caterpillar brows. I can't see his face at all.

I can only see his boots.

CHAPTER TWENTY-FOUR

A Web of Wishes

Turns out, hospitals don't let kids visit the ICU no matter how long you wait or how many times you ask.

Sometime long after sundown, as Scotty lies curled up asleep on a waiting room chair, the doctor tells Mom the procedure went well—something about a blockage and an angioballoon thing. He says Grandpa has a will to survive and a strong heart.

But we know that already.

Mom asks Asher to take us home. When we get there, Hutsi is waiting for us. She enfolds us in her warm, wrinkled arms and tucks Scotty into bed. I watch the moon rise past my window, thinking I'll keep watching till the sun takes its place. But when I open my eyes again, dawn has come and gone.

I can't remember the last time I woke up so late.

My hand aches, numb and prickly from being held tight against my chest all night, and I uncurl the fingers one by one, revealing the wishstone pressed to my palm. If whispered wishes could be spun like threads, they'd weave a web to hold us together. Grandpa, Scotty, me, Mom, Milkshake, T-Rex, all of it.

My farm. My world.

A dirt bike buzzes past the house, and I press my hands against the window as Mateo rides away down our lane.

Why was he here?

I change clothes, pull my boots on, and walk downstairs.

"Good morning, Paige." Hutsi looks up from her Sudoku puzzle and waves her pencil. "There's eggs on the stove, if you're hungry."

"Thanks. Did Mom call?"

"She did. She says she'll stop in later this morning. Your grandfather is resting now. And Kimana called too—says she'll be home tonight."

I nod. Best get chores done before Mom comes home. Wouldn't want to miss her. I pile eggs on my plate and wolf them down, partly because Hutsi is an amazing cook and partly because I've got a big day ahead with Grandpa gone.

"Thanks for breakfast. I'll be back after chores." I reach for the door.

"Young Mateo already did them," says Hutsi.

"What?"

"He stopped in before you came down and said he'd done all the morning chores. Animals are fed and watered, pipes moved. You don't have to worry about it."

"But—" I hang onto the doorknob, not sure what to do.

"Why don't you go on upstairs and lie down, or read a book? Rest while you can."

That seems sensible enough, but walking upstairs in the daytime without lifting a finger for chores is as foreign to me as pointy heels and frilly scarves.

Instead of turning right at the top of the stairs, I turn left to check on Scotty.

With curtains half drawn, the room is cozy and safe, filled with pinpricks of light slipping across his ceiling from a galaxy night-light that flickers on his bedside table. Snoring softly, he is curled on his side, small under the enormous patchwork quilt.

I watch him sleep. The rise and fall of the blankets, the flicker of his eyes beneath his closed lids. His mind is so very busy. It never rests during the day, and it seems his dreams are just as busy. He feels more, sees more, senses more than most people. Sometimes, the more excited he is, the less he shows it. And at times like that, the tiniest of smiles lights up my whole world. At other times, all that emotion runs bubbling out of his mouth in words and facts and chatter, flooding out like the headgate inside his brain has burst wide open.

He didn't deserve to be yelled at.

He deserves to be protected and loved.

I brush the hair from his eyes and tuck the blanket close around him.

"Daddy?" he mumbles.

I ignore the sting and smooth his hair back. "Just me, Scotty. It's Paige."

His lids flutter open, his sleepy eyes focusing on me.

"I'm sorry for yelling. Really. I shouldn't have. I'm sorry I hurt your feelings."

His gaze fixes on me for one heartbeat, then two, then . . . "Did you know peahens have four to eight eggs in a clutch?"

"Nope." I smooth the covers over his shoulder.

"Did you know peafowl like Royal are almost four feet long with tail feathers?"

I squeeze his shoulder. "Yeah, I knew that one."

He looks at the window, covered with stickers of planets and stars, and takes a deep breath. "Is . . . Is . . ." The rocking starts real slow. "Where's Grandpa?"

"Hutsi says he's resting."

His palms slide over his ears, his gaze fixed on the window. "Resting in heaven with Daddy?"

"Oh, Scotty. No." I gently pull his hands down and lean over so he can see me. *Really* see me. "Grandpa is resting— sleeping in the hospital. He's okay."

He chews his lip, the tautness in his body relaxing bit by bit. "How do you know?"

"Hutsi told me. She says Mom will be here later, so you don't have to worry."

"Okay. Okay." He nods. "Did you know the peacock symbolizes eternal life?"

"Nope."

Now that he's talking again, he's got days of facts to catch up on. "Also, they represent rebirth for Easter."

"I did not know that." I shake my head. "Is it because they live so long?"

"No, it's 'cause they thought the feathers never faded away. And did you know the eyes on a peacock's feathers were supposed to mean that God is watching?"

"Watching us from inside those eyes?" That sounds a little creepy.

"No, just . . . watching over us all." He yawns.

"Go back to sleep, smart boy." I kiss his forehead and tuck the covers closer. "You can teach me more things when you wake up."

He yawns again. "There's a lot to learn."

"You're right." Standing, I step toward the door.

"Do you think I'll ever learn everything?"

My hand on the doorknob, I look back one more time. "Probably not. But I think you'll try."

I try not to let Scotty's words bother me as I go back to my room, but they do. If God really is watching over us, then where is He? It sure didn't feel like anyone was watching over us in September. And what about now? Why do bad things happen at all? What about Grandpa? And Royal? Heck, we can't even find him, and *he's* the one with the fancy feathers in the first place, so who's watching out for him?

I sit on my bed like Hutsi said, but my foot twitches inside my boot, and I'm as restless as a weather vane in a windstorm. I scan the puzzles on my bedroom walls. Dad did every one with me, and always teased that I was the fastest in the West at finding the next piece and putting it in place. I wish that was true. In my real life, I can't keep any of the pieces where they belong.

I thought I knew what my life was supposed to look like. It had a dad and a mom, and Scotty, and our friends. And when pieces fell out of that picture, I tried to figure out how to put them together in a different way. Tried to make it all work without the Dad piece, with the Mom piece being broken. Now the Grandpa piece is missing too, and it just doesn't work. There aren't enough pieces left to make me whole.

Once upon a time, puzzles and robots kept me happy for hours, but the only place I feel normal anymore is when I'm outside, keeping my promise.

I pace the room, a fox in a trap, and every minute, the air grows thinner, and the walls press in. If I stay inside, I'll suffocate.

With Grandpa in the hospital, I should be doing more, not less. I gotta work enough for both of us—for all of us.

Worn and rounded with age, the wood stairs creak under my boots, and Hutsi hears me coming long before I step into the living room. "How's our Scotty?"

"Tired, but good. I'm gonna walk around till Mom gets home." I wait till she nods, then step outside.

True to his word, Mateo did all the chores, and I feel strangely useless as I stand with my elbows on a fence rail, watching Milkshake and her calf play in the sun. Usually, we only name the mommas because the calves go to sale—I think that's so it hurts less when we have to say goodbye. But this year, I'll be lucky to keep anyone at all, so what does it matter? Named or not, it's gonna hurt.

After playing with the other calves and drinking his fill of milk, our little curly-haired prince lies down in a clump of alfalfa and falls fast asleep. So that's what I name him: Prince.

"Heyo!" A distant cry pulls me right off the fence, and I turn my head, listening.

Was it Royal? With all the roosters, cows, and everything else, there's no quiet to hear one soft voice. But that makes no sense. Royal's so loud when he cries, he'd have to be awful far away for his call to be so soft that I can't tell which direction it's coming from. "Come on, Royal. Do it again."

Instead, Mom calls from the house. "Paige!"

"Coming!" I get to the porch just as Hutsi drives off.

"Hey, honey." Mom gives me a one-armed squeeze while Scotty tromps down the stairs with his backpack.

She rubs my back. "Grandpa's awake. Sore and very tired, but awake."

I wrap both arms around her and squeeze, 'cause sometimes words aren't big enough to say what I feel. When Grandpa comes home, I'll put him in his favorite chair, help him put his boots up, and tell him all about the stuff we get done every day. He won't have to lift a finger till he's all better.

"We're having a sleepover!" Scotty hoists his backpack up for me to see. "Hutsi's gonna feed us."

"Wait, what?"

Mom nudges me toward the stairs. "Get what you need to spend a few nights with Hutsi."

"But what about the animals? What about the watering?" How can she think I can leave? Sure, Mateo did chores today, but he's got his own herds to look after.

"Javier said he'll take it on this week."

"Mr. Rivas and Mateo are doing it all?" That's like letting someone cut your meat for you when you've got a perfectly good set of hands and a sharp knife.

"Asher has offered to help too. He says it will give him experience."

"When did that happen?" I thought Mom had been at the hospital, not off visiting with the whole town.

"He was worried about your grandpa and texted me this morning. He probably saved your grandpa's life, calling 911 as fast as he did. I had no idea, and by the time I got home, the ambulance was already on the way." Mom walks down the hall. "I'm grabbing a few things, and then we'll go. Pack a bag, and I'll run you over."

"To the hospital?"

"No. I'll go back after I drop you off." Her phone chimes, and she stops to read a text, but I don't move.

If we don't get to see Grandpa, I can wait for him here as well as anywhere. There's no reason for me to go.

Mom glances up at me, a small smile on her lips. "Looks like I got the job."

"What?"

"Helping Hands Home Health liked my interview. They say I can start as soon as I'm available. I'll need a few days because of Grandpa, obviously, but—"

"Available? Mom! I don't want you to get another job. You're already gone most of the time."

"I know it seems that way, with my school and everything, but I need to look to our future. We need the stability."

"But you already have a job. Right here. On the farm with us. We're supposed to stick together."

"Paige, I know change isn't easy. It's hard on all of us, but we can't keep going like we have been. We need this." She slips her phone into her pocket and walks to her room, me following behind.

"But we don't have to sell the farm. I'm doing all the chores. I can cook *and* clean up. I don't ask you for anything except seeds and starts, and if you don't wanna help with that, I can figure it out on my own." I stop in the doorway to Mom and Dad's room and try hard to ignore the empty nail on the wall, where Dad's hat is supposed to be. "Dad said it was my job to look after the farm. I gotta be here to do that."

"I need to know you're safe, or I can't focus on your grandpa. The farm will be fine with the Rivas family looking after things for a few days. It's okay to ask for help."

A few days? No way. "I can't just leave. I need to stay here. I gotta work." What would Dad think of me just walking off the job? He's counting on me. "I can't stop."

She puts some clothes in a bag on the bed. "Paige, you'll have to stop. We all do. We can't keep the farm. You know that."

I flinch. "Why do you keep saying that? I know how to do

everything. I drive the truck and tractors. I move pipe, straw, and hay. I can do it on my own."

She stuffs socks into her bag, her voice soft, resigned. "You can work till your arms fall off, and it won't change anything. There are bills we can't pay and a foreclosure notice. Bill collectors call every day. It's just a matter of time before we have to leave the farm."

"No, Momma. Stop saying that." If I was Scotty, my hands would be over my ears. "We gotta save Daddy's farm. We have to."

She breathes in real sharp and looks at me. "We can't."

"Don't say that!"

"I'm only saying the truth. Pretending something's different doesn't make it so. Yes, we planned on living here *forever*. It was our dream together—your dad's and mine. But Grandpa's heart can't take the load. Yes, I *know* you work, but you *can't* do it alone. You can't change a tractor tire, or hook up a three-point like the plow, or drive the semi up to Tetonia for seed potatoes, or load wheat into the grain drill with the crane . . ."

Can't she see that I'm trying? I'm trying so dang hard. And the jobs she's talking about—I *know* how to do them. If I was bigger I could do all of them. My nerves prickle like I'm teetering on the edge of a badger hole, but she doesn't stop, and every word pushes me farther in.

"You can't pick up an eight-inch mainline. Half the time you can't get the mainline apart. You have to call—well, of course, *you* don't call—but you go get Grandpa because it's impossible for you to do it on your own. And now Grandpa can't help anymore because the work *will kill him.*"

"I won't ask him for help anymore. I'll figure it out. I promise." I hate the way my voice cracks, the way my breathing is too fast. I turn for the hallway, but Mom grabs my arm and touches my face with her other hand.

"It's okay to ask for help—that's not the point. What's it going to take to get it through your head?" Her words dig in like spurs. "No matter how much you want it to be different, you can't run the farm on your own. Your dad wouldn't want that."

I look past her to where Dad's hat should be and close my eyes, but the empty nail is still there, clear as day on the back of my eyelids. Sharp. Piercing. Accusing. I can't breathe, and I try to yank out of her hands. "You don't understand. I promised. I told him I'd take care of the farm, and I have to. I said I'd watch over things."

"You are twelve years old. No one expects you to run the farm on your own, least of all your dad."

"He does!" The walls tremble, and I need to be outside, need to work, need to keep my promise. "I said 'no' one time. Once! And it got him killed! He *died* because I said no."

"Paige, honey—" She drops to her knee in front of me, holding my arms, but I'm twisting and pulling. I *need* to go outside. "What happened isn't your fault."

"It is!" My voice rises, and I can't stop yelling. "It is! It's my fault! If I had been there, I coulda seen the truck. Coulda warned him. He'd still be here. He's gone because of me!"

"No, baby. No." She pulls me tight against her and wraps her arms around me, but I push and fight. "Shh, Paige. This is not your fault. None of it's your fault."

I feel her warm breath against my hair, her freckled cheek pressed to my forehead.

"If you had been there, I would have lost you both. Thank God you weren't. No one expects you to do this on your own."

I want to say she doesn't understand, that my promise is all I've got, but my throat won't work, and an animal cry wails from my lips instead. I shudder, and it's not just the walls closing in, but the weight of the whole farm settling hard on my shoulders, pressing me down and down. It crushes me. Strength drains from me faster than a sieve, and my knees buckle, and then it's Mom holding me, keeping me upright.

In the darkness of my mind, I hear her whisper, "None of us can do this alone."

CHAPTER TWENTY-FIVE

Down a Well

Sometimes, when Mom has one of her fragile days, she's more delicate than dried rose petals, and I fear the next hard gust of wind will break her in two. But then there are times like now, when her gentle arms grow strong as iron.

We stay like that, curled up on the hallway floor while thistles tear me up inside, but no matter how I thrash and cry, she never lets me go.

Scotty pulls his heavy blanket from his bed and tucks it around us both, the weight grounding me as much as my mother's arms. She holds me for a long time, and after awhile, we move to the couch—and that "rest" Hutsi talked about sneaks right up and steals me away.

When I wake, Mom agrees to let me stay home alone during the day only if

#1. I promise to keep the cell phone with me at all times—charged *and* with the sound on, and

#2. I promise to let Hutsi pick me up before dark for dinner and bed.

With no chores to do, I work on Mr. Collier's report out on the porch. I start out on the porch swing but end up scooting a chair beside T-Rex's nest so I can tuck my bare feet under his warm side as he sleeps.

Scuzbag decides he needs some loves too and jumps onto my lap—right on top of my homework.

"Hey!" I wiggle my papers under his feet, but Scuzbag yawns and lies down across my whole notebook. "How am I supposed to write like this?"

Purring, he rubs his face on my hand, ready for the petting to begin. I swirl a finger around each delicate ear and trail down and under his chin for a good, long scratching. Pretty soon, I've got both hands rubbing his neck and belly, and he's starting to drool when Mr. Ferro's red Dodge turns onto the driveway.

After he parks, and closes and locks the door, he waves. "I didn't expect to see anyone home."

"Mom let me stay for the day."

"How's your grandpa?" He strolls up the walk and sits on the top step in his jeans and tennis shoes.

"He's resting and tired, but okay."

"Excellent. I'm glad to hear it. I came to check the outbuildings again for Royal. Maybe see if there's someplace we missed."

I wish it was that easy to find him, but it seems like things have a way of staying lost on the farm. "Go ahead. But we checked them already."

"I know. But it's the strangest thing—yesterday, when the ambulance was coming, I swear I heard a peacock cry."

My fingers still. "I heard that too."

"And yet he's not in any of the surrounding trees or buildings. I can't help but think I'm missing something."

I like the way he looks across the fields. It's not like those other guys who looked *through* the trees and buildings. It's more like Mr. Ferro sees them and wants to know what they're made of, right down to the ground. I suppose reporters have to understand things like that.

Scuzzbag hooks my finger with a claw to make sure I continue petting him proper again, so I do, and his purr box starts up again, full throttle.

"So, why do you have peacocks if you live in the city?" I think he might have told me before, but it didn't stick. "I never heard of a journalist with a peacock before."

"True. I grew up with my parents on the East Coast, but my grandparents had an acreage with an exotic bird aviary on the Tyhee Flats near Chubbuck." He waves a hand to the west. "Pheasants and peacocks were a labor of love for my grandfather, and after he passed, my grandmother cared for the birds out of love for him. Some of the peacocks are almost as old as I am, but your Royal is one of the newer ones. Grandfather's records place him at around four years old."

"Are they happy there?" I always imagined Royal running away from someplace awful, but now I'm not so sure.

"I think so. I've contracted with a local vet to be sure the birds receive proper care, but I suspect some neighborhood kids threw sticks at Royal and scared him off."

"Who would do that?" Anyone who throws things at animals deserves to take a long dive into the manure pile, head-first.

"I was too focused on watching Royal fly to pay attention to the fleeing kids, but with all the houses packed in around the property now, it could have been anyone. I remember there being fields all the way around my grandparents' home, but the only field left is theirs. The rest of the peacocks are okay, though. Would you like to see them?" At my nod, he jogs to his truck and returns with a tablet, taps the screen, and passes it to me. "I took some pictures last week to send to the sanctuaries and zoos for possible adoption. You can scroll through them, if you like."

Two white peacocks sit on a branch while brown peahens lie in the grass at the foot of the tree. In the next picture, a blue peacock fans his tail beside a half-eaten watermelon. I stop on a picture of a giant painting. "What's this?"

He leans closer. "Ah, Grandmother's mural. She painted her life story on the side of the garage. Not everything that happened, just the highlights."

I zoom in on the tablet to see the details better. It starts with a boy and a girl holding hands beside a peacock, whose tail trails up and around them like a picture frame. Behind them, a tractor puffs smoke on its way across a field dotted with peacocks and quail, who fly and peck the earth.

"Your grandma was a real good artist." I follow the landscape as it escapes from the peacock frame and spills into scene after scene of farm and family.

He points to a little boy about midway across the landscape, holding onto a woman's hand. He has a letter in his other hand. "That's me. Back then, we wrote letters. Now, I mostly do emails, and phone calls, but all my writing started by hand."

Toward the end of the mural, houses begin to dot the landscape, and a skyscraper with two kids standing on top reaches up to painted clouds.

"Are these your kids?" I point at the girl and boy.

"Yes."

"Why aren't they here with you?"

"They have school and obligations at home in Boston. I'm only here for a couple months to take care of my grandparents' estate and rehome their birds. Besides, my kids prefer to stay with my ex, where the Wi-Fi is good." He takes the tablet back and gazes at the two figures on the screen a moment before closing it and standing up. "If you catch Royal, please call."

"Okay."

It's not long after he drives off that I'm in my mudboots, walking past the wheat field with T-Rex, on our way to the corn.

Another month, and this wheat will be taller than my knees, with feathery wisps on each head. Then weeks of sun will bake it till the wheat seeds dry in the heads, and the crowns turn to gold. It always looks the softest then, but it's a trick—the dried heads are the prickliest to the touch.

I can't help but wonder who will be here to run their fingers through the fresh-cut grain when it's time for harvest.

If that foreclosure letter Mom talked about is right, it won't be me.

At the cornfield, I get to work while T-Rex supervises.

Grandpa and me laid out the pipe last week, but we didn't have time to hook it all up, so the corn's looking a little thirsty. It's the only thing I can see that Mateo hasn't already done.

Line after line, I ease the pipes together and get them to latch. Sometimes the sprinkler birds fall over—and when one goes down, they all do—just to spite me, but I get it done anyway. Mostly, I'm glad to do something useful and finish what Grandpa and me started.

When I get the last line hooked and ready, I walk across the field to the corn pump on the far side.

Nestled in a thicket of quakey trees, the silver turbine pump perches atop a square cement casing, sort of like a shallow well that burrows down into the canal bank. Green pipes run from the pump to the irrigation lines that feed water to the corn.

Leaves and things float on the canal, but an underwater wire mesh keeps most of the junk out of the cement square and away from the pump. The water level seems high enough, so I reach for the power switch to flip it on.

A small splash sounds from inside the cement beneath the

pump. At least, I think it's a splash. Could be I'm imagining it—except T-Rex stands beside the cement, his nose twitching.

"What is it, boy?" Water splashes again, and I warily peek over the cement ledge. With my luck, it'll probably be a skunk. Below, dark and swirling water circles the intake pipe for the pump, but nothing treads water. Could it be a fish?

Brown leaves on the surface shift unnaturally, as if an impossibly large hand scooped them up all at once and moved them over. I can't understand what I'm seeing until a dirty, but elegant neck swivels from its place in the corner and something looks at me with bright black eyes.

My peacock!

"It's you!"

My yell startles Royal, who thrashes to get free, but his long tail is deep beneath the muddied water and drags his whole body down. It's all he can do to keep his head above water, with his wings spread to the sides like flimsy, sinking rafts.

In the time it takes me to understand what's happening, the water slips over the base of his neck, submerging his back entirely.

He's going to drown right in front of my eyes.

I search frantically for something—anything—to prop him up.

A couple of thin branches lie between some trees where Grandpa put weeds he pulled from the canal, but when I hurry around, I see Grandpa's pitchfork propped against the far side of the cement.

Even better.

I grab it and gingerly lower it into the water. If I can get it under him, he can ride it up like a backhoe. He flaps when it nears him, and when I finally get it into position, he slides off again and again when I try to lift him. The angle's too steep. I can't get him out like this.

Tired from fighting my attempts to help him, Royal sinks a little more.

"Oh gosh!" I ease the tines underneath the bird, but instead of trying to lift him, I press the sharp ends of the pitchfork against the cement with all my might. Then I wedge the top of the handle against the other side. It's not enough lift to get him out, but at least he can stand on it and rest. Once he gets his feet under him, he's high enough out of the water to draw his muddied wings closer to his body.

If it weren't for his tail, he could jump out. It's holding him down as sure as any chain. What did that plate Mr. Ferro gave me say? *"The sparrow is sorry for the peacock at the burden of its tail."* I bet Royal's wishin' for a sparrow's tail now instead of the elegant one he's got. If only he could let go and jump free of it.

Getting him out on my own is impossible, but I don't dare leave him to go find help. What if the pitchfork falls in? He's so exhausted, he'd drown for sure. I pat my pockets and find the wishstone in my right, and the cell phone in my left.

I pull out the phone, my thumbs hovering over the screen. Grandpa can't help, and Mom's in town. Neither of them can help us.

I begin dialing.

Mateo's voice mail picks up after three rings. *"Bueno, hablame."*

Short and to the point. But if his phone rang for that long, either he left it on the charger, or he watched it ring and didn't pick up.

His last words echo in my head—*Text you later*. An invitation and a challenge.

Fine.

As my thumbs press the letters on the screen, a familiar panic creeps up inside my head, but I shove it down. This time, things are different. This text could *save* Royal.

I need you at the pump by the corn. Found Royal in the pump hole. Bring something to help. Hurry.

Send.

I watch the road toward Mateo's house as if he'll instantly appear, but he doesn't.

I wait.

And wait.

But as soon as I start to think maybe I should have called Hutsi or someone else, I hear the most beautiful sound that ever was—the growl of Mateo's dirt bike.

He doesn't have a net, but he does have his lasso over his shoulder.

"Where is he?" He props the bike up.

"Down there." I tilt my head toward the hole. "But be slow or you'll scare him off the pitchfork and he'll drown."

He peers down the hole. "Look at all that mud on him. It's a miracle he didn't sink."

"He almost did." I shudder. "I almost turned on the pump."

"With his tail feathers down there, he'd have been toast for sure. Good thinking wedging the fork under him like that."

"It was all I could think to do."

Studying the hole, he shakes his head. "I thought maybe I could get a rope around him, but I think he'd spook and fall in again. We need a real net. Mr. Ferro had one, didn't he?"

"Yes! Do you have his number?"

Mateo turns away, his fingers flying on his phone. "On it."

Ten minutes later, the red Dodge Ram spits gravel down the road toward us and skids to a stop.

The door flies open, and Mr. Ferro jumps out. "Where is he?"

"He's down there." Mateo points at the hole. "Paige saved him from drowning. You got the net?"

"Absolutely." Mr. Ferro slams the door and pulls a net with a long silver pole out of the truck bed.

Together—Mateo using a stick, me holding the pitchfork, and Mr. Ferro working the net—we catch Royal in the net, with the opening against the cement. The only part of him not contained is his sad and drooping tail, which hangs out the side, the feathers all broken and muddy.

"Mateo, can you grab a blanket from the truck, please?" Mr. Ferro asks.

"You got it." Mateo runs, and I peer at the shivering little body. If it weren't for the head, I'd never know a peacock was under all that muck.

When Mateo gets back with the blanket, we drape the corner of it over the net and carefully swap the net for the blanket, always keeping Royal's wings tucked tight against his body. At last he's in my arms, an extra-muddy bird burrito.

Mr. Ferro passes Mateo the net and adjusts a few things with Royal before taking him from my arms and cradling him against his chest. "Paige, can you get the door?"

"Sure."

Mateo drops the net in the back of the truck while Mr. Ferro places Royal carefully on the floor behind the seats and tucks another blanket around him.

"I'll call after the vet checks him out. I can't believe we found him again." He flashes a grin at us and then speeds away.

With one more look to be sure nothing else lurks in the water—and a couple of swishes with the pitchfork just to be sure—I pull the lever and start the pump. The loud whine fills the air, and we watch for a few minutes as water leaks from every joint until the line pressurizes.

"So." Mateo rocks back on his heels. "You texted me."

"Yeah, and? People text, right? Isn't that what you guys keep telling me?"

His smile is a slow, mischievous thing, and I want to smile back, but first, I need to set things right.

"I'm really sorry about your mom's plant."

"I know."

"I'll make it up to you."

"Accidents happen." With a shrug, he walks his bike beside me and T-Rex, waiting now and then as I jam a wire down

253

inside a bunch of clogged Rain Birds and pump the nozzle till mud and grass spit out, freeing the line. Normally we have one or two clogged birds, but today, there are almost ten. Royal musta been fighting for his life a long time to kick this much mud into the lines.

Details about Mom and Grandpa and the foreclosure letter spill out of me as we go, and for once, Mateo listens without interrupting. At last, he says, "So you have to sell or the bank will take it anyway."

"Mom says if that happens, we won't have a choice. It's move or get kicked out. The bank doesn't care that my family's been here a hundred years. When it's money, nothing else matters. And when the bank takes it, it'll get developed for sure. I don't know. Maybe Mom was wrong to turn down the people Dolly found last time."

"Maybe if we bring in a bunch of farmers, someone will want to buy it," Mateo says.

"Yeah, because that worked so well last time."

He raises a finger. "All you need is an open house that we *don't* sabotage."

CHAPTER TWENTY-SIX

Kiss a Skunk

When Kimana's bike growls down the driveway, I break into a run and meet her at the gate. With Grandpa, Royal, and everything, it seems like months since I saw her instead of days, and I almost tackle her when she swings off her bike. Her hair tickles my nose with the scent of woodsmoke from her cousin's cabin. With one more good squeeze, I let her go as Mateo catches up to us.

"How's the baby?" I ask.

"Cute and fat, with black hair as thick as his brothers'— two inches long already. You should see the boys argue over who gets to hold him next. What about you? I'm sorry I couldn't be here, but I finished a surprise for you." She digs into her pouch and pulls out the peacock lanyard.

"Oh! Wow." At the base of the leather necklace, a peacock fans its tail, the feathers sparkling like shattered crystals, each bead a prism of captured light. Lines of long, gold beads branch from the feathers and twine up the leather necklace like molten sunshine beside the blue-and-green vines. "It's beautiful."

Mateo whistles. "That's your best one yet."

"Thanks. I think it turned out pretty good." Kimana lifts the base. "And there's a clip here so you can hang a key or something from it, if you want."

"But what about your jingle dress?" I slip the necklace over my head and touch the peacock again. "You shouldn't have wasted time on me when your regalia isn't done yet."

"Maybe. But after I heard what happened, I couldn't work on anything else until I got it done. When I make something like this, I think good thoughts and prayers, so it kind of carries those things with it for you. And it brings good things back to me too. You needed it, and it was something I could do."

I blink hard and swallow a couple times so my voice will work. "Thank you. It means a lot."

With Kimana back home and Mateo by my side, we come up with a pretty good list of things that need to be done. It's kinda weird to plan an open house without sneaking around, hiding plans, or smuggling in fart spray and soup bones, but we do our best.

Near as we can figure, for an open house to work, we gotta pick a date, advertise, find farmers to come look, and sweet-talk the heck out of them.

But if the bank gave Mom a final date, she never shared it with me, so snooping that out of the mail pile's the first step. The bank letter blends right in with the other envelopes, a rattlesnake hiding in the piano basket, but eventually I find it. I open it up, skim the letter, and find the words I need: "Make all payments and fees by 11:59 p.m. on April 30."

I grab my calendar. That's Friday—over a week away. We've still got time. Just to be safe, I pick Monday for the big day, so if it doesn't work, we've still got till Friday to try again.

Mateo calls Mr. Ferro to see if he'll ask the *Idaho State Journal* to write something about the open house. And Kimana's dad helps her make a list of farmers on the north side of the county—ones he knows from his patrols—who might want to come.

And me? Well, it's my job to call Miss Dolly. I shudder. Mateo's and Kimana's jobs don't sound so bad, but I can think of a whole list of things I'd rather do than mine:

- Lick a cow
- Wear a dress
- Read an encyclopedia
- Kiss a skunk
- Or even send a text

Asking for her help feels akin to inviting a black widow into my bedroom to catch a couple flies, but if we want to catch buyers in our web, who better to help than her? Besides, if she's half as good as she says she is, she'll make this work. She picks up on the first ring and promises to bring as many people as she can.

Mr. Ferro's willing enough to help, but he still holds a pitchfork like it's a broom. His city apartment must've been at the tippy-top of some cement skyscraper, 'cause I could fill ten calendars with all the things he doesn't know. At least he told us the vet said Royal will be fine soon, so that's good.

Every day after school, we clean, organize, and mow. Milkshake even gets a bath—which she doesn't mind—though Prince is pretty sure shampoo is pure torture.

The doctors let Grandpa come home Sunday night, and we settle him in his room. He's supposed to be resting, but he keeps sneaking out of his room, so Mom hides the truck keys and promises Scotty a subscription to *National Geographic* if he'll keep an eye on Grandpa.

"If he steps foot outside this house, you call me immediately," she whispers.

"I can go where I please," Grandpa grumps, his sheepskin slippers peeking from under his striped pajama bottoms.

"Of course you can, as long as it's inside." Mom kisses Scotty's head. "If he sneaks out, and I don't answer, text me."

"Got it."

෴

When Monday rolls around, we cross our fingers and toes while we wait for folks to arrive.

Instead of fancy cars like last time, trucks roll down our lane filled with people wearing baseball caps and cowboy hats instead of slick hairdos.

A husband and wife jump out of an older truck and a couple little kids in boots and John Deere shirts spill out of the jump seat behind them.

"Daddy, I see a tire swing! Can we swing on it?" the girl says.

"Not right now. Let's see what's happening first." The dad is wearing leather boots, a silver belt buckle, and a long-sleeved work shirt. A low ponytail keeps the lady's long, curly dark hair out of the way while she holds onto her husband's arm as they take in the house, the pump house, and all the outbuildings. I'd peg them as cattle ranchers, if I had to guess.

"This your place?" The man squints up at us from under a straight-brimmed black hat. He waves while the lady and two kids pet T-Rex, his tail wagging in lazy circles.

"Yep," I say with a nod.

"I love the porch." The lady stands and leans against the man with her arm around his waist like Mom used to do with Dad. "Wouldn't the kids love that?"

"Yes, yes!" The brown-haired girl runs up beside us, leans over the rail, and waves at her younger brother.

"How are the riding trails? Any way to get up into those hills from here?" the man asks.

"We used to ride up there all the time." I hitch a thumb at Kimana and Mateo. "And we got good neighbors here too."

"There's good pasture." The lady gazes across the fields. "We could run a sizable herd from here."

Other people enter the yard, but I keep watching that same little family. Before last year, that was us: Mom, Dad, Scotty, me. Excited about our farm. Wishing for an extra turn on the tire swing, or planning a ride up in the hills. We had nothing but time, and no one better to spend it with than each other.

"May I have your attention?" Miss Dolly claps her hands from the porch steps and beams at the crowd. "Thank you all for coming. We'll begin with a tour and take your questions as we go. Hope, would you lead the way?"

The family follows Mom and Miss Dolly. Scotty and me stay on the porch. We've done all we can do. All that's left is hope.

"What do you think?" Mateo straddles the porch rail, his feet dangling off either side. "Any of them look like good neighbor material?"

"I dunno. Good neighbors for normal people? Or for you?" I tease.

"For me." Mateo scowls at me. "Hey, wait."

"Kidding! Totally kidding."

My thumb slides over the wishstone in my pocket as the strangers disappear into the chicken barn, the place where we first found Royal and where I promised I'd fight and never let this day come—except I helped make this happen 'cause it's the only way for my family to survive.

"Mateo, why won't your dad buy the farm? You said you guys wanted more space to run cattle. Why not here? We could rent from you—work for you and stay here."

"We talked about it, but we can't. Dad says we have too much to pay on our place now. We can't get any more loans until we pay off more stuff. I wish we could."

Dolly's group pokes around the farm for a good thirty minutes before they gather by the porch again. Some go right to their trucks and drive off, and others stay a while and talk.

The family of four is one of the last. Mom leads them into the house.

"Do you think you'll move into town, or find someplace to rent out here?" Kimana swings on the porch swing, and I shrug.

"I dunno." She may as well ask if I'd rather live on the stars or on the moon. I can't imagine either one. This is the only world I know, and even if I don't get to live here anymore, I'm just hoping I can keep it from disappearing.

"Dolly has papers!" Scotty squints through the front window into the house.

"What?"

We jump to our feet and cup our hands to the window.

The dad sits in Grandpa's chair while Miss Dolly points at one page and then another, with him signing right behind her. Then Mom leans over and adds her signature. They shake Mom's hand and Grandpa's, and Dolly slides the papers into her briefcase and flips the locks shut.

Sealed. Locked. Done and done.

"We did it," I breathe.

We sold the farm.

The kids come bursting out of the screen door, thunder down the steps, and race for the tire swing. "It's mine!"

"No, it's mine. I saw it first!" Then the girl drops the swing rope and runs for our tree fort. "You can have the swing. I get the fort!"

Their squeals wake T-Rex from his nap, and he thumps his tail, hefts himself to his feet, and takes a few steps toward them before he stops and whines. The wrong kids are on our toys and in our fort.

Dolly steps out, holding the door for the new owners. "I'm so glad this worked out."

"We've been looking for a place to move our operation so we can be closer to her parents. The house is older than we'd like, but you can't beat the location." The man tips his hat to me and Kimana on his way past us.

"Close to town, but still in the country. It's the perfect place to raise a family," the lady agrees.

She's not wrong. It really is the perfect place for a family.

Just not *our* family.

Not anymore.

We watch Dolly and the family drive off, and Mom pats my back. "I'm real proud of you, honey. Thank you for helping this happen."

My lips part to say "No problem," but the words get stuck somewhere in my throat, so I just nod.

I don't want this change, but like it or not, it's the only way for my family to go on.

After everyone leaves and Scotty goes upstairs, I sink into T-Rex's sleeping bag nest and run my fingers down his side as he snores, his paws twitching from the chase inside his dreams. Whatever he's dreaming must be real exciting 'cause he huffs a few times and twitches a little faster.

I kiss the top of his head and go inside.

A faint whir sounds from inside Mom's room as she works on something behind closed doors. I pass her by.

At the back of the main floor hallway, Grandpa's door sits ajar, like it has almost all the other times I've checked on him since he got home from the hospital. He sits dozing beneath a floor lamp, in Grandma's upholstered armchair, a doily at each elbow. Whatever book he'd been reading lies facedown on the floor where it fell from his sleep-numbed fingers, the pages curled against the red shag rug.

A black, oval frame with Grandma's picture stands beside the bed, which is made up tight as any military bunk ever was. Under the foot of the bed, two sets of slippers wait side by side.

Did he always have that many wrinkles? Sunspots smatter over the tanned, thin skin on the backs of his hands, which are curled around one of Grandma's embroidered throw pillows where he fell asleep hugging it.

It's like he's stuck in a time loop in there. None of it changes, but Grandpa gets older every day.

And now, how's he gonna let it go?

Everything in me wants to hang onto the farm with all my might, but all that would do is drag us down—same as Royal in the pump well. He couldn't jump to safety, and he couldn't fly free, 'cause he was stuck, caught by his own beautiful feathers. And who could blame him with something that wonderful to hang onto?

But is that what the farm is for us? A beautiful weight to pull our whole family down?

Even peacocks shed their tail feathers once a year.

Maybe it really is time to let go.

What did Dad always used to say?

It's like shaking hands with God—I'll do my best, and you do the rest.

Peacocks grow a new tail, don't they? Maybe that's what this will be like. We'll grow and change, and someday what we carry will be just as good as what we had before.

Just different.

Mom's phone chimes from the kitchen, and she hurries from her sewing room to answer it. "Hello? Oh, hi, Dolly."

I drift to the kitchen doorway, where Mom stands with her head bent to the phone.

"They were denied? Can't they appeal?" She rubs her face. "I see. Okay. Then we'll do what we have to do. See you tomorrow."

She sets the phone down and leans against the counter, shoulders slumped.

"Mom? What's wrong?"

With a sigh, she turns around. "It was a good try, but it's not going to work. The bank denied the family. They can't buy the farm."

Is that all? We found that family; we can find more. We've got time to do it again.

"So we'll try again. I saw the letter. We've got till Friday to sell."

"No, honey." Mom shakes her head, an awful sadness in her eyes. "Today's the twenty-ninth. The deadline is tomorrow."

CHAPTER TWENTY-SEVEN

Best Part of His Day

Her words make no sense. "What do you mean it's tomorrow?"

"Tomorrow is the thirtieth." The date glows on Mom's phone screen.

"That's not right. Tomorrow *can't* be the end of the month. I checked." I snag my calendar off the piano. "See? April 30 is a Friday. It's only the beginning of the week."

Mom takes the calendar from my hands and turns the pages, pausing to touch a note Dad scribbled up the side. "It *was* on Friday years ago when your dad first made this calendar. This year, the thirtieth is tomorrow."

The dates change every year. I know that. I *know* Dad's calendar isn't from this year—that the dates are all wrong—but with everything going on, I forgot. "Tomorrow is the last day? The day the bank gets the farm if somebody doesn't buy it?"

"Yes, but one of Dolly's clients from the first open house

still has an offer for us. If it's between the bank and that offer, we'll take the offer. Whatever happens, we'll be okay. Please don't say anything to Grandpa. I'll tell him tomorrow, after he's rested." Her arms enfold me in a tight hug before dropping the calendar on the counter and then stepping into her sewing room. A moment later, she returns with a big blanket in her arms.

"I was going to save these for a special day, but I think I'd rather you both had them tonight." She shakes out the blankets—there are two—and holds the top edge up so I can see the pattern. Fabric cut from my dad's shirts and jeans fills every square.

I reach for a corner, run a hand over the material, and lean close to take a big whiff. It might be my imagination, but I think I can still smell him. I pull the blanket from her arms and bury my face in the folds.

"I've been working on them for months, whenever I couldn't study or think. I thought maybe it might help, for when you need one of his hugs."

"I love it." I lean into her shoulder. "Thank you."

"I've been thinking." Mom folds the quilts into neat piles. "Maybe we should invite Asher over for breakfast in the morning. It might be good to have a reporter document what this is like. That was his story, remember? People losing their farms."

"I don't want to be in that story."

"But you are in it. And maybe, someday, you can look back and remember something you forgot because of something he wrote."

"Maybe." With her kiss on my cheek, I grab Scotty's quilt and mine to take them both up to our beds.

       ❦ ❧

Long after Mom closes her door to study, the calendar mocks me. Every puzzle has a key, a legend, a map as to what it should look like, or how to solve it. Every engine has a manual listing all the parts, directions for how to use them, and maintenance for how to keep them running.

Dad's calendar is the only manual I've got, and I've followed it a thousand times. And every time, it was right—except this time.

I followed it too close and missed the bigger picture.

I lean on the kitchen counter and cup Kimana's beaded peacock in my hand.

So, was the calendar my guide, or my tail? Did it ever show me the way? Or has it only been pulling me down?

Maybe sometimes things can do both at the same time if we cling to them too tight.

My gaze drifts from the peacock to the wall, where me and Scotty smile back from a dozen silly pictures pinned to a bulletin board—from back when things were easier. When we did chores together because we wanted to, not because we had to. Back when Mom used to sing—when she had a reason to sing.

And suddenly I see all the faces I've trained myself not to see over the last nine months. There, on the board beside Scotty, me, Grandpa, and Mom, is Dad.

He smiles in every photo.

He laughs while holding Mom's hand.

He reaches for me from the saddle.

And he waves from the seat of his tractor, with laughter in his eyes and a smile just for me. I know, because I took the picture. He wasn't smiling before; he was just working. But then I came, and he smiled. He said I was the best part of his day.

Staring at the pictures, I realize that, somewhere in the middle of all the work, I forgot about Dad's smiles.

Would he be happy or sad we were selling the farm? Would he think I did enough to keep my promise? Or would he only care that we were still together?

I tap the chair backs as I walk around the table, but I stop a seat early, my fingers resting on the edge of Dad's chair.

Prickles zip up every fingertip, like someone hooked a low-volt electric fence to the chair, but instead of pulling away, I grasp the chair, slide it away from the table, and sit down.

My skin tingles everywhere it touches the chair. I've been trying to take Dad's place for almost a year. Seems right to sit here now. Besides, if not now, then when?

I pull my wishstone out, set it on the table, and close my eyes. What would Dad say if he were here? He'd smile at me and say . . . he'd say . . .

I spread my fingers over the arms of the chair, as if I could pull his words from the wood, but nothing comes to me.

With a sigh, I open my eyes and focus on Kimana's note cards poking out of the napkin holder in the center of the table. She'd left them in the barn the other day, and I'd meant to return them to her, but then she was gone and things just got crazy. I reach for them, my peacock necklace clicking against the table when I lean over.

One after the other, I read them all. But the last few I read aloud, and I swear my dad's voice echoes every word.

"'It does not do to dwell on dreams and forget to live.' J.K. Rowling."

Dad would say, *"Stay in the moment."*

I set the card aside.

"'It's no use going back to yesterday, because I was a different person then.' Lewis Carroll."

"What's done is done. I'll do my best, and God can do the rest"—'cause none of us is perfect, and none of us can do it alone.

"'Don't cry because it's over. Smile because it happened.' Dr. Seuss. "

"Focus on the smiles, the laughter, the love."

As I set the cards back into the napkin holder, my necklace clicks against the table again, and an idea sprouts in my head. Like any crop worth growing, it's my job to tend it.

Grabbing the wishstone off the table, I stand up and slide Dad's chair back into place. It might be that this'll work, or it might be that I'll fail, but at least I know I'll be okay either way. All that's left is to try.

I've got one more big job to do here on the farm, and this time, it's a work of heart.

CHAPTER TWENTY-EIGHT

Report

The next morning should be a school day, but I argue that if the farm is selling, I should be there, so Mom lets us stay. She's in the middle of making bacon when Mr. Ferro pulls up to the house.

The screen door creaks open as I step out and wave him inside. At the table, I pull out a chair for him. Grandpa gives me a look, but I pretend not to notice as Mr. Ferro settles down beside him.

"Thank you for inviting me. It's been a long while since I shared a meal that wasn't at a restaurant."

"When there's a big job ahead, a home-cooked meal adds a little steel to the spine." Grandpa passes a plate of hash browns and eggs. "You've got that article to write, and we've got papers to sign as soon as Miss Dolly comes. At least we can face the work with full bellies."

Mr. Ferro peers at my necklace. "Did you always have that peacock medallion, or is it new? Such fine workmanship."

"Kimana made it." I hold it up so it catches the light. "It's Royal on the front, see?"

"I do. Your friend is very talented."

"You bet she is. Kimana can bead and program and code better than anyone I know. She makes pieces like this to earn money so she can buy her jingles and other things to finish her regalia—that's a special dress she needs for competitions like her cousin's powwow that's in a few weeks."

"How's Royal?" Scotty asks.

"He's good." Mr. Ferro pulls a picture up on his phone of Royal standing beside a peahen, and shows it to us. "The vet gave him a clean bill of health, but the way that bird paces the edge of the aviary, I have no doubt he'd fly off the second I opened the door if he got the chance."

"Would he fly here?" Scotty holds his glass while I pour orange juice into it. "He likes our trees. Peacocks roost up high to protect themselves from predators and to watch for intruders, just like guard dogs."

"Your guard dog barely opened an eye when I pulled up." Mr. Ferro grins. "The cats, on the other hand, came right over. That little orange one—Scumbag, was it?"

"Scuzbag," Scotty corrects.

"Right. Scuzbag and the black one wouldn't let me up the porch steps until I gave them both a good scratch."

Mom sets the bacon plate on the table, and it's Scotty's

turn to say the prayer before everyone dives in, but my plate stays empty.

"I finished my report for school." I tap my papers on the table beside my wishstone. "Wanna hear?"

"Sure, honey." Mom peppers her eggs.

I stand, slide my chair in, and take a breath. "There are lots of people who made a difference in my life. Famous people that got me the right to vote when I'm old enough. People who explored and invented things. But until this year, I didn't really understand that I'd built my whole world to begin and end with one man: my dad."

Scotty grabs a bacon strip and chomps down, but the others are watching me, so I keep going.

"See, my dad taught me how to fix things, and when he saw I was good at it, he told me I was smart and gave me tricky things to troubleshoot, and when I fixed all that, he gave me new puzzles to solve."

I glance up from my report. Everyone's still listening.

"Because of him, I know that there's a season for everything: a time to plant, to grow, to work, and to harvest. It's all connected with family, 'cause in the middle of all that hard work, there's times to laugh and love—and family holds it all together. Trying to run our farm alone is like running an engine without any oil. It might go for a little while, but all the parts wear out and everything seizes up." I sneak a glance at Grandpa.

"Hey," Grandpa says, rubbing his chest, "I'm not worn out yet."

I smile. "I was talking about me, Grandpa."

"Bah." He chuckles. "You're still a spring chicken."

"No. I'm like our peacock." My eyes flick to Scotty and Mr. Ferro as I turn the page. Might as well skip ahead. "Peacocks protect their territory against intruders. They sound the alarm when there's danger, and they fight to protect what's theirs."

"I told Paige that," Scotty whispers to Mr. Ferro.

"Peacocks carry a long, beautiful tail—maybe the prettiest tail in the whole world. It makes them feel safe and helps them find love, but it can trap them and weigh them down if they don't let those feathers go."

I slide the page to the back of the stack. It's not the order I meant to read things, but it feels right. "I used to know exactly how I fit in the world, but when Dad died, *nothing* fit anymore. I tried to fix the puzzle by doing more, by taking on all his jobs and stretching myself thin to fill the space he left behind, but I couldn't do it right. And I pushed other pieces out of place."

"I tried my hardest and worked till I was dead tired, but wishing for things to be the way they used to be is like ramming straw down a bolt hole and hoping it holds. It can't hold, because the piece you need is gone. And it seemed like my life would never be okay again because the pieces I knew didn't fit in this new picture."

I meet Mr. Ferro's gaze. "But I learned some things from Royal, and then you showed me pictures of your grandparents' peacocks and the painting on the garage. See, my life isn't just a puzzle picture stuck inside a frame. There's not just one single way to make all the pieces fit—and that's okay.

"My life is a mural.

"The picture of my family that I love so much? It's in the corner, at the start of my life. It's my beginning."

I set the papers down beside the wishstone. "But the cool part about a mural is that we don't leave our beginnings behind. Because of Dad, I know how to help a newborn calf come into the world, and how to lose a crop and move forward anyway. And I'll never have to ask someone what's wrong with my car, 'cause I'll know how to fix it. I know how to solve problems and work hard, and those things matter—no matter what happens next."

Dad's picture is taped to the next page—him smiling at me from the seat of the tractor when he said I was the best part of his whole day. Scrawled across the page beneath him are big, bold leters that say, "Don't cry because it's over. Smile because it happened."

"I thought our home here was perfect, and maybe it was, but that season is over for the farm. There's a new season starting, and I'm not full of holes and missing pieces like I thought. Our roots are still connected—my family, my farm—all painted in the corner of my mural. All I gotta do is paint the next scene."

The moment hangs there quiet between us, a butterfly perched on a blade of grass, its delicate wings open. Then Grandpa breaks the spell. "I find duct tape does wonders for holes—if'n you still have any left."

I laugh. "No, Grandpa. I'm okay."

"You forgot to say that peacocks symbolize eternal life and rebirth." Scotty pours ketchup on his eggs. "Will your teacher let you have more pages for your report? How about three? I can tell you three pages of peacock facts." He scrunches his face up. "Maybe five. Yes, you need five more pages."

"Her report is perfect just the way it is." Mom pats my hand as I sit down to eat. She has tears in her eyes, but I think they are happy tears this time. "Thank you for sharing it with us. It's nice to think we can begin again. Focus on the positive, right?"

"Where did you say you live?" Grandpa asks Mr. Ferro.

"I've got an apartment in Boston."

"An apartment, eh?" Grandpa points his fork at Mr. Ferro. "How do you sleep with your neighbor snoring so close to you?"

"Grandpa snores every day. So does T-Rex." Scotty stands with his plate. "Can I go?"

After the plates are cleared, Mom and Grandpa hover near the windows like bees on a Coke can, waiting for Miss Dolly and that buyer of hers. I hope she takes her own sweet time in coming.

Mr. Ferro sits on the porch swing and taps on his tablet, writing his report.

I perch on the seat beside him, slip Kimana's peacock off my neck, and cradle it in my hands. "You can look closer if you want. It's even prettier out here in the sunlight."

As he tilts it, shafts of light reflect off the peacock beads and dance across his face like freckles of sunshine. "Amazing."

"It's not just a necklace. It's a lanyard. See the clip on the bottom? It's great for holding a key or a press badge."

"What use would you have for a press badge?" His thumb rubs small circles over the beads, like I do with my wishstone.

"None at all. But *you* need one. See? Then you'd have your grandpa's peacocks with you all the time when you work. It's like a piece of your roots that you get to carry with you."

"With me?" His thumb stills. "But this is yours."

"It *was* mine, but I feel like it belongs with you, like maybe it was meant for you all along. So I'm giving it to you."

"Don't you want it?"

I hold a hand up to stop him from giving it back to me. "I do love it, but Kimana says it carries good thoughts and things with it, and I think you need it more—to remind you of home."

"Well, then." He lifts the lanyard over his head. He doesn't even have to remove that silly hat of his. "Sounds like we need to agree on a price."

"But it's a gift," I protest.

"No, this is too fine a gift. I can't accept without a fair price."

Since he insists, we haggle back and forth like a couple of ganders, and when we shake hands, it's all I can do to keep my smile under control. With the money Mr. Ferro paid, Kimana should be able to have everything she wants for the powwow for sure—not that I'm cheating him; her work is worth every penny.

I tuck the money into my sock for safekeeping. I'll run it right over to Kimana as soon as she's out of school for the day.

We swing slow for a few minutes before I point at the trees.

"Remember that day you sat on the grass and watched Royal playing up in those trees?"

"Mm-hmm."

A breeze teases red strands across my nose, and I brush them behind my ear.

My boots click on an uneven board as we swing back and forth.

Click, click.

Click, click.

"Would it be so bad if he got to do it again?"

The swing stops, and my fist tightens around my wish-stone, but I don't dare look at him yet.

Gravel crunches under tires as Miss Dolly's black Cadillac turns down the drive. Her tires spin faster than chain saws, eating the distance in no time at all.

"Hello!" Miss Dolly waves as she steps out of the car with a man in a suit, then laughs at something he says. With his sunglasses and pinstripes, I can't remember if he was here before or not. They all looked the same to me. No hats, dress shoes on every one. One gray rat looks an awful lot like another.

"Come on in." Mom opens the door, and I flinch at every step Dolly's heels take as she prances inside, the man right behind her. I know Miss Dolly is just doing her job, but now that the moment is here, it's hard.

Minutes.

I've got minutes left till our farm is gone forever.

"What do you mean?" Mr. Ferro asks. "About Royal?"

I tear my gaze from the door. "Wouldn't it be better if all your grandpa's peacocks stayed together, instead of being shipped off to a bunch of different places? They've lived their whole lives together as a pride—that's what peacock families are called—and they could live here. In our trees. All safe and protected. Then you'd always know where they were, and you could see them anytime you wanted."

He takes his hat off and runs his fingers along the tiny brim. "Of course I'd like to keep them together, but I'm no farmer, Paige. I might like to learn new things, get my hands dirty now and then, but I could never take care of all this."

"That's the thing." I hear Dolly's tittering laugh from inside, and I stand in front of Mr. Ferro. "You don't have to. Mateo's dad wants to expand their herd, but they can't get financing, so all they can do is rent. Why not have them rent from you? If they took care of the cows, you could split the profits from the herd, but they'd do all the work."

"I—" He starts to shake his head, but I hurry on.

"If they take on the cows and pastures, and we lease out the other fields, the land wouldn't be lost. And you could keep the garden, the greenhouse, and the horses."

"What would *I* do with horses? I live in an apartment in Boston."

"Remember how you said you wish your kids could experience what this is like? How they could use some time away from their phones? Maybe we could figure out a way so that lots of kids like yours could come and learn how to garden and ride horses. Then folks from town could come and buy the vegetables the kids have grown. They'd learn how to work and loads of other important things. You wouldn't even have to be here all the time—you could hire someone to help. My family could teach them."

"Mr. McBride, I heard you had quite the health scare. I'm so glad to see you up and around," Dolly says from inside. "This is the gentleman I told you about . . ."

"I see the appeal," Mr. Ferro says. "And it's a fine idea, but realistically, I don't see how—"

My fingers tap like Scotty's. "If you don't like that idea, we can think of another, but after today, your chance to change things is gone. When land is lost, it takes something away from all of us because it can never be put right again. You know it matters, or else you'd have sold your grandparents' place right off—but you *didn't*, because you know those birds are a part of your legacy, your heritage. This is your chance to put down roots instead of cutting them off. Heck, maybe you could even bring your grandma's mural here, brick by brick, and rebuild the garage. It doesn't have to disappear."

"You're a smart kid, Paige. I appreciate that, but it's hard to put down roots when I travel so much for my work. Our worlds are just too different."

"You're wearing the proof that they can work together."

I point at his chest. "Look at your lanyard. It can hold your reporter badge, but it's got your grandpa's peacock right in the center. It's part of us here on the reservation, part of your family, and part of your job. All of it works together to make something beautiful. And if we can rent the house from you, we can stay and care for your birds. And then you'd have a place to come home to. A place where your grandpa's legacy lives on."

I step back as he walks to the house and stares through the screen door. When Scotty thinks about things, his brain zips like a hummingbird flitting from one flower of facts to another, but Mr. Ferro's mind rolls more like a steam engine, steamin' and thinkin', turning things over slow, then gaining speed.

My words tumble out, one after the other. "If your grandma cared for those peacocks out of love for your grandpa's legacy, wouldn't she like it if you carried on the same tradition? You'd be connected to the land like him, and you wouldn't even have to be a farmer. You say you don't have roots, but you do. Maybe not in a farm, but in your family."

His hand opens and closes, and I feel him teetering, a water skipper on the brink.

"I gotta believe Royal came to us for a reason. It's the only thing that makes sense. He needed a new place to put down roots, and he picked here. Right here." I nod toward the screen door. "Can't you trust him a little? Believe for one moment that maybe something bigger than all of us brought us together?"

With his face in shadow, peering through the screen door,

I can't tell what he's thinking. Can he feel it? Can he see the way through as clearly as I do?

"We just need to go over a couple more things and get a few signatures." Miss Dolly's voice drifts through the screen. "Almost done."

I touch the back of Mr. Ferro's wrist. Then I lift it and press my last hope into his hand. "Sometimes, you just need to follow your heart, choose to believe, and make a wish."

Swaddled in all my hopes and dreams, and worn smooth from a thousand wishes, Dad's heart-shaped wishstone seems to glow in his open hand.

He stares at the stone, and his gaze cuts to mine, but I don't hide. I open my soul, letting all the hope and fear inside me shine through as I will him to *feel* what I feel, *see* what I see, and *love* what I love.

"It's my Dad's wishstone," I whisper. "Please, please . . . make a wish."

Dad's stone disappears as Mr. Ferro's fingers close around it.

I hold my breath and hope.

He opens the door. "Wait!"

CHAPTER TWENTY-NINE

Wishfire

Change can come in tiny packages like a cocoon or a butterfly chrysalis, or it can sweep over the land and remake the whole world with seasons of sun or ice.

Mostly though, change is more subtle—a tiny root sprouting from a seed, burrowing down into the earth, growing stronger, and then pushing the rest of the seed upward till it opens to the sky and become leaves.

It's hard to look at the towering branches of a giant cottonwood and remember it all started with a tiny seed small enough to hide in a puff of cotton. It doesn't matter if seeds fall down deep cracks or are buried under a pile of thorns. They can take root and grow into something wonderful, if they remember to always follow the light.

Tufts of white cotton float on the breeze, catching on my lashes and gathering in swirls at my feet like snow, but it's a warm, sunny day. The *swish, swish* of my boots sends the miniature drifts whirling, each cotton puff spinning around its precious seed.

A few white bits of fluff settle on the rim of the pot I carry, and I blow them away. I need this for more important things.

Grandma was the one who was good at flowers, and she'd probably have gone for the poppies, or maybe the irises, but I am a farmer's daughter, and I'd rather give Mateo's mom something more useful. So I transplant a whole potful of strawberry plants, deep green leaves with tiny white and yellow flowers, and press the dirt around the roots to keep them safe. I don't worry about the holes I leave in the berry patch, 'cause with a little love and care, flowers and berries spread out. Love shared only grows—everybody knows that.

It's not the bouquet Mr. Rivas picked out, but it's something to last through all the seasons. Something that can give her berries again next year.

Next year.

It's still a thrill to say that and know I'll be here.

Scotty says peacocks symbolize rebirth, so it's fitting that when Mr. Ferro sat in Dad's chair for the second time that day, he had Royal's picture beaded around his neck. And when he signed those papers, he changed all of our lives for good.

Our farm was reborn.

With Mr. Ferro's purchase of the barns and surrounding fields, Mom was able to pay our debts and still keep the house and ten acres—including Queenie's barn.

As for the other seventy acres, Mr. Rivas, Mateo, and Mr. Ferro's new farmhand have been moving cattle to new pasture and fixing fences all week. It would have been done already, but Royal's new home needed to be finished first.

Scotty said we needed to celebrate the new farm by lighting the wishfire to welcome new friends, restart our year, and reset our wishes. We wouldn't change the tradition for always, but just this once, we wanted to celebrate the change and show our hope for the future. Like Mr. Ferro's pride of peacocks, we all get a second chance, and that's worth celebrating.

"Ha! Ha! Heyo!" Royal's neck rolls as he calls from his high perch inside the newly completed aviary.

"Is that so?" I say to him with a smile. I set the strawberry pot down and slip inside the aviary. I close the door, grab a couple apples from the treat bucket, and roll them onto the grass, where a few peahens walk under Royal's watchful eye.

He flaps down, and they scurry away, still nervous from their move. With his long tail folded behind him, he pecks the apple, eyes the door behind me, then peers at me as if to scold me for my rudeness.

"Not my fault." I back toward the door. "The vet said you need another few weeks of rest before we turn you loose. You'll be out soon."

"Paige!" Mom waves me over to the horse barn.

Inside the biggest stall, Mr. Ferro has his hands all tangled in Queenie's mane as Mom talks him step by step through a simple French braid. "Not that way. Twist these other two right here."

"How can you possibly tell that that bit of hair is any

different from this one? They're all the same. Look, there's some hair. Here's some hair. It's all hair."

"Here, let me show you again." Mom reaches for Queenie's mane, and the smile on her face warms me right down to my toes.

"She's really digging that," Mr. Ferro says. "If she could talk—"

"She'd boss me around all day. We don't call her Queenie for nothing." Mom's skilled fingers fly through the braid, and she spies me at the stall door. "Paige, is everything ready?"

"Yep."

"You've got hoses and buckets?"

"Yep."

"Where's Scotty?"

"Counting marshmallows, to make sure everybody gets exactly the same amount." It's a good thing we have a chocolate bar for everyone or he'd probably cut them all up, square by square, and make them even too.

"You're not even watching what you're doing." Mr. Ferro tsks. "Now you're just showing off."

"Oh whatever." Mom ties the braid off with a band and rubs Queenie's neck. "You don't look at your keyboard when you type, right? It's the same thing. Just practice; you'll get there." She opens the back panel to Queenie's stall. "Okay, off you go."

Tossing her head, Queenie blows hot air and trots outside with her tail high. Her ears swivel toward Milkshake's pasture, where Prince bucks and frolics beside his mother, his little tail flapping behind him.

The stall door creaks as Mom pulls it shut. "When Kimana comes, can you two roll some logs over for seats?"

"Sure." I'm too excited to sit still anyway. Might as well be useful. Our bench logs always start pretty far out at first—to keep them safe—but we roll them closer as the roaring heat fades and gives way to coals.

By the time Kimana rides up, I've already got one log rolled into place.

She hops off her bike and joins me at the next log. We brace our hands against the heavy log, digging our heels in to push it into place.

"One more," I breathe.

We walk to the last log, closest to the pile, and give it a good shove, but it rolls back, hung up on something.

"It's probably a rock. I'll get it." I step over the log and toe the grass with my boot. I hear a metallic *clink* and kneel to brush the grass aside.

A thin, curved blade is wedged against the log, its long wooden handle disappearing beneath the load.

"Roll it back!" I shout, barely waiting for Kimana to get out of the way before I roll the old tree. One push, two, and then it's off.

I lift Dad's shovel from the tall grass, and bits of dirt fall from the handle. Last year, under the snow and ice, we never saw it here. Not once.

"It was waiting for us." I grin at Kimana, clutching the handle with both hands, as if the shovel might disappear again.

The only way Dad's shovel would be here is if he worked here on that last day. I always wondered what he'd done while I played inside, working on my robot design, and now I know.

Dad was looking after our wishes.

By the time Mateo and his family come by, I've buffed the rust off the blade, sanded away the few slivers winter raised on the handle, and shoveled a few thistles into the pile, just for fun.

"I've got something for you," I say to Mateo's mom. I hurry to Royal's aviary and grab the strawberries. "They're not fancy, but I hope you'll like them."

"*Gracias.*" Mrs. Rivas fusses over the plants and nods her thanks.

"*De nada,*" I say as Mateo takes the pot from his mom and carries it farther from the pile.

He shoots me a wicked grin. "You already roasted one pot of flowers. Let's keep this one back here, so you don't cook another."

I make a face at him, but we both grin.

"It's my turn to light the wishfire." Scotty kneels beside a pile of shavings, cardboard, and papers jammed beneath the branches.

"Want some lighter fluid?" Mateo asks, but Scotty scowls as though Mateo asked if he wanted to light his own hair on fire.

"No cheating allowed."

"Okay." Mateo smirks at me and Kimana, then looks past us. "Check it out."

Royal stands beside a peahen, his tail fanned wide in an arc of green-and-blue feathered eyes.

The hen bobs her head, and Royal shakes his wings, his tail rattling softly.

"I think he's feeling better," Kimana says, then waves at her dad and Hutsi, walking up from the house with hot dogs and buns.

T-Rex thumps his tail to greet them, but stays a good hundred feet away. Scuzbag and Magic Cat doze by his side.

A crackling rises behind us, and Scotty dances back from the flames. "I did it. I did it!"

"You sure did." Mom pulls him close for a squeeze as fire licks the sky and roars beneath the branches. He squirms free and runs to the log where Mateo's parents sit beside the marsh-mallow sticks and s'mores supplies.

"Not yet," I warn. "Let it burn down enough for hot dogs, then I'll make s'mores with you."

I stick Dad's shovel upright in the dirt, and then jump on the edge with both feet so it's buried deep into the earth. I don't want to lose it again. Besides, we'll need it to put the ashes out before the night is through.

The wishfire burns hot, sparks drifting on the smoke like dancing fireflies. When the last branch catches fire, I pull a round stone from my pocket. "Does everyone have their wish-stones?"

Most everyone pulls a rock from a pocket, but a couple people pick one up off the ground.

"Make your wish!" I cup my stone in my hand, ready to make my wish, but Mr. Ferro touches my arm.

"Trade me. I think you should use this stone." He plucks the round rock from my hands and drops Dad's heart-shaped stone in its place. "That's better."

"Kimana wishes you'll be on the robotics team again," Scotty says, and Kimana whirls.

"Hey! You're not supposed to listen."

"Wish granted. I'll be there." I laugh, and smile wide as she grins back at me.

"Can we wish for food?" Mateo stands over the hot dogs. "I'm starving."

I run my thumb over the twin bumps at the top of my stone and circle the smooth hollow in the center, tracing the same lines my Dad did a hundred times before. Gently, I bounce the stone in the center of my palm, feeling the weight of it.

So much lost, and so much found.

None of this is how I imagined it would be, or ever wanted it to be, but now that it's all fallen into place, all the pieces fit. And joy fills in the cracks.

Cupping my stone to my lips, I whisper my wish.

Mom holds her stone toward the fire. "Everyone ready? Stay back in case one of them pops out of the fire."

"Ready," we chorus.

I squeeze Dad's heart in my hand, a last hug for the way things were and a hope for how things might be.

"Aim," Mom says.

We draw our hands back, a circle of friends and family.

"Wishfire!" Mom sings.

I swing my arm, open my hand, and let go.

Acknowledgments

I'm so thankful for everyone who helped this story grow from wishes to reality. First and foremost, my brilliant editor, Lisa Mangum, and my product manager, Heidi Taylor Gordon, who helped me find the story I wanted to tell, and bring it to light. A huge thanks to everyone else at Shadow Mountain who worked so hard on this story: Chris Schoebinger, Troy Butcher, Callie Hansen, Richard Erickson, and Malina Grigg. Working with you is a joy, and I'm so very grateful.

To my wonderful agent, Stacey Glick, thank you always for believing in me and going on this journey with me.

Thanks to my writing group for putting up with my crazy world, listening to my stories, and loving me anyway. You guys are the best. Special thanks to Nicki Stanton for slogging through the mire with me; to Marcy Curr for writing all night with me; and to John Roscher, our host with the most. To Daniel Noyes for sharing his brain, and to Seriously Gina for sharing her cabin and heart. To writing coach Ali Cross and her StoryNinja academy for helping me flesh out the original outline, and to all my writing friends with Storymakers, Snake River Writers, and elsewhere, my sincere thanks. Love you guys.

To my beta readers and sensitivity readers of awesomeness who answered my many questions and offered wonderful suggestions, thank you for sharing your world with me. To Moses Collier for letting me reimagine him as a teacher and giving me pointers. To Georgette Running Eagle for answering texts at weird hours with odd questions. To Tonia Anthony Countryman; the Toane family: Kerwin, Melody, Natasha, Feather, Dakota, Little Man, Tamina, Aspen, and LakotaRose, and Baby; Lisa Eddington; Talysa Sainz; Ximena Martinez Bishop; Caterina, Tomas, and Mateo Bishop; Courtney Weaver; Courtney Hartley; and Heather Warren.

Huge thanks to my family: Mike and the kids, to Brian and Sue Foster, and Janiel and Jerry Swore, as well as the many friends and neighbors who support me and this crazy writing thing I do even when it conflicts with farming season.

Thanks to the talented Brandon Durmond for the beautiful cover. I love it. High fives to Chris and Kimmel Dalley and kids for thinking up mischevious and rotten things to do on the farm. And to Tina Petersen for sharing her talents with me.

I'm sure there are some I'm forgetting, and please forgive me if I have. It takes a village, and I am grateful for all of you.

To Uncle Steve, we miss you every day the sun is shining.

And a special thanks to all my readers out there. Thank you for stepping into my world and sharing this story.

Author's Note

For the last twenty years, it's been my privilege to live and farm on the Sho-Ban Reservation where my husband and children were born and raised. Prior to writing *The Wish and the Peacock*, I asked some of my Shoshone-Bannock friends and neighbors what they'd like to see in a fictitious Shoshone-Bannock character, and they responded that they wanted to have their love for beading and dancing at powwows reflected in a story.

I've invited them to explain in their own words why these skills, talents, and events are important to them.

Georgette Running Eagle said, "Dancing matters because to dance is to heal, to be in connection with the healing spirit, if only for a brief moment. I feel connected to a higher power through my regalia and my eagle feathers. Dancing can take away any worries or burdens that I may be carrying that affects my well-being. After I am done dancing, I feel rejuvenated spiritually, though my physical being is exhausted.

"In today's modern society, there are two types of Jingle dancers, old style—which is more traditional—and contemporary. Old-style dresses often have 365 cones on them to represent each day of the year.

"There are different versions of the story of the jingle dress, though they share many similarities. This is the story as I learned it:

"The jingle dress, it has been told, evolved from a dream. The daughter of an elder man was very ill, and he was given a dream in which four women were each wearing a jingle dress and dancing. In the dream, he was given instructions on how the dress was to be made, along with a specific song that needed to be sung. When he woke, a ceremony was conducted for the ill daughter in which the women danced and sang. Throughout the night, the daughter regained her strength, and upon the end of the night, she joined the women and began dancing. That is why the jingle dress is also known as the healing dress.

"We are a bartering people and trade often, and when we work on projects such as dressmaking, beadwork, or hide tanning, we are supposed to think good thoughts or prayers for the individual whom will eventually wear or use the items. So in the story, when Kimana puts aside her own projects to work on a medallion for her friend who is struggling, it is an example of how my people will sometimes create something beautiful as a service to have prayers and blessings go with the handmade item to bless the life of a friend in need."

Feather and Natasha Toane said, "The Shoshone-Bannock people are especially well-known for their high quality bead-work, and we use two needles at the same time to do it. Beading connects us to our ancestors and the skills they had. It's vital that we carry on those skills from generation to generation so they won't be lost. When we bead, we put good thoughts and prayers into our beadwork. In our tradition, when someone buys our beadwork, they also get all our good thoughts and energy that goes into our work. As a signature for our work, we put one oddball bead into the piece to represent ourselves."

Tonia Anthony Countryman of the Eastern Shoshone, Northern Arapaho, and Navajo Nation said, "We are a spiritual, humble, and grateful people. The Shoshone-Bannock reservation is the only reservation that allowed women to dance in the annual Sun Dance, a spiritual event and honorable tradition where dancers fast from Friday evening to Monday at noon and offer prayers for the land, crops, water, the people, and other important issues. The Northern Arapaho tribe has one of the largest Sun Dance in North America. We love to hear our songs, listen to the drums, and tell our stories."

I'm grateful for all my dear friends who helped me honor their culture and traditions in this story, and who taught me about their history. And for those readers who are curious, "Hutsi" is the Shoshone word for paternal grandmother, and "Kimana" means butterfly.

Discussion Questions

1. Paige makes a promise to her dad to always take care of the farm. How does she do that? In what ways does she take that promise too far?
2. Paige is proud of her knowledge of how a farm works. What things did you learn about farming that surprised you? What kind of work do you do that are you proud of?
3. Kimana's skill in beadwork is something she was taught how to do by her family. Does your family have traditions that have been passed down through generations? What is something you know how to do that you could teach to someone else?
4. Scotty tells Paige that peacocks symbolize eternal life and rebirth. How are those two ideas woven into the story?
5. Mr. Collier assigns Paige's class to write a report on someone from history "whose story speaks to you, someone

we don't hear about every day." If you had to complete that assignment, which person would you choose to write about? Why?

6. Friendship is an important part of this story. In what ways is Paige a good friend to Mateo? To Scotty? To Kimana? To Mr. Ferro? In what ways is she not such a good friend? How could you be a better friend to the people in your life?

7. Paige realizes that her life isn't just a puzzle where the pieces only fit one way. It is more like a mural—a story that continues and gets bigger and bigger over time. If you were to draw a mural of your life—and what you hope your future holds—what things would you include?

8. If you had a wishstone, what would your wish be?

Compassion Makes Us Human

I must be a monster.

But if I can gather the right feather, the right shell,

and the right crystal, I can make a wish . . .

. . . and be human again.

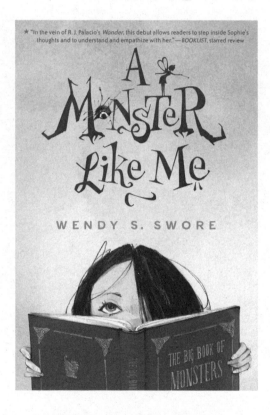

★ "In the vein of R. J. Palacio's *Wonder*, this debut allows readers to step inside Sophie's thoughts and to understand and empathize with her."—*BOOKLIST*, starred review

A Monster Like Me

WENDY S. SWORE